PENGU
WHO LET T~~~ ~~~~ ~~~~

Sidin Vadukut's bestselling debut novel *Dork: The Incredible Adventures of Robin 'Einstein' Varghese* was published in January 2010. The second book in the series, *God Save the Dork*, was published in 2011.

Born in a small town near Irinjalakuda in Kerala, Sidin spent most of his growing years in Abu Dhabi eating falafals. Once even with sambar. He is an engineer from NIT Trichy and an MBA from IIM Ahmedabad. Over the last decade he has made auto parts, developed online trading platforms, worked as a consultant and once had a sizeable portion of a tree fall on him. Sidin is currently a columnist and editor with the business newspaper *Mint*, a cricket columnist for www.cricinfo.com and a full-time freelance Twitterer.

He lives in London with his remarkably patient wife, a plethora of Apple products and a growing collection of Buddha statues. He blogs at http://www.whatay.com and tweets with the handle @sidin.

# WHO LET THE DORK OUT?

## SIDIN VADUKUT

PENGUIN BOOKS

PENGUIN BOOKS
Published by the Penguin Group
Penguin Books India Pvt. Ltd, 11 Community Centre, Panchsheel Park,
New Delhi 110 017, India
Penguin Group (USA) Inc., 375 Hudson Street, New York, New York 10014, USA
Penguin Group (Canada), 90 Eglinton Avenue East, Suite 700, Toronto,
Ontario, M4P 2Y3, Canada (a division of Pearson Penguin Canada Inc.)
Penguin Books Ltd, 80 Strand, London WC2R 0RL, England
Penguin Ireland, 25 St Stephen's Green, Dublin 2, Ireland
(a division of Penguin Books Ltd)
Penguin Group (Australia), 707 Collins Street, Melbourne, Victoria 3008, Australia
(a division of Pearson Australia Group Pty Ltd)
Penguin Group (NZ), 67 Apollo Drive, Rosedale, Auckland 0632, New Zealand
(a division of Pearson New Zealand Ltd)
Penguin Group (South Africa) (Pty) Ltd, 24 Sturdee Avenue, Rosebank,
Johannesburg 2196, South Africa

Penguin Books Ltd, Registered Offices: 80 Strand, London WC2R 0RL, England

First published by Penguin Books India 2012

Copyright © Sidin Vadukut 2012

ISBN 9780143414094

Typeset in Georgia by SÜRYA, New Delhi
Printed at Thomson Press India Ltd, New Delhi

ALWAYS LEARNING                    **PEARSON**

*To K.*
*Who is the best manager in the whole world.*

# Author's Note

Date: 11 January, 2012

From,
The Right to Information Officer,
Ministry for Urban Regeneration and Public Sculpture,
Patel Chowk,
New Delhi - 110008

To,
Sidin Vadukut
Mint
New Delhi

Ref: RTI Request No. 120912/000051/1 dtd April 30 2011

Sir,

In response to your above mentioned request for information, please find attached the following information requested:

1. Copy of all purchase orders issued to Messrs Fundango Ltd
2. Copy of all service purchase orders issued to Messrs Lederman India Ltd
3. Copy of inter-ministerial requisitions issued to National Informatics Centre, New Delhi
4. Universal Serial Bus drive provided by Raghu Khanna, Messrs Lederman India Ltd, containing creatives, design outlines and

merchandizing plan drafted for Allied Victory Games 2010. Drive contains miscellaneous personal documents which are being submitted as-is.

The following information request could not be processed:

Nature of information: Minutes of meetings conducted between Hon. Minister Badrikedar Laxmanrao Dahake and Robin Varghese, Messrs Lederman India Ltd.

Reason for inability to convey information: During animal control operation conducted in ministry premises in October 2010, following unexpected ingress by monkeys inhabiting ministry compound, several documents in Hon. Minister's office was destroyed accidentally by water, fire and explosives. All efforts made to recover documents were unsuccessful. The ministry regrets to decline information request.

Yours sincerely,
Vallath Kavitha
Right to Information Officer
MURPS, New Delhi

# BOOK ONE

# TITLE

## 3 October 2009

### 3.14 p.m.

This is the life, Diary. This is the life.

Can it get better? Maybe. There is room for some minor improvements. After all whose life cannot get better in some small way here and there? People always want bigger car, bigger house, more salary, different girlfriend who does not want to talk about marriage every second of every bloody day from morning to night even when you go to meet her at her apartment in Sector 7843 in Gurgaon despite having spent the whole day at office handling an entire national team, and then when you say 'Come, Gouri, let us stop fighting about marriage and order pizza' she gets even more upset. Because apparently she does not want to eat carbohydrate at night as if she will become Ms India if she loses just half kilo. BUT THEN BLOODY EVERYTHING NORMAL PEOPLE CAN EAT HAS CARBOHYDRATE YOU STUPID WOMAN!

But otherwise, frankly speaking, what more can I ask for?

Right now I am looking outside my window into the middle of the office building tower and I can see all these poor low-level and middle-level fellows in other companies sitting and slogging in front of their computers. Look at their faces, Diary. What do you see? Exactly. Frustration, disappointment, disillusionment, fear, negativity, hopelessness, anger and regret. (Except for Fundango Ltd. God only knows why they are so happy always. Must be some insider trading.)

Many of these poor fellows must be thinking: How can I also become vice-president and interim CEO of the Indian subsidiary of an international investment and advisory firm? How can I also get

3

paid in British pounds in India? How can I also get invited to give alumni guest lecture on Managing Across International Cultures at the Institute? How can my Jet Privilege status also go from Blue to Platinum in just three months due to extensive business class travel?

How can I become what Robin 'Einstein' Varghese has become?

Hard work, Diary. Hard work, commitment, intuition, ingenuity, originality, solidarity and a little good luck. All these things are required. Also people skills and leadership. Only then can you be where I am today. Also strategic vision.

Who would've thought a few years ago when I joined Dufresne Partners as a mere business analyst that today I would be just one review committee meeting away from becoming full-time CEO of the India office? Or that I would be summoned to the offices of a cabinet minister for important business discussions?

Too much, Diary, too much. (Also communication skills. Refer skills list for success above.)

In just two hours I will be meeting Sivraj Tiwari, cabinet minister for sports and culture. I have a one-hour dedicated appointment during which I will take him through a comprehensive overview of what Lederman's International Sports Finance practice can do to help conduct the 2010 Allied Victory Games in New Delhi.

As you are already aware, Diary, AVG2010 is a complete and utter shameful mess. (They completely forgot taekwondo till two months ago.) Everything is behind schedule and already international media is beginning to laugh at the situation. This is exactly the kind of business problem Lederman can help with. The ISF team is superb at handling the accounts of huge sporting events and making it look as if everything is profitable for the purposes of audit and media.

It is, of course, a huge responsibility on my shoulders. Lederman first tried to get AVG2010 work four years ago when Delhi beat Tripoli by just one vote to win the hosting rights. But at that point they got outclassed by the usual criminals: McKinsey, Goldman, BCG. Even Dufresne got a little piece of useless work like overseeing parking or something. Amateurs! Must have made some PowerPoint presentation called 'Park2.0: Rethinking the stationary vehicle'.

But back then Lederman didn't have an India office or a local guy who really got India. Someone with an intimate sense of how this huge, complicated, diverse market operates. Someone who could tell the great opportunities (microfinance) from the terrible ones (ecommerce).

Now they do. (Wink, 'Einstein', wink.)

So day before yesterday when the Prime Minister admitted that AVG2010 was a mess, needed more help, and was looking to hire fresh advisers I didn't even waste one second. As a country head I have direct access to the people who matter in this company. I immediately sent an email to the John in Tokyo, who replied with a CC to Nicola in Milan, who organized a call with the business leadership team in Boston that immediately—within fifteen minutes— agreed that my idea was excellent and could be forwarded to the CEO. Within twenty-four hours he asked the leadership team to convey to Nicola his approval, who forwarded the email to John in Brussels, by mistake, who sent it to John in Tokyo who instantaneously asked me to meet Tiwari.

The first challenge, of course, was to get an appointment. This is a cabinet minister, Diary. Not some shady Gurgaon real estate broker. (Actually Tiwari used to be a real estate broker before he went to Tihar jail for some minor murder problem in 1987. There he met the current home minister's mother and decided to enter public service.)

Thankfully Johnson Uncle (Kuwait) is married to the daughter of Sebastian Uncle, the principal secretary in the rural development ministry, who, it turns out, was in the same batch of the IAS as Tiwari's personal secretary. Within fifteen minutes the appointment was fixed. Networking, Diary!

So now, in just two hours' time, a little boy from a small village in Kerala will spend an hour talking to a cabinet minister of the largest democracy in the world. It sounds like a scene from a heroic Spielberg film like *Braveheart*. But it is true.

It is on days like today that the story of my own life truly astonishes me. How can this happen to Robin Varghese? How?

Amazing.

Must send a brief note to the Varghese Samajam for inclusion in my profile in the *Varghese Annual Gazette*. Not for showing off or anything. But I want to inspire the next generation of Roman Catholic Vargheses in Thrissur.

**8.01 p.m.**

Meeting with minister cancelled. I don't want to talk about it.

**10.12 p.m.**

Met Gouri for dinner. We went to that tiny Italian place inside Hotel Hans Plaza. I have no idea what is the restaurant's business model. Whenever we've gone there to eat we are the only people there. But still somehow they have a fully stocked bar, several waiters and imported items on the menu. Like truffles.

But for whom? Maybe like Abu Dhabi Towers hotel in Guruvayoor there is a brothel in the gym.

We've been meeting less than we used to these last few weeks. As you know, this marriage thing is causing a lot of tension. Tonight I could sense that Gouri was trying not to make any references at all to the 'Great Marriage Crisis'. For most of the dinner we spoke about work and work-related issues in a jovial manner. Like me she is also doing very well indeed.

But it is inevitable. Anything we speak about eventually comes round to 'us'.

Look, Diary, it is not like I don't care. Or I have doubts. Or I am not sure. Or other women have not tried to proposition for long-term or short-term interactions and I have said yes because I am not sure or I am unfaithful.

I have no doubt at all in my mind. Gouri is the one for me. And Einstein is the one for her. She knows this. This is why when I moved back to India from London two years ago to take over Lederman she moved as well. She loved Mumbai. But she was prepared to give up all that comfort and safety and culture and sophistication and move to Delhi. For me. Only for me. Even her parents didn't like it.

Which is why I understand her need to constantly worry and get upset and nag about this marriage thing. Gouri thinks we've spent enough time together and made enough sacrifices to justify the commitment.

YES BABA I ALSO AGREE.

All I am saying is that just wait for me to move from interim to proper CEO. For two years Lederman has been fucking around with my patience. For two years they've been finding random reasons to not settle it once and for all. When I left London they were very clear about the fact that I would take over as vice-president. And if everything went well for the first twelve months they would consider elevating me to CEO.

And we had a mind-blowing first twelve months. Purely because of my effort we took that 15 per cent stake in Subhiksha Retail. Today it is worth billions, Diary, billions.

So what did the fuckers do? They promoted me to interim-CEO pending 'confirmation from our regional and global leadership teams'.

It has been nine months now. And I simply don't want to make huge life commitments before getting this out of the way.

Gouri, unfortunately, doesn't see it that way. Her parents are vaguely aware of our relationship. And they've been asking to meet me. And I've been resisting.

You know how these parents of north Indian girls are, Diary. You chumma go to their house for dinner and then suddenly they will ask you to marry their daughter. Say yes and they will lock you in the bathroom till you finalize date and content on invitation card. Say no and they will take you to Rajasthan in the dickie of a car and behead you.

I am not prepared for that now.

Let me deal with Lederman first, please?

Anyway towards the end of dinner she again asked me when I would meet her parents. Apparently some important relative is coming from abroad in two days. And apparently I have to impress him without fail.

I said I would try. And then she thought I was being too

unenthusiastic. And then we got into the same loop of emotional blackmailing (her) and serial apologizing (me).

Excellent tiramisu.

## 4 October 2009

### 1.16 p.m.

Leaving for the ministry of youth affairs. Long, tragic story. But at least this time the minister is aware of my arrival and has personally guaranteed a one-hour appointment.

The government is complex. But then otherwise, Diary, what is the challenge?

### 5.32 p.m.

Just finished watching *Devasuram* DVD on the laptop once again. Minister is still in a meeting. I am sitting here inside a waiting room. There is one other man here with me. At around 2 p.m. he sat and ate some horrible-smelling lunch (Bengali?) and then fell asleep.

Diary, I have heard many people snore in my life. But this man is truly extraordinary. Every time he inhales it is like *Saving Private Ryan*.

Even my Panasonic headphones are useless. But who knows? Maybe he is some IAS officer.

### 6.56 p.m.

Fuck. No sign of minister so far. Tired.

Thankfully Snorendranath Tagore has left. At 6 p.m., on the dot, not one second before or after, he suddenly woke up. One moment he was Idukki Dam during monsoon water release. Next moment he was standing, packing his tiffin box and leaving. Miraculous. No watch or alarm clock or anything. How many years of training are required for such accuracy? Must be very senior in the IAS.

Fucker.

MINISTER IS COMING BYE! Wait ... who the fuck ... LATER.

### 6.57 p.m.

Minister, BASTARD SHAMELESS INSULT TO THE NATION, has asked me to approach the ministry of urban regeneration for all

9

consultancy offers as youth affairs has already hired ... RAHUL GUPTA. (Vomiting sensation is coming.)

In fact the minister had postponed my meeting because he spent the whole day sitting through a Rahul Gupta presentation. They have decided to immediately hire his new company, The Braithwaite Group, under the Prime Minister's urgent Allied Victory Games 2010 directive.

Rahul walked out with the minister, shook my hand, gave me his new card and then left with the minister in his car. IN THE MINISTER'S CAR! (Sexual favours? Possible.)

Diary, why does this happen to me always? Why? Why, at every possible moment of personal success and achievement, does that man have to enter my life? I am fed up of Rahul Gupta.

Also, what is THE Braithwaite Group? Nonsense. As if there are other Braithwaite Groups. Original Braithwaite Group. New Improved Braithwate Group. Deluxe Braithwaite. Nayyinte Mone Braithwaite Group. Bastard.

One more time I go to a ministry and then I give up. I can understand some amount of bureaucracy in government. But what nonsense is this?

## 8.44 p.m.

Finally managed to get an appointment with the minister for urban regeneration. Day after tomorrow.

Tomorrow early morning I have to go to the airport with Gouri to pick up her uncle. Ex-military type who now lives in New Zealand doing some major family business. Everyone in the family calls him Colonel Kalbag. Even his own mother, Gouri's grandmother, calls him Colonel. Apparently he fought in one or two wars before taking retirement and moving to Auckland. The family treats him like some war hero. Gouri told me several times to call him only Colonel and not Uncle.

Not once or twice. But 16,000 times. As if I am a child. I love her very much and all. But if after marriage she keeps repeating everything 20,000 times one of us will fall from the balcony.

## 5 October 2009

**11.07 a.m.**

Colonel Kalbag landed at Delhi airport exactly on time. As soon as he saw me he asked me some polite questions about my family and my professional accomplishment. I humbly and respectfully answered everything.

In the beginning things were a little cold. But as we spoke in the car to Gouri's house things began to get more casual and friendly. When we got out of the car Colonel had his arm around my shoulder and insisted that I stay for breakfast. I protested, telling him I would be late for office. But he simply would not relent, Diary. In the end I called office and told Sugandh that I would be at least two hours late.

By the time I left Gouri's house the Colonel and I were swapping jokes and talking politics like good friends. He was very nice and friendly and really made me feel welcome in the Kalbag family. Of course I didn't get informal at any point. That would be taking too much liberty. But both Gouri and I left him with a feeling of extreme happiness at how things turned out.

Colonel Kalbag's sign off is crucial if our wedding plans are to proceed. But I think we have started off on a good note.

All this sounds excellent no, Diary? No? Are you happy? Yes? Okay.

Well, I have some news for you.

COLONEL KALBAG IS MAD DIARY! FUCKING INSANE! AND THAT IS NOT AT ALL HOW THINGS TURNED OUT. NOT AT ALL. IT WAS A DISASTER. UTTER COMPLETE DISASTER.

Let me explain.

Now as you know one of my personal codes of conduct is that 'Irrespective of what elderly people do, however stupid it is, however narrow-minded, uneducated or stubborn they are, even if one day one of them by mistake decides to proactively clean your room upstairs and sells all your old newspapers and magazines along with

11

your laptop to a waste-paper fellow for a sum total of Rs 176, you must always treat them with respect and not deposit the iron box on their head.'

So even though I don't see the point in calling people by their professional titles, I still immediately went up to Gouri's uncle and said: 'Hello Colonel Kalbag, hope you had a good flight, I am Robin Varghese.' (The airport security in-charge was an ex-colleague of the Colonel's from Bangladesh or something and let us inside till the baggage area.)

He didn't smile, but shook my hand briefly and walked away talking to Gouri. His wife ran behind him looking terrified. (I later realized that she permanently has a look of terror on her face. Poor woman. But with a husband like this it probably saves time to look terrified all the time as a precaution.)

He continued to ignore me throughout. Then Gouri started doing that Kathakali with her eyes, silently asking me to go up and talk to him. So I loudly asked him how the weather in Auckland was this time of the year. He didn't say anything. And then, just as one of his bags came down the conveyor belt, he asked me which part of Kerala I was from.

He asked me this question at the exact same moment that I politely bent over to pick up his suitcase from the belt.

The rest is still a blur, Diary. But let me remember as much as I can.

So now this suitcase was a normal, large Echolac or Samsonite or something in dark blue plastic. The Colonel had wrapped it entirely in plastic film, leaving only the handle exposed.

Usually all this is not a problem for someone who is a Jet Privilege Platinum. I know baggage conveyors all over India like the back of my hand. And I have a proven technique for whipping bags off the belt.

Most people bend at the waist. This is an amateur mistake. You must, instead, settle down on your knees, keep your back straight, to avoid strain, and then use your upper arm strength to pull the bag off the belt in one smooth movement. If the handle is away from you, simply rotate the bag on the belt with a flick of the wrist.

Unfortunately Colonel Kalbag, like typical classless NRIs, had packed at least two refrigerators and one Adnan Sami into his suitcase. I flicked. It did not move. I nudged with my arms. Not even a millimetre of movement. By now the bag was slowly moving away into the personal space of the next passenger with his trolley. So I reached over the suitcase to get at the exposed handle. I grabbed it and began to pull.

Simultaneously I was also saying: 'Colonel, I come from a small village of some 3000 families midway between Guruvayoor and . . .'

At this point I tripped over the trolley next to me and fell over the belt. Even from this situation I am usually capable of exiting gracefully using physical comedy and self-deprecation.

BUT ONLY IF I CAN LET GO OF THIS MILITARY MADMAN'S FUCKING SUITCASE NO? Unfortunately my cufflinks (Shooting Stars) got snagged on the bloody plastic wrapping paper and wouldn't let go.

The next ten seconds or so are undoubtedly the most embarrassing in my life, at least in an airport environment. Slowly, along with the belt, I got dragged along the floor of the airport. Along the way I left a line of toppled trolleys, upset bags and several scattered small children. Meanwhile, I still valiantly tried to reply to the Colonel: 'Thrissur. THRISSUR! THRISSUUUUR! . . .'

At this point one of the staff members hit the emergency stop button and the belt, along with me, slowly came to a stop. Gouri helped me to my feet and when I got up there was a continuous line of conveyor belt grease from my neck to the crotch of my pants. I nonchalantly pulled the suitcase off the belt and jovially asked Colonel Kalbag 'if we should go through the Green Channel or had he bought anything illegitimate into the country!' And then I giggled alone.

By then all of them had turned around, out of embarrassment perhaps, and walked away. I followed them all the way to the car park, dragging the fucking luggage of the devil behind me. I resolved that I would at least put the suitcase in the dickie without making a complete fool of myself. While Gouri, the Colonel and his wife settled into the car I got into an optimum suitcase lifting position.

This time there was no room for error. I stood right up close to the suitcase, lowered myself at the knees and firmly gripped the handle. Already I began making a mental picture of where in the dickie I would place the suitcase. The technique is to lift and swing in one fluid motion, such that you don't have to nudge or push the object later. I took a deep breath, calmed my nerves and lowered myself. At which point the Colonel came out of the car, picked up the suitcase, flung it into the dickie, and then went back and sat down again.

I got up, shut the dickie, and then went and sat in front next to Gouri.

For the first few moments there was utter silence. But then you know how sometimes when something embarrassing happens there is a moment of self-appraisal after which everyone simply bursts out laughing?

Once again it did not happen.

Gouri drove quietly. Then somewhere near Subroto Park the Colonel said to nobody in particular how 'youngsters these days had no focus at all on physical fitness and can't even do minor menial jobs'. His wife, looking like something was electrocuting her underneath her salwar kameez, agreed immediately.

Immediately I sensed the obvious: He was trying to gauge my personal approach to physical fitness. An understandable criteria when choosing a prospective groom for one's niece. I told him that while I could not speak on behalf of other young people these days, I personally believed in treating the body like a temple.

He asked me if I went to a gym. I reminded him that a gym was just one of many ways of maintaining fitness. He asked me to limit my answer to a yes or a no. I told him that depending on how you looked at it my answer could be a yes or a no. By now the Colonel was beginning to look irritated and Gouri's face was a blur of Kathakali signals.

He then asked me if I did running or jogging. I was beginning to get fed up of this nonsense conversation. So I said yes. I loved running. He asked me how much I could run. I told him that I routinely ran 5 kilometres for time pass.

He immediately asked Gouri to stop the car. A little voice in my head said: 'Behenchod.'

The Colonel told me that we were now approximately 5 kilometres from the Taj Mahal Hotel at Dhaula Kuan. They would drive to the hotel immediately, and I would run/jog/walk and meet them as soon as possible. On no account was I supposed to take an auto or a taxi or the metro. He asked me if I could be trusted. I laughed to myself in a complex way and told him that trust was one of my personal strengths. He looked at his watch. And then asked Gouri to drive.

Think about this for a moment, Diary. I am standing on the side of the road near Subroto Park. There is conveyor belt grease and airport floor dirt all over me. I am humiliated, dirty, hot, dusty and unbelievably pissed off. Also, I have not had breakfast because the plan was to have a joint dhokla swallowing session with the Kalbags. All because of some shady third-rate relative of Gouri, impressing whom was the point of this entire trip to the airport.

FUCKING FUCKRUDDIN ALI AHMED.

Diary, you kindly note the following down: One day I will make that insane Colonel Kalbag rue the day he decided to fuck around with Robin 'Einstein' Varghese. One day, after Gouri and I have settled down, I will make that crazy kakkoos Colonel beg and plead in front of me for forgiveness. At which point I will drive to this same exact point, throw him out of the car, and tell him to jog to Auckland you bloody fool!

You note this time. I swear I will do this.

I slowly jogged for two minutes, till their car was out of sight, and then got into an auto. I told the auto fellow to take me to the ITC hotel next to the Taj. The plan was to wait at the ITC for 45 minutes or so, before walking over to the Taj to meet them. A solid plan. If they asked me why I didn't look tired, I would tell them that I had freshened up at the Taj restroom.

Brilliant.

For a change I found an auto fellow who kept quiet, used the meter and drove safely. Why can't this auto fellow be Gouri's uncle? So well behaved. The drive helped me to cool down a little bit, even though the traffic was truly horrible. Still it wasn't too warm or humid, and I was able to get some work done on my BlackBerry.

And then suddenly there was a very loud banging sound. I crashed into the back of the driver, and then fell down to the floor of the auto. I carefully looked up and immediately saw the accident. My auto had crashed into the rear right side of a metallic blue Maruti Baleno. All the lights were broken and there was a huge dent in the metal panel.

My first thought was: 'How ironic! Gouri has the same car in the same colour!' My second thought was: 'The irony mounts! Gouri's car has the exact same picture of Ganesha on the rear windscreen.' My third thought was largely along the lines of: 'FUUUUUUUUUCCCCCCCCCKKKKKKKKKKKKKKKK'

Gouri and the Colonel stepped out of the car and immediately began shouting at the auto driver. I tried hiding in the back till they reached a compromise. But then the Colonel decided to call the police. I couldn't spend the rest of the day in the back of an auto, and I had to go prepare for the ministry of urban regeneration meeting tomorrow. So I took a deep breath, got up, stepped out of the auto, nodded at Gouri, who looked utterly astonished, got into another auto and went home.

Since then I have not had any contact with Gouri, the kakkoos Colonel or Wonder Woman. This is not good. According to Gouri's First Law of Conflict, the longer her initial silence the louder her subsequent interactions. I have started mentally preparing.

Went home, changed, and came back to office. Back to work now. So much to do. But if this meeting doesn't work I give up. The Government of India can plan the Allied Victory Games without Lederman's expertise.

**10.23 p.m.**

Still no word from Gouri. I hope her bloody uncle doesn't call off the marriage plans because of this.

Or what if he does? I am a man. I can deal with it.

**11.23 p.m.**

I've been thinking about it. And there are at least fifteen different things Lederman can do for the Government of India through our bespoke financial advisory and cash flow practices.

But right now, Diary, patience is key. First, we will help them actually make some money from these Allied Victory Games nonsense. And then, once I have my tentacles inside the highest echelons of government, I might even help radically change the way this country is run. And unlike consulting firms, our focus is on money, not bullshit. And who needs sound financial advice and strategy more than a booming economy like India?

When the country hits 10 per cent growth next year and is minting money, who will tell them how to spend all that cash? Robin 'Einstein' Varghese, special adviser on financial policy to the Prime Minister with cabinet rank.

Too ambitious, Diary? Maybe. But from great ambitions are born great visions. And from visions, success.

**12.05 a.m.**

Text message from Gouri: 'How could you humiliate me like this?'

What I really wanted to send in response: 'Gouri baby, I am so sorry you humiliated yourself at the airport by cleaning the floor with your Rs 12,500 Reid & Taylor suit and then got thrown out of a car outside Subroto Park. I know nothing I can do to heal these deep deep wounds, but will you let me treat Colonel Kalbag to dinner where I can mix some potassium cyanide into his paneer butter masala so we can both sit back and watch him initially struggle for air, and then later choke on his own vomit and die? Just a thought. Please say yes.'

What I really sent: 'Gouri baby, I am so sorry.'

Lying just saves so much time, Diary.

Big day tomorrow. Goodnight.

# 6 October 2009

**11.34 a.m.**

Where the heck is the ministry of urban regeneration? How the heck do I reach there on time? According to Google Maps there are at least four locations all over Delhi. The ministry's website is entirely in purple. And has no address.

Called up Sebastian Uncle. He told me to go to the building opposite the post office at Patel Chowk. Fingers crossed. I don't think I can handle one more cancellation. It shouldn't be this hard to help your own country no?

Sometimes, on days like today, I feel that I should have taken up that offer from Abu Dhabi Commercial Bank last year. It would have been nice to work in the same company as Johnson Uncle, Thomas Uncle, Joby, Jebin, Simon, Anilkumar, Saiju and Perpetual (both of them).

But that option is always there. Plan B!

**8.45 p.m.**

No time to write, Diary. Just popped into the office to show Minister Dahake the Lederman facilities.

What? Excuse me? How come? Where? Why? Who? For what purpose is the minister in the office? Settle down, Diary. No need for all this alarm and consternation . . .

You may have forgotten that old saying they have in Lederman: 'WHEN THE GOING GETS TOUGH, THE EINSTEIN HAS ALREADY FINISHED GOING!'

The ministry of urban regeneration is now OFFICIALLY A CLIENT OF LEDERMAN INDIA LTD!!!!!!!!

More details later tonight.

**12.37 a.m.**

Adipoli whisky mone! Fully frunk. Tomorro . . .

# 7 October 2009

## 7.13 p.m.

SOOOOOOOO tired. I am still in office. Everybody else has left. Diary, have you ever heard of a company where the boss is the last guy to leave? What to do? The price of sustained excellence.

As you know the moment we close a new client there are so many things I have to do. First of all I had to inform Tokyo, Milan, Boston and finally the CEO. This is a big deal for Lederman. The first public sector client we've signed on in emerging markets since the business risk quantification project for Fukushima Daichi last year.

And now the ministry for urban regeneration and public sculpture. And Minister Badrikedar Laxmanrao Dahake. The story of how we won that deal last night will go down in Lederman legend. But only if I am allowed to repeat it in public. But that would be a violation of client confidentiality.

But what confidentiality is there between a man and his Diary? So let me share it with you.

First of all things started very badly. The ministry for urban regeneration and public sculpture (MURPS) is located inside a dingy, dirty little building near Patel Chowk. My first feeling was: 'Deivame! How can Lederman possibly find a client in this horrible, horrible place.'

Diary, do you remember many years ago when I had to go to the University of Calicut office to get a copy of my pre-degree mark sheet? I was sitting in a dirty waiting room when someone discovered that a cow had entered an open godown nearby and started eating BSc geology II year answer sheets. I helped to chase away the cow. Afterwards grateful university employees gave tea and samosa to everybody. Later when I came home I developed amoebiasis from tea/samosa/cow-contact.

Compared to the ministry, the University of Calicut is Buckingham Palace. If there was any location in the entire building that had three pieces of concrete meeting each other there were paan stains. The following are the smells I encountered on each floor:

1. Ground floor including reception area: Hint of synthetic lemon over a full-bodied hit of urine.
2. First floor comprising offices: One or more dead animals.
3. Second floor comprising meeting rooms and computer centre: Beef curry made last year and henceforth left inside a humid room.
4. Fourth floor including minister's office: Clean and air-conditioned with slight hint of 'Kodaikanal horse' that turned out to be only one peon and not a general characteristic.

I arrived there a full forty-five minutes ahead of my meeting just in case the government bastards or people like Rahul Gupta tried to screw me over again. As usual the minister was in a meeting when I arrived but his principal secretary, a small mysterious man called Joyyontoh, asked me to wait just outside the minister's cabin. This room was also air-conditioned and comfortable in a 1970s kind of way. Every bloody thing in the room was made of plywood.

While I was waiting, Joyyontoh (North-East? Bengali?) kept entering and exiting the minister's office. And once in a while I could hear the minister shouting at somebody or the other.

After some twenty minutes Joyyontoh asked me if I wanted to have tea or coffee. I said I would like tea. He said he would send someone. After five minutes another fellow came and told me Joyyontoh had sent him, and he wanted to know if I wanted tea or coffee. I told him I would like some tea. Then five minutes later an office boy came and gave me coffee.

Then suddenly, before I could even sip the coffee Joyyontoh exploded out of the minister's room and frantically waved at me to come in. I leapt up and ran inside.

The minister's office was also clearly designed in the 1970s. But everything had been meticulously cleaned and polished. His table reflected so much light that for a moment I couldn't see him at all.

And then without any warning, Minister Badrikedar Laxmanrao Dahake came jumping out of a side room, stood in front of me and asked me whether his hair looked okay. Then he started turning from side to side to show me his head from various angles.

For the briefest nanosecond I wondered if this was some kind of special test to see what kind of professional I was. What if the minister was testing my observation skills? My honesty? My spontaneous on-the-feet thinking?

Meanwhile I played for time by seamlessly transitioning into my signature 'thought leader' gesture (Clasp my palms together in front of my chest, look intently at his head, and then make gentle 'mmmm mmmm mmmm' sounds. Same as my photo on Lederman India website).

But then I realized: It was unlikely Kedarji thought that deeply about such things. During the previous Lok Sabha, I found out while doing deep background research, Kedarji had picked up the wrong printout from the table in front of him and asked the home minister what he had done to 'extradite known terrorists from Pakistan such as Varun Kantilal Shah, Jacob Kurien, Owais Ali Farooqi and A.C. Alagappan being the recently deceased sitting members of this august house. I have no more questions, Speaker sir.'

I told the minister that it was a dignified hairstyle befitting his position. Kedarji looked happy and bounced along to his table. He then sat behind his chair, inserted a hearing aid, and then told me to sit in one of the armchairs on the other side of the table.

I took a deep breath. And launched into my proven sales pitch.

'Minister sir, I will make you this offer once and only once. What if I told you that with some help from one of the world's top eighteen investment banks and financial advisers, you could turn the Allied Victory Games from an international humiliation into a global success story, that also makes you crores in profits (conditions apply)?'

Kedarji looked intently at his computer monitor and then said: 'I cannot hear.'

So I started again but much louder. 'MINISTER SIR, I WILL MAKE YOU THIS OFFER ONCE AND ONLY ONCE ...'

At which point he picked up a little metallic bell, used to call peons, and threw it at me. It hit me in the chest, impacting an area already sore from the previous day's developments of Colonel Kalbag's Death Case.

The bell made a clear sound and Joyyontoh came running inside. The minister first pointed at the screen. And then at me. Joyyontoh came and whispered in my ear from an extremely uncomfortably close distance: 'Please be quiet. Minister is talking on the Skype.com to British Broadcasting Corporation.'

I nodded silently, pulled out my phone and made sure it was on silent. Then I carefully replaced the bell on the minister's vast desk.

Meanwhile Joyyontoh checked the minister's headphones, removed them and switched the audio to speakers. After that he sat on the chair next to me, leaned over and whispered again: 'Any tea or coffee?'

I vigorously declined the offer.

And then, Diary, I proceeded to listen to the most ago-fucking-nizing, meaningless, depressing, pointless words ever to emerge from the mouth of a human being.

The BBC journalist would ask a question about the Allied Victory Games. Kedarji would think for two seconds. And then say something that was basically a string of English words assembled in random order. It made no sense whatsoever.

Let me give you an example. BBC reporter would ask: 'So Minister, are you admitting that the Allied Victory Games are behind schedule but the Government of India still does not feel that it has to go into panic mode to deal with it? How does that make sense?'

The minister after thinking (About what? Idiot!) would then say something like this: 'See the Government of India has a commitment to make to the people about the sports and youth and culture. The potential is huge and it is a long path that we have to cover on this journey. Allied Victory Games is a flagship event in the history of our nation with its rich culture, diversity and spirituality. In a nutshell.'

Obviously the BBC reporter kept trying to clarify what the heck this guy was trying to say. Joyyontoh simply sat there with his face in his hands, looking contemplative. And Kedarji was beginning to sound increasingly uncomfortable.

It was quite clear to everybody that the minister was making a fool of himself. And it was clear from the BBC's line of questioning that they were mocking not just the minister but the entire country itself.

SORRY. BUT THAT IS NOT SOMETHING EINSTEIN CAN JUST STAND AND CHUMMA WATCH. ENOUGH IS ENOUGH!

Einstein had a plan. Einstein pulled out his laptop. Einstein switched it on. Einstein noticed low battery and connected it to a power point. And then Einstein began to type like the wind. Each time the BBC finished asking a question I would furiously type an answer and then point the screen at Kedarji. The minister caught on to my plan immediately.

He would meticulously read each answer, but then he also acted as if the answer was coming spontaneously from his mind. Commendable presence of mind for an elected representative.

Let me give you some examples:

BBC: Don't you think this reflects poorly in the West on India's ability to deliver on big projects?

Kedarji feat. Einstein: Our responsibilities as a government are primarily to fulfil the wishes of the people of this country. Not the people of your country, your blatantly biased media, or anybody else in the West. Can we spend more money and finish it faster? Sure. But that is not our way. That is not the Indian way. Unlike in the West money is not our solution to everything. Instead we are being slow, thorough and responsible. Forgive me if the West does not understand the value of patience. Kindly do not force your methods on us. We suffered that for many centuries.

BBC: Minister, no doubt patience is a virtue. And perhaps your method will eventually work. But the Allied Victory Games Federation is very concerned. And they have received no reassurances from any of the ministries involved on timelines.

K & E: You want reassurances? I will send you by email in ten minutes. Reassurances are worth nothing. Didn't every single Lehman Brother reassure the public they were safe before they went bankrupt? The British government reassured the people of the Middle East in the 1950s that everything would be fine after they left. Please let us focus on ground realities.

BBC: What are the ground realities, Minister?

K & E: As per the latest data from the Delhi Public Works Department over 85 per cent of our work is approximately within 5 per cent of scheduled targets. Five per cent is delayed by 35 per cent or more, but the remaining 10 per cent is well within our emergency alert levels of 45 per cent overall completion for October 2009.

BBC: Thank you, Minister. I hope your confidence is justified and we will be able to see a successful Allied Victory Games next year.

K & E: Of course. Jai Hind.

After disconnecting the Skype call there were a few moments of silence. And then Joyyontoh patted me on my back a few times silently. Kedarji got up, took a few minutes to walk around the table and then picked me up and hugged me very, very tightly. He thanked me profusely.

One second, Diary.

### 9.52 p.m.

Sorry about that. The housekeeping staff came and did not notice me sitting in my cabin on this side of the office. Criminal bastards. The first thing they did after coming was go to the coffee machine, make coffee for all of them and then relax in the conference room. After that while three fellows were cleaning, one fellow opened the coffee machine, stole half the beans and most of the milk powder, and shut the machine again.

I went screaming out of my cubicle. Within forty-five minutes their manager came with replacement staff.

Can't trust anybody these days. Not one person. All thieves.

Ah. So where was I?

Apparently, Diary, this BBC reporter has been calling Kedarji on a daily basis since the Prime Minister's confessions of AVG2010 delays. Every evening she calls up demanding a progress report or some nonsense about why this stadium is not ready and why that stadium is not ready and such insignificant micro-management details.

Normally, Kedarji told me, he does not take any media except

India TV seriously. Everybody in his constituency Akola North, including his mother Bhavani Devi Dahake, apparently only watches India TV for news. But the Prime Minister, it seems, is a huge BBC fan. So now he has no option but to accept all BBC requests.

(Amazing, Diary. I've met a minister only once. And already I am being given insider gossip on how things operate in the highest echelons of government.)

Personally I've never really been a fan of the British Broadcasting Corporation. When I was in London a few years ago I used to have a TV with only ten channels, half of them BBC. At any given moment three of them used to show that horrible Top Gear show and the other two some form of Hitler documentary. The British are OBSESSED with Hitler, Diary.

If Britain was still ruling India today we would have good roads, hospitals, pubs and better women and all, but also hundreds of documentaries about villains like Nathuram Godse, Jallianwala Bagh and that fellow who killed Siraj ud Daulah. Something something Jabbar. Thank god for freedom fighters like Mahatma Gandhi and Pattom Thanu Pillai.

Personally I think CNN is the best media channel in the whole world. Good graphics, good presenters, good production value and rarely any Hitler.

Then the minister took me to a set of sofas in one corner of his vast office and we all sat down. Joyyontoh asked me if I needed any tea or coffee. I told him that anything was okay. The minister suggested the very good filter coffee made by a 'madrasi' fellow in the canteen. I humbly accepted. Joyyontoh called someone on an intercom and asked them to send the peon. Who then came and took our orders.

Q: Diary, how many people does it take to make a cup of tea in a ministry?

A: One second, let me ask Ramesh to ask Ramu and give the answer to Santosh who will then send it to your office through Kishore. Nonsense.

No wonder Allied Victory Games is in such a mess.

Kedarji asked me how Lederman could help them with AVG2010. Out of the corner of my eye, subtly, I noticed Joyyontoh taking notes.

The peon came with three glasses and one large jug of orange juice. While sipping on the juice I quickly arranged my thoughts into my usual mental analytical framework. Why tamper with a method that has been proven to work for so many years, Diary?

After profiling Lederman's Sports Practice Expertise and overall international finance horsepower, I told Kedarji about how I had a three-point plan to help him make serious money from the Allied Victory Games 2010. Enough revenues, I told him, to harvest serious political mileage for the ministry, the minister and the Prime Minister.

You should have seen the look on his face.

I then unveiled my three-point plan: 'Repurpose, Receive and Retail'. Or the '3R Plan'. Joyyontoh stopped me and asked me why it was called the 3R Plan.

Maybe the IAS examination paper leaked in his year. Idiot.

I quickly clarified.

Then I took Kedarji through each of the three Rs one by one.

Repurpose refers to efficiently using the facilities and infrastructure created for AVG2010 in a revenue-generating manner. For instance the Mahatma Gandhi Memorial Aquatics Centre could be converted into a high-end members-only aquatics club. Meanwhile at least 30 per cent of the seats and 75 per cent of the non-arena spaces could be converted into a highly lucrative conference, retailing and office complex.

Such a conversion, carried out with some specific inputs from Lederman's India team, could provide the AVG2010 with crores in revenues over several years.

At which point Kedarji told me that all the infrastructure created for the Games will be handed over to the Delhi PWD and respective sporting bodies after the Games. The ministry of urban regeneration had nothing to do with facilities. So revenue potential was zero. 'Big zero,' reiterated Joyyontoh the bastard.

Which is why, I said, we should particularly focus on my second R: Receive. With some time still left for the Games there was huge potential for Kedarji to generate tremendous revenues from the Games in the form of Games-specific visitor traffic and spending. For instance the ministry could set up an exclusive air ticket and hotel booking website for AVG2010 that athletes, their friends, families and other supporters could use to make all their bookings. In addition this website could also offer value-added services like tourism, bespoke luxury packages, car hires, chauffeurs, events, wine tastings, yoga sessions, Dharavi tours, etc. According to my rough estimates the potential was worth tens of crores.

The minister said this was very good and that he would share my plans with the Delhi Tourism Development Corporation which was exclusively in charge of all visitor interface and bookings.

Exactly, I told him with commendable nonchalance, this is why what the ministry really needed to do was focus on our final and most important R: Retail. In other words: AVG2010 was a unique opportunity to sell truckloads of superb merchandise.

I paused for a second to see if this stupid, nonsense, urine-smelling ministry at least had the rights to sell merchandise. Simultaneously I did some self-brainstorming and came up with a few backup Rs:

Reputation: Using the global opportunity of the Games to reach out to foreign trade delegations to visit Delhi during the period and thereby creating FDI worth crores upon crores of rupees.

Rejuvenation: Develop sports participation programmes for Delhi citizens thereby improving local health, reducing local dependence on public and private health care and creating crores upon crores of savings for the government.

Rehabilitation: Blah blah blah crores upon crores of something.

After all this bloody effort I wasn't going to leave this bloody ministry without getting something or the other. What is the point of living in a democracy, Diary, if you can't even get a small contract from your government? This is why China is progressing so much while we are still sending illegal immigrants all over the world.

The minister said that this was a very good idea. PRAISE THE LORD DEIVAME! One of the few revenue-generating opportunities given to the ministry was to sell AVG2010 merchandise. Kedarji said that someone in the ministry was supposed to work on a retailing plan. He asked Joyyontoh who it was. Joyyontoh immediately called someone on the intercom and asked them to investigate.

By now it was already 8 p.m. The minister looked at the time, got up and said that he had been very impressed with my performance during the BBC interview. He was prepared to hire Lederman to handle the merchandising planning process. But there was a condition: He wanted me to personally help him deal with the media and public relations.

COMPLICATION!

Getting a contract from the ministry is one thing. But sitting in this fellow's office helping him answer interviews every day is different. First of all how can an office function without the constant overseeing and leadership of the interim CEO? Also, this is the first year Lederman will be hiring summer interns in India. Head Office will be watching very closely. Annual offsite is also there. Who has the time to teach the minister public outreach and business communications?

Certainly not Einstein. Even if he is quite possibly the man best suited to the job.

Secondly, given the fact that Lederman still hasn't decided on a full-time India CEO, it is extremely unsafe to be away from office for long periods of time.

Now most of my colleagues are decent fellows and there is 95 per cent unanimous opinion in the office that I am the natural choice to lead Lederman India into the next stage of our growth and development.

But sometimes I get the vague feeling that perhaps one or two of them try to undermine me in office. Not that I have tried to figure out who these people are. Who has the time for petty politics when there is a business to run, Diary? But once in a while Sugandh has a casual look at their email inboxes. He had suggested that I keep an eye on reimbursement-fraud-superstar Raghu Khanna and Internet-misuse-maestro Rajeev Rao.

Last week, during our morning meeting, I asked Raghu what the telecom sector was looking like. He looked up at the ceiling for ten seconds and then looked at me and said, 'The sector looks like this.' And then burst out laughing. Everyone else also laughed.

BASTARD! THIS IS COMEDY? YOU ARE TEACHING ME SITUATIONAL COMEDY?? BASTARD THINKS HE IS JAGATHI SREEKUMAR.

But for the sake of team morale I laughed along with everybody else. And then asked him to urgently send me a sector profile of telecom in the standard Lederman 150-slide sector profile format. I casually phoned John in Tokyo and informed him that Raghu would send him the profile in twenty-four hours.

HOW IS THE SITUATIONAL COMEDY NOW? LAUGH NOW BASTARD.

Just because we are both technically vice-presidents . . .

Anyway.

In such a tense and highly uncertain atmosphere it may not be wise to leave the office unsupervised. So I told Kedarji that personally attending to his press duties may be very difficult given my time commitments and leadership obligations.

Kedarji asked Joyyontoh how much the proposed merchandise finance plan was. Joyyontoh picked up the phone, asked somebody, then cut the phone and said: '43 crore minimum . . .'

Immediately, I reminded the minister, the sign of a modern company is that leadership is a state of mind rather than a physical paradigm. Over the last three years I had built a team more than capable of taking care of themselves. Therefore I had no hesitation in offering my full services to the nation in general, and the ministry of urban regeneration and public sculpture in particular. If Lederman India was going to be affected . . . well, so be it.

Kedarji looked extremely pleased. He shook my hands, hugged me, said 'romba nalla romba nalla' four or five times. And then asked me to join him for dinner at Bukhara. I immediately accepted.

(I only need expenditure of 12,000 more rupees this month to get free Rolls-Royce test-drive on my American Express points. Fingers crossed.)

Minister might look like some country zamindar type. But apparently he drinks only Pinot Grigio. And that too by the bottle. But then last moment he insisted that he would pay for dinner.

(Fuck.)

Spent the whole day today drawing up paperwork. The minister has asked me to visit him at 9.30 a.m. tomorrow to go through some press releases and then close the assignment.

Very, very tired. But also very satisfied.

Diary, what can I say? Now not only am I running the Indian office of a major international financial services behemoth, but I am also genuinely making a difference to how this country itself is being run. Who knows how this MURPS project will turn out? If it goes well, and AVG2010 are a success . . . who knows?

But first things first, I need to get this contract signed. Now I know that the ministry is full of 100 per cent potential Vigilance Department cases like Coffee Peon, Horse Peon and Joyyontoh. (That is his full name, Diary. Joyyontoh. He does not have a surname. I am not joking. His legal name genuinely has only a first name and no other name. Kedarji calls him 'Principal'.)

But I have a feeling the minister himself is a decent chap. Frankly I was expecting to meet some kind of seventy-year-old dinosaur who believes in child marriage and honour killing. (Or even honour killing during child marriage. God only knows what happens in rural Haryana and Maharashtra.)

But this fellow is a nice, knowledgeable forty-six-year-old. I have a feeling that this could be the beginning of a very, very mutually beneficial relationship. It took a week's worth of humiliation to get through to Kedarji. But it seems utterly worth it.

I want to tell you how pleased I am. But I don't have the energy.

Back to work. So much to do. So little time.

Sometimes I wish for the simpler times back at Dufresne when all I had to do was make bullshit PowerPoint.

Real work is so hard.

Talk to you later. I also need to draw up a vision document for our summer internship strategy for this year. Thrissur Pooram is going on in my email inbox. So many people to respond to.

**10.23 p.m.**

Diary, you know as well as I do that I am not an expert on the topic of love. After all how many bilateral relationships have I been in? Just this one with Gouri.

But even with limited exposure to the inner workings of the female mind I am beginning to come to grips with it.

Today I said to myself: 'Okay fine, Gouri got upset. She thinks I have humiliated her. But we are not children. Give her some time and she will become okay. Sometimes it will take two days. Sometimes it will take two weeks. Sometimes, when you spend the entire weekend at her house talking to her slightly younger but vastly more athletic squash champion cousin, Jesal, from Baroda while Gouri is suffering from viral fever, it will take two months.

But eventually, after her anger has cooled down and her biological processes have returned to normal, she will revert to her normal state. Eventually love will triumph.

Therefore I was not worried too much initially about the ongoing Colonel Kalbag fiasco.

But this is now getting out of hand. Four times today she called me up, screamed at me for exactly seven minutes. And then cut the phone. And each time she screamed exactly the same thing.

My family blah blah humiliation blah blah you have no respect blah blah how will I convince them blah blah south Indian blah blah you don't understand blah blah. Ente deivame.

Fed up.

What is that stupid confusing movie in which that fellow gets hit on the head or something and keeps forgetting things and then suddenly the entire movie is playing backwards but also forwards and also motherfucking sideways and everybody dies and you want to burn the theatre down for wasting your time?

Right now my love life is like that movie. Except in the movie the lucky fellows all died peacefully. Here I have to hear Gouri scream over and over and over and over again.

Then five minutes ago Sugandh called me about some latest developments in Raghu's email inbox and I instinctively picked up the phone and started saying, 'Sorry Gouri, I can see how this has hurt you. It was entirely my fault. Is there any way I can make this up to you . . .'

Sugandh just laughed and laughed.

Note this down, Diary: At least 25 per cent of love is apology.

Okay, phone is ringing again. Gouri only.

**12.03 a.m.**

Had a long two-hour chat that has helped to calm both of us down.

She is still very upset. But even she had to accept that I had absolutely no motive in pissing off the Colonel, embarrassing myself or embarrassing Gouri at the airport and afterwards. No motive at all. And besides, I told her, if I had wanted to sabotage the meeting I would have done it in a much more professional manner.

Maybe I would have shaken hands with the Colonel and then pointed at his wife and said: 'But there was no need for you to bring domestic help with you! We have plenty of good help here already . . .'

Or I would have come wearing my world famous metallic purple shirt with the yellow flowers and the large pineapple on the back.

Even in her agitated state of mind just the mention of the shirt made Gouri laugh. She hates it very much.

I told her that there was no conspiracy here.

We've decided to plan a proper meeting with her family. But not immediately. I want to let things cool with the Colonel. He doesn't seem the kind of guy who forgets things easily.

## 8 October 2009

### 7.43 a.m.

EXCITING DAY! CONTRACT SIGNING DAY! AVG2010 PROJECT
FINALIZING DAY! SO EXCITED!

### 8.34 a.m.

Inauspicious start to the day. But that is to be expected in this office
full of idiots.

Walked into my corner office, opened the door and immediately
tripped over a stack of massive yellow packets kept just on the other
side of the door. I went flying through the air and landed with my
face slapped flat on the desk. For a few moments I just stayed still,
waiting for the pain to subside and the feeling to return to the right
side of my face.

And then I slowly got up. Lightly checked for fracture or stroke.
Sat in my chair. And contemplated upon this unexpected turn of
events.

Why, in the name of Sergei Bubfuck, was there a massive stack of
packets on the floor in front of my desk? This was not something
Raghu or Rajeev would do, it was not public enough. They prefer to
humiliate me only in front of other people.

I called Sugandh. He said the packets were delivered by Amol. I
told him to send the office boy right away.

Amol came and told me that the packets had been sent to me for
immediate checking by our new HR intern in the Mumbai office.

I asked him why he left them on the floor.

He told me that he had to leave them somewhere where I would
notice them immediately.

I pointed at the table.

He reminded me that I had banned him from leaving things on
my table. (I had gone for a long weekend break to Ranikhet with
Gouri. Amol left a client gift on the table. The packet had some
imported cheese or something inside. By the time I came back the

33

whole office was smelling like Chennai airport. My keyboard had hair growing from it. Took almost a month for the smell to go and the 'K' button to work properly.)

So he decided to leave it right behind the door so that I would notice it as soon as I entered.

I asked him why he didn't just leave a note for me and leave the packets somewhere in one corner.

Amol asked me where he would keep the note. On the table? But that is banned.

On my table I have a small Statue of Liberty that Gouri brought me as a souvenir when she went to Singapore for training. (Clarification: It has Statue of Liberty body but Buddha face. I like it. Has a nice East-meets-West vibe.) I swear to god I was THIS close to picking it up and inserting it into Amol.

I called Sugandh into my room and told him to never let Amol enter my cabin again. If there were things to be delivered Sugandh would do what was needed.

So now, Diary, I have a stack of dozens of summer placement résumés from all the institutes to process as well.

When do I take a break?

Off to the ministry now. Talk to you later when I return in triumph having secured yet another client.

**11.23 a.m.**

Even more paperwork. Also Joyyontoh is not what it seems. More soon.

**3.17 p.m.**

For the last three hours, Diary, I have been trying to arrange for quotations. FOR THREE HOURS. Running up and down the building trying to pull favours from all kinds of shady people. Thankfully Sugandh and the guys at Fundango were able to help.

So in the morning I went to the ministry. The minister was not available but Joyyontoh as usual was ready to help me. I handed him a copy of the contract and asked him when he could get it signed by the minister. He looked at me and then giggled for a few seconds. He asked me if I had ever done work with the government before.

I honestly told him that I had not. And that Lederman had been trying to break into public sector projects for years.

He then sat down and told me how to proceed. First of all, he said, no contract was accepted without some sort of a competitive bidding process. Even if the minister concerned had already chosen who to give the contract to.

I asked him how long this took. He said it could take anywhere from three to six months. (Sudden vomiting sensation came.)

But AVG2010 itself would take place in that time! I told the buffoon there was no way we could take care of the financial plan, pricing strategy, inventory management plan and all the other things required to get merchandising off the ground in just six months. WE HAD TO START RIGHT NOW!

He thought about it for a while. And then said that given the Prime Minister's urgency perhaps the ministry could approve the paperwork at high speed.

But the competitive bids were a must. Otherwise the ministry would be seen to have given the project without transparency.

And transparency is essential.

Joyyontoh then outlined a plan. He would put out a tender for financial and advisory services for the merchandising as soon as possible. With a deadline of one or two weeks. In the meantime I would go and arrange for at least three bids including Lederman's. Of course Lederman's had to be lowest.

If all went according to plan the ministry would only get my three quotes, I would get the contract and then things would proceed as planned.

It sounded like a good plan. I asked Joyyontoh if he was absolutely sure that everything was legal in this process. Ever since Jeremy Jones took over from Tom as global head, Lederman has been very strict about our ethics. (Except in China.)

Joyyontoh looked at me quietly for a second. And then told me something that I don't think I will ever forget.

Mr Varghese, he said, do you know why people want a government?

Joyyontoh was looking out of the window, his eyes glazed, his face a portrait of somewhat mystic introspection, looking at a very large monkey on the tree outside. The monkey was looking elsewhere.

'People choose a government to do things they don't want to do themselves. Do you want to clean a road, maintain a toilet, construct a railway, kill Pakistanis or torture terrorists? Do you, Mr Varghese?'

No, I said.

'Exactly. Government only has to do all this. But this is a very tough job. Why?' Joyyontoh got up and walked to the window while talking.

'Why is this hard? Because on the one hand you want us to function according to rules and regulations. But on the other hand you want us to do all your dirty work for you. How is this fair, Mr Varghese? How?'

He slowly opened the window.

'Voting or paying taxes is the easiest thing. But making government work with all these rules and regulations is extremely difficult.' There was a small bowl of decorative marble balls on a table under the window. Joyyontoh slowly picked up one.

'These rules are there because the people are afraid. The people are afraid of the same government they bring to power.' He kept talking while still looking out of the window.

'They are saying to us: We want you to be powerful. Powerful enough to kill the enemy or hang criminals. But not so powerful that you will turn on us. We want to control you. Like an animal in a cage. And we want to constantly remind you that you are an animal in a cage.'

He raised the arm with the marble ball in it. By now the monkey was looking at him. Eyeball to eyeball. Monkey to Joyyontoh.

My heart began to pound wildly.

'So all this tender and quotation and all . . . simply the public's way of putting us in our place. They know. They know very well that if every government office in India followed these rules properly . . .'

He slowly, gently withdrew his right hand, the marble ball still caressed in his fingers.

'Then nothing would ever get done in this country. Even today we will be organizing the 1982 Asian Games.

'So my duty is to look at these rules and say: Thank you Public. I am aware of your superiority and your power to tell me what to do. Duly acknowledged. Now will you please fuck off while the government gets down to work?'

He released the marble ball like a bullet. The monkey did not even have a chance. It hit him exactly over his left eye. The ball bounced off at an angle. The next moment the monkey fell like a stone on top of a small Mahatma Gandhi statue in the ministry garden outside.

'I hate monkeys,' Joyyontoh said as he came and sat down. 'Do you want any tea or coffee?'

I refused politely.

He then told me to go arrange for three quotes as soon as possible while he got on with the tender process. Joyyontoh told me to get them from anywhere. Later, if required, he would draw up a qualification criteria to disqualify other bidders. I left the office in a daze. By the time I got downstairs to the garden, the monkey had vanished.

I had underestimated Joyyontoh. To me he looked like a buffoon. But inside that soft Bengali exterior is a shrewd, smart, ruthless operator.

By the time I reached office I had made up my mind on next steps. I called in Sugandh for a secret meeting. When it comes to creative business concepts like fake quotations and clearing couriers through customs Sugandh is the Lederman India point person.

He said that this would be very easy indeed. Most companies in Delhi, he said, were well aware of the government tendering process. In fact some of them in our own building might be open to the idea of helping us out. He said he'd ask around using the building IT engineer network and figure out who'd be up for it.

So for the last three hours both of us have been slogging away like animals. But finally we've solved the problem. Sugandh discovered that the dry cleaning guy downstairs has an uncle who owns a chit fund in Faridabad under the name of Indo-European Financial

Services Corporation. We had to pay him some money. But we will receive a box of IEFSC letterheads in two days.

Meanwhile I had to personally go to Fundango and spend an hour there talking to their CEO. I still don't completely get what they do. Some kind of online sales or marketing or consulting or something. Nobody looked like they were working in the office. Most of them were on Facebook.

In fact Harish doesn't even have a cabin. He just sits in a cubicle like everybody else. Weird socialist culture.

Harish, like me, seemed bothered about the legality of the whole thing. But in the end he agreed to help if I would later put him in touch with my extensive business contacts network and help him find 'social strategy projects'. (Who knows?)

Hopefully by the end of the week I should get all the quotes prepared. John in Tokyo has already started working on the bona fide Lederman proposal.

I must admit that I am not as pumped up as I was in the morning. Delays are so painful, Diary. But that is the government for you.

Now off to read résumés. I know I make it sound like hard work. But in reality I enjoy it. Feels like peering into the lives of utter strangers.

Gouri update: Her cousin in Baroda just sent me a Facebook friend request. I have accepted. Better to consolidate all piss-offy things when it comes to Gouri. Saves both of us time and energy.

## 9 October 2009

**1.54 p.m.**

I thought I'd take a five-minute break to update you on some troublesome developments. But I am too hungry, Diary. And I don't have the patience to order something from Subway. Will go there directly.

Back in a flash.

**3.13 p.m.**

Guess who I spotted while walking to Subway?

Gouri.

You should have seen what she was wearing. Fed up.

Diary, I have seen that woman wear some very very disturbing clothing in the last few years. When we went to Goa for Amba's wedding I told her a thousand times that we should wear normal ethnic clothes and go for the ceremonies. But no! We are in Goa no?? We should dress like bloody British people and go no?

In the end I wore a proper formal suit and she spent half a month's salary on a purple gown by that unbearable designer fellow who works out of a toilet in New Friends Colony market. (But my Bose headphones I can only buy later because we are saving for marriage. Feel like punching the wall.)

Of course Amba and Gautam decided that they wanted to have a traditional Iyengar wedding in Goa. The only other people at the entire function wearing Western formals were the catering fellows. Even bloody Gautam's friends from Boston came dressed in Fabindia kurtas.

It was so embarrassing. They even asked the photographers to specifically leave us out of pictures.

So far, thank god, she has never worn that embarrassment again. Horrible dress. Starts without a problem at the shoulders and maintains normalcy till the waist. Then suddenly it falls vertically in three layers of silk, lace and satin all mixed up together in one purple tornado as if the layers of fabric were engaged in a death struggle.

But today was even worse. She was wearing an extremely tight fluorescent yellow top, with a pair of extremely tight knee-length purple exercise pants and running shoes. And just standing without shame near the Subway at Outer Circle.

She was just about to enter Fighting Fit gym when I ran into her. Everybody was looking at her and I quickly pulled her into the Subway. I asked her the meaning of this nonsense. She told me she had just joined the gym, that it was very expensive, that she had a personal training session, that she had to go back to office as soon as she was done and that she would explain things later.

I told her she could have saved money by just standing outside Subway dressed like that, wait for one or two rapists to come and then run for her life thereby getting excellent cardio training.

She just laughed at me, told me that she was doing this to somehow get Colonel Kalbag to calm down.

Then she insisted she come with me and order my sandwich for me. Six-inch kakkoos sandwich with greens, paneer, some mustard and oil.

I walked back to office. And then bought a Kit Kat (small) from the building canteen.

Back to work.

**7.43 p.m.**

I am terribly upset, Diary.

Now I know that Lederman India is not the biggest name in business school recruitment in this country. We are a small firm. We are a new firm. All that is okay.

But nothing can explain this rubbish they have sent us in the name of candidate profiles. The quality is very very poor. So far I have read 360 profiles. And not even fifteen are engineers from IITs. Not even fifteen, Diary!

Might as well just go to Connaught Place and randomly pick up people as summer interns no? Instead of all these dreadful fellows from . . . one second . . .

HOW MANY PEOPLE WITH ANY SELF-RESPECT OR AMBITION STUDY CIVIL ENGINEERING THESE DAYS? THAT TOO FROM SANTHANAGOPLAN EDUCATIONAL SOCIETY IN CHAKAN, PUNE???? WHAT DID HE SCORE IN ENTRANCE EXAMINATION? MINUS 79 PERCENTILE?

Diary, you will not even believe the quality of some of these idiots. One fellow's greatest passion in life is 'Pink Floyd'. No, seriously. He has a sub-section on his résumé called 'Passions' and it has seven bullet points on Pink Floyd. He is even planning to write a semi-autobiographical book on growing up with Floyd. As if his uncle is the lead singer. Fool.

Also one girl from Calcutta has given the Prime Minister as a reference. The actual Prime Minister. With phone number and all. HA HA HA HA. Boss, you lie on your résumé. That is natural of MBA students. But this is too much. (Still, I have shortlisted just in case.)

So far I have shortlisted a total of around fifty or sixty people. The best of the worst. Some ten to twelve of them are Malayalis. But I am not keeping track or anything.

Many many more still left. Will read tomorrow. I should have delegated this to some of the other vice-presidents like Sharmila suggested. But how did I know that these students would all be such lying, incompetent, illiterate fucks.

## 11 October 2009

**12.12 a.m.**

Anushka Sharma is the Raveena Tandon of this generation. Just an observation.

*Rab Ne Bana Di Jodi* is excellent. That is how you wear exercise clothes. Should somehow subtly indicate to Gouri.

**2.12 p.m.**

Okay, so this year, for the first batch of Lederman India summer interns, I've decided to interview around 100 people across the top five campuses.

Not me personally. I will die if I have to interview all of these underachieving morons. But I will probably handle Ahmedabad and Calcutta. And let Raghu and Rajeev handle the rest. They will try to play politics there also. But what is the worst that can happen. We only need five or six interns this year. And they will only be around for two months.

In any case by summer next year we should have a full-time CEO whose name will rhyme with 'Rockin' Fine-style Parties'.

Ha ha. I am still nervous about this whole CEO thing though. All is in Joyyontoh/Kedarji's hands now.

**2.15 p.m.**

'Rockin' Fine-style Smarties'. More balanced I think.

**6.10 p.m.**

Had a long chat with Sharmila about why the quality of résumés was so poor.

She reckons it is a matter of visibility. Lederman India simply isn't a big enough name on campus to draw the cream of the crop. Sharmila thinks it will improve dramatically next year when the current set of interns go back and give good feedback.

But I am wondering if the secret to visibility is a couple of big bang interactive events held on campus that will really draw in the best of the batch and get them to experience the real Lederman.

Diary, I can feel the wheels in my head turning. I can feel some superb sparks of brilliance forming. If there is one thing I am good at it is high-calibre, high-intensity communication. A huge campus event is exactly the kind of thing I can execute out of the park.

## 14 October 2009

**9.06 a.m.**

All three quotations have come. And will be sent to the ministry this afternoon. At 12 per cent of total revenue from merchandising, Lederman's quote is by far the best. Wink. Nudge.

**11.12 a.m.**

Where the heck is my Montblanc pen? I am very pained.

**4.22 p.m.**

Tomorrow is going to be a traumatic day. Joyyontoh is coming for a meeting after lunch. And Gouri wants to meet for dinner. (Stir-fried lettuce with lettuce salad and lettuce pickle served with lettuce sauce.)

Which means I won't be able to eat in peace the whole fucking day. Must try to have a very large breakfast.

## 22 October 2009

**10.22 p.m.**

Sit down somewhere comfortable, Diary. We have a LOT to talk about.

A few days ago Joyyontoh came to office for a meeting. And he brought two pieces of very bad news.

First, Kedarji is suddenly not as enthusiastic as he used to be. He is now sitting on the quotations without any urgency. Joyyontoh said that there was nothing to worry. It is just that the minister has so many things going on. And he makes so many commitments to so many people that you should not take everything he says at face value.

The second piece of bad news is this: Joyyontoh has my Montblanc pen. I remember taking it to the ministry last time, when he assassinated the monkey. I used it to take notes in Joyyontoh's office.

No doubt, Diary. It is the same pen. He used it to make some minor corrections on the quotation documents and I noticed the 'REV' engraving on the pen. I casually asked him where he got the pen.

Joyyontoh said that his son who worked for Wipro in Geneva bought it for him last Diwali. (Bastard! Joyyontoh I mean. Not his son. But son also most probably.)

In which case, I asked him, what did the initials stand for?

Joyyontoh looked at the pen for five seconds and then said that the initials stood for the three people who had the most influence on his life: Rabindranath Tagore, Vivekananda and Eknath Solkar. (Solkar is a real person. I checked.) Joyyontoh is such a bastard.

But thank god this fellow is on my side.

While leaving the office Joyyontoh gave me a very useful piece of advice. Despite having moved into the building nine months ago we still haven't decided what to do with the pedestal outside reception. I want to do something with modern art. But corporate policy only allows us to put up sculptures and art of locally significant real people or places. And nothing religious. So now, for the time being we just keep a bouquet of flowers on it.

Joyyontoh suggested that I could do something with the pedestal to make the minister happy. Maybe a new statue. I could then invite the minister to do an 'official' inauguration of the office and unveil a suitable sculpture. 'Out of sight is out of mind, Mr Varghese,' Joyyontoh said looking very very evil as he got into his car.

Perfect job for Sugandh. He is now doing background research on Kedarji's taste in art.

That evening I had dinner with Gouri. We went to some Japanese-cum-Chinese-cum-Thai place. I had chicken stir-fry. She had soup and salad. (I bought KFC on the way home after dropping her.)

Frankly, I don't get the point of stir-fry. A dish with a lack of commitment. Is it a starter? Is it a main course? Is it a sandwich filling? But she wouldn't let me order any proper food.

Gouri has come with a new plan for me to impress the Colonel.

The Colonel is passionate about physical fitness and discipline. And has already joined Fighting Fit for the two months he is here in Delhi.

Gouri, of course, is already going there every day, laminated in plastic. Now she asked me also to sign up immediately, start working out, and bond with the Colonel at the gym. That is the only way, she said, I could meet him regularly, impress him, and eventually get his approval for more serious family-level discussions about our alliance.

I agreed immediately. Her plan, as usual, made little practical sense. But KFC closed at 11.30 p.m. and I didn't want to waste time.

WHOA. One second.

**11.22 p.m.**

I am back.

Gouri's cousin in Baroda, Jesal, put up a Facebook photo of her playing squash. I started looking at that and other photos and then time just started flying. Sorry about that.

Anyway. So yes. I have joined the gym and went for two free trial sessions. It is a decent gym. Lots of machines and all kinds of complicated classes. I don't want to go.

But then what is love if not a lifetime of doing irritating things for other people to prevent them from getting even more irritating?

I will most probably sign up for membership tomorrow.

As usual Sugandh has done a splendid job. The minister, he has discovered, has been a lifelong devotee of Maratha hero Sivaji. Who, of course, is a real person and of Indian relevance.

If that is what it takes to get the minister to sign the bloody contract, so be it.

Sharmila is commissioning a small statue from our central art fund in New York. I've told them to get it done as soon as humanly possible. Even if it means modifying some existing statue to make it look like Sivaji.

Bloody headaches at work and at home. When do I get the time to do any actual work? Fed up of leadership.

## 27 October 2009

**8.16 p.m.**

OH YEAH BABY! OH YEAH! PUMP IT UP PUMP IT UP PUMP IT UP.

TOO PUMPED UP TO TYPE. LATER BITCH!!!!!

**9.53 p.m.**

Sorry about that, Diary. The last few days have been the most physically active week in my life. I've been hitting the gym every day after work and burning through hundreds of calories. Running, spinning, weights, cardio.

I'VE NEVER FELT BETTER ABOUT MYSELF!

There was a lot of tension in the beginning when I went to sign up. Fighting Fit has six levels of basic memberships with a further seven levels of additional special packages. And then there is a further surcharge for off-peak and on-peak use. Which means every new member has to choose from eighty-four different types of membership plans.

UTTER FRAUD. Fuckers thought they could get me to sign up for an unnecessarily expensive plan by confusing me. Been there! Done that! Fuck off!

I told them to give me whatever membership Gouri was using: Rs 6700 per month for full on-peak use plus sauna/steam and three free personal training sessions per month. The Fat Burner Plan.

The girl at the counter (excellent physique, tragically asymmetric face) told me that Gouri's offer was no longer available.

So I told her to sign me up for the most basic scheme: the 'Simply Sweat' plan at Rs 3500/month for use of all machines during off-peak hours. She asked me if I wanted roaming facility in case I wanted to use the other Fighting Fits in Delhi. She said that this made sense for busy corporate professionals like me who were always on the road.

Of course it did. So I moved up to the 'Simply Sweat and Roam' plan for a minor surcharge. I was just about to sign the contract when suddenly she stopped me.

She asked me how frequently I would visit the gym. I told her that since I was paying so much money I would come at least four days a week. Often more.

In which case she said I should really not be wasting time with all these amateur plans meant for housewives and instead go for a proper frequent user plan which came with rewards and cash back offers.

The 'Ultra Sweat and Roam' deal was actually very good. Every time I completed ten visits to the gym I would get a coupon that I could exchange for training or classes. And every month I visited the gym more than twenty times I would get a 15 per cent discount on the next month.

Just the kind of incentive I need to really take the whole thing seriously.

And then just before I was about to sign she asked me if I had ever used a sauna to detox my body and refresh my skin.

I swear to god I wanted to pick up the small decorative dumb-bell on her table and restore symmetry to her face. I told her to shut the marketing and complete my contract.

At which exact moment Jesal walked into the gym and came and stood next to me at the reception. The last time I met her was when Gouri and I threw a Navratri dance party last year. She only popped in for a few hours and left for what must have been a much cooler party. But I didn't notice her much because of soooooooo many backless blouses. (Why is this trend not taking off in Kerala?)

But this is the first I'd run into her after that evening.

Diary, at that very moment the rest of the world faded into black. It vanished. Only Jesal remained.

Only perfect, athletic, toned Jesal. With her endless legs, muscular yet feminine biceps, tiny delicate wrists and that high, high, impossibly high ponytail.

And she was dressed exactly like Anushka in *Rab Ne Bana Di Jodi*. Exactly. Blue top. Blue headband. White pants. Spotless sneakers.

It took me several seconds to get my breath back. Jesal punched me on the shoulder and said hello. She was in Delhi to see Colonel Kalbag and the family. She was also trying to find an internship somewhere. Because she was already a member of Fighting Fit in Surat, with national roaming facility, she'd come down for her daily workout.

Now I had several challenges to overcome. First of all I had to make complete words in my mouth and say them. Secondly I had to look her in the eyes while saying them. Simultaneously my brain was already making scenarios of how there would be a terror attack at Connaught Place while both of us were in the sauna during off-peak hours and we had no option but to stay inside the gym wrapped in turkey towels for safety. But she is scared. Very scared. And so she comes to me and asks me if I think both of us will die. I reach up and hold her bare shoulders, sparks flying in my brain as my naked palms caress her smooth yet firm flesh. 'Don't worry, Jesal. If we die, we die. Let us at least be happy while we are alive.'

And then the receptionist intervened and asked if I would like to sign up for the Gold Medal Ironman Package with National Roaming facility like my friend Jesal.

BLOODY CHARLES SOBHRAJ RECEPTIONIST.

Jesal held me by the upper arm and shook me vigorously screaming: 'Sign up, Robin! Sign up! It is the best! It is the best package ever!'

I wavered.

'And then both of us can be gym partners whenever I am in Delhi and do couple's exercising . . .'

I handed the receptionist my credit card immediately. She told me I could start the next day itself.

Diary, the last few days have been a delightful haze of health and Jesal. I have rarely been happier.

It would have been nice to have Gouri around as well. Of course. That would have made me immensely happier. But she always exercises during her lunch break, while I prefer working out after work. And what is the point in unnecessarily shifting our schedules for such a small matter?

Gouri is thrilled I am working out. I haven't seen the Colonel in the gym yet. But Gouri has informed him of my new venture.

Meanwhile Jesal's motivating presence is helping me do justice to my expensive membership. So far we've worked out together three times. And tried three different training sessions.

The woman has the energy levels of a nuclear weapon. Personally I find it very hard to keep up with her pace. But she is not snobbish about her fitness levels at all. Yesterday, for instance, we decided to do interval training on the treadmill. Both of us took adjoining treadmills, plugged in our earphones and started.

Usually I like to run at a reasonably challenging pace of around 8.5 to 9 kilometres per hour. I can do more, of course. But the idea is to train the body. Not kill it. Jesal usually goes off at 12 kilometres per hour. Today I thought, why not push myself a little more. So I set the speed at 11 kilometres per hour. Then I did a brisk five-minute warm-up walk. And started running.

The treadmill got faster. And faster. And faster. And faster. And by now I was running with the grace of some large animal giving birth.

Which is when I noticed a small notice on the wall opposite the treadmill. The handwritten note said: 'This treadmill only, setting in miles NOT kilometres.'

FUCK.

The next few moments are still a blur.

I reached up to hit the emergency stop button when my hand got entangled in my iPod headphones. The iPod popped out of my pocket and fell on to the treadmill. Instinctively I bent down to reach for the iPod. By which point my feet were no longer in sync with the treadmill itself. The iPod went shooting out into the gym, my feet following it.

I began to fall forward. I looked to my left to see if Jesal had noticed the suboptimal turn of events.

She had not. She was looking straight ahead, intensely concentrating, and pounding away on the treadmill. Satisfied, I calmly waited as my face smashed into the emergency stop button on the panel.

I rested there on the control panel for a few seconds. Waiting for the pain to subside. And then I got up, picked up my iPod, went to the water cooler, took a glass of water, came back to the treadmill, drank some of it, and poured the rest into a small slit on the side of the panel meant for ventilation.

When the screen stopped working I moved to another treadmill where I jogged slowly while checking for any swelling. Jesal came over after a few minutes and gave me some motivation. 'No need to push, Robin. Keep going at your own pace! Come on! Five more minutes!'

After that we went for a spinning class.

Today when I went to the gym there was an 'Out of Order' sign on the treadmill.

Don't. Fuck. With. Einstein. Stupid machine.

Tomorrow is aerobics day. If Jesal moves like a dream on a treadmill, imagine her doing aerobics, Diary. I am getting goose-bumps everywhere, except side of face, just thinking about it.

A young artist from Valencia who uses CNC machines is making Sivaji for us on express order. I want this to be out of the way in another week, two weeks maximum. Then Kedarji can cut a fucking ribbon and sign off on the contract.

Have some interesting ideas for campus events. Must chat with Sharmila this week.

Rajeev wants me to take a call on the new Kingfisher Airlines financing project. I have 700 pages to read now. Later, Diary.

Having a tuna wrap for dinner.

## 30 October 2009

### 3.56 p.m.

Rahul Gupta makes a presentation for The Braithwaite Group at Ahmedabad. Twenty-four hours later seven shortlisted guys from Ahmedabad withdraw their Lederman summer internship applications.

This means war, Rahul. War. You have been warned.

### 4.33 p.m.

Emilio, the Spanish artist, has sent a sketch of the drawing. Sharmila thinks it looks odd. I don't have the time to do fucking fact-checking for an artist. Told the fucker to el shippo el sculpturo el soono as el possiblo bloody fool.

Joyyontoh says that the paperwork is perfect. Now all it needs is the minister to sign off. It is sitting on his table.

Dropped the minister an email asking him how he was coping with media queries. Told him that I look forward to working with him closely on a regular basis as soon as possible.

No reply so far.

Fucker was all 'I love you Robin! Marry me Robin! Do me slowly bent over this table Robin! Pour the dal slowly over my back Robin! Rub your face into the dal Robin!' at Bukhara.

And now he is giving attitude.

## 2 November 2009

### 10.23 a.m.

Just got a call from the ministry. I had just started to punch the air with joy when Kedarji said that he wanted me to urgently double-check a press release that the MURPS was going to publish this evening. He told me to revert latest by 2 p.m. But before I could ask about the quotation he cut the phone.

Then two seconds later Joyyontoh called me again and reminded me of the 2 p.m. deadline.

Chooths. But powerful chooths. What can I do?

### 1.47 p.m.

Finished. Sent. Under the circumstances, superlative end result.

Diary, this is actually a little humiliating. For the last three years I have worked on some of the most important projects in India. There are companies in almost every sector in India that are in operation today because Lederman India and Robin Varghese helped them raise money, place debt, etc. etc.

Who else could have secured what is wildely believed to be the most lucrative assignment in India: Project Gandhi Market. We raised capital for Kingfisher Airlines in exchange for a stock-cum-profit arrangement. Five or ten years from now, when the airline is so profitable that it serves caviar parathas to economy class passengers even on short-haul flights, Lederman India could be the most lucrative division of the company globally.

And how much did we charge companies for each hour of Robin Varghese's time? Starting from Rs 69,000 and going all the way up to Rs 1.5 lakh when we did work for that Qatar oil company whose stupid accountant used to ask us for exchange rate information.

And now I just spent more than two hours salvaging the worst press release written in the history of press releases. For free.

First of all, Diary, the press release was 1000 words long. As if journalists are sitting around India all day waiting for someone to send them long articles which they can just copy-paste.

The trick with press releases is focus, brevity, humour, accuracy and simplicity.

Kedarji's original release had the following distribution of ridiculous words:

Esteemed: 17 times

Honourable: 32 times

Inclusive: 11 times

Nodal: 46 times

Capacity-building: 9 times

It also contained this line which, by itself, is enough to win the Nobel Prize for Literature:

> The immediate challenge in the case of the Allied Victory Games 2010 is to appropriately calibrate the organizational and coordinative policies for addressing the risks from preparatory shortcomings that may spill over into the inter-ministerial understanding on cooperation that has been active since the Allied Victory Games were notified appropriately in 2004.

Diary, if you want I can stab you with a pen or something to end the agony.

WHO. THE. FUCK. WRITES. LIKE. THIS?

I spent half an hour trying to make edits on the document. Then I gave up. I was so frustrated that I called one of the new analysts and told him to make a report on leveraged finance opportunities in the sugar cane industry. I told him to do it in two hours. You should have seen the poor fellow's face.

(I can see him at his workstation. Slogging away. Poor fellow.)

That cheered me up. And then I sat down and wrote a new one.

Total waste of time actually. This is a press release about future press releases. Seriously.

Anyway sent it off.

My calendar is full of things to do. Summer hiring. Statue (puke). Gym. AVG2010. CEO politics. Wooing Gouri's family. And except the gym everything is just hanging in the air.

Anyway time to start reviewing all our open projects and pitches. No point in letting day-to-day work suffer because of one stupid minister.

**4.01 p.m.**

HA HA HA HA HA HA. Poor analyst came running just now with a massive sugar cane sector overview. Chumma I asked him if he had also included sugar beets and corn-based sweeteners. He looked devastated. I told him to urgently go and include that information as soon as humanly possible.

He ran away, Diary. Ha ha ha ha. Poor fellow.

Very satisfying.

**8.12 p.m.**

Still at work. Still reviewing reports. The good news is that Emilio has sent a prototype of the statue in plastic by courier. If it is good enough I am going to just get the minister ass-licking done with as soon as possible using the prototype.

The press release was sent out to the media as is. Of course.

I am pasting a copy here. Not my best work. But not my worst either.

### MINISTRY OF URBAN REGENERATION AND PUBLIC SCULPTURE

**Ministry of Urban Regeneration and Public Sculpture (MURPS) Announces Comprehensive Reporting and Media Coordination Plan for Allied Victory Games 2010**

INTRODUCTION AND BACKGROUND: The Allied Victory Games were first held in Coventry in 1948 as a celebration of the sports and games of the Allied powers in the Second World War. What began as a symbol of the return of peace and prosperity to the world in general and Europe in particular, quickly became one of the most important sporting events in the world. Today the esteemed Allied Victory Games are fourth only to the Olympics Games, Asian Games and Commonwealth Games as the largest assembly of international sportspersons in one place.

The next edition of the Games, to be held in Delhi in 2010, is a special one. It will be the largest Allied Victory Games since the Toulouse edition of 1968 which is the last one in which the United States took part. The US withdrew that year in order to focus on the Olympics. Subsequently, after many years of financial instability, the Games received a boost in 2002 when both Germany and Japan joined as full members of the Allied Nations Games Federation.

Delhi will witness the first time that both countries will send teams for the Allied Victory Games. This makes the 2010 edition significant for many reasons. It will be the largest sporting event ever held in India. Thus underlining India's role as a global emerging power with an enviable GDP growth rate of well over 8 per cent. It will also showcase a long-overdue emotional unity between nations and the healing of old wounds.

The successful conduct of the Allied Victory Games 2010 is a matter of immense importance for both our country and the world.

NODAL AGENCY: In 2002 Delhi beat Tripoli to win the bid to hold the 2010 Games. Subsequently the Government of India and the esteemed Indian Olympic Association formed a joint Empowered Committee to oversight the planning, execution and conduct of the Games. At the time it was decided that the MURPS would serve as the nodal agency for inter-ministerial coordination, oversight and public relations for all non-sports-related activities.

RENEWED URGENCY: Subsequent to the Prime Minister's address to the Lok Sabha on 3 October 2009 concerning the status of AVG2010 projects Shri Badrikedar Laxmanrao

Dahake, the minister with oversight of the nodal agency, initiated a new reporting and media coordination plan called the Mahatma Gandhi Media Games First Initiative (MGMGFI).

Henceforth the MURPS will publish monthly MGMGFI updates on AVG2010 progress comprising status reports from all non-sports ministries and departments. From May 2010 these reports will be issued on a weekly basis. An exclusive MGMGFI website will be set up on the Internet to enable access to all the reports.

In addition, on a case-to-case basis, the ministry will convene press interactions in order to convey the state of preparedness to the esteemed Indian and international media.

We hope this MGMGFI initiative will help to make the Allied Victory Games 2010 a rousing success.

For further information kindly contact the undersigned:

Joyyontoh

Principal Secretary, MURPS and Nodal Oversight (AVG2010)
Email: joy_tagore_mohunbagan-illichmaach@yahoo.co.uk
Website: http://murps.nic.in/mgmgfi

**10.11 p.m.**

SMS from Gouri: 'Hope you are enjoying the gym sessions. This is why I know despite all issues you really do love me very much. Thank you Goosey.'

Diary, you note this down: Women are the easiest things in the world to handle provided you don't have any self-respect.

Jesal wants to try some dance-fitness-type thing tomorrow. Why not?

# 7 November 2009

**12.09 p.m.**

Statue has come. I am off to the ministry to plan the fraud ceremony as soon as possible. Not a single phone call or email from the ministry after I salvaged that press release. Thankless fucks.

**4.32 p.m.**

Kedarji will come to office day after tomorrow. You should have seen his face when I gave him the invitation and courtesy gift (Longines watch). As if I bloody gave him Anushka Sharma to take home.

Sharmila is organizing some fraud party items and photographer and everything. Statue will remain under a curtain till the inauguration.

**5.15 p.m.**

Imagine if I could take Anushka Sharma home ...

**5.36 p.m.**

She probably comes one Saturday evening wearing something casual and comfortable. Because she is a casual kind of girl. So casual that you think when you see her: 'This Anushka! Just throws things on before leaving home. How classless!'

But, Diary, you are so, so, so wrong about her. Because behind that casual effortlessness is a method. A technique. A genius.

That evening she comes in a pair of worn jeans and a thin, pink cotton pullover. And a pair of well-used tennis shoes. Athletic yet chic. Sporty yet relaxed. Sweet yet very very sexy.

And that ponytail. High, Diary, so, so high.

When my doorbell rings my heart stops suddenly. The anticipation, Diary. The anticipation. When I open the door she is slightly surprised. 'Where is Gouri, Einstein?' she asks looking around.

Gouri, of course, knows about Anushka visiting. But she has gone for some particularly complicated gym session. And will not be back for at least two hours.

'Oh how sad,' she says. 'I was so looking forward to meeting her.' Anushka's words indicate disappointment but her eyes ... they tell a different story. A story of hope and opportunity. And delicious tension. A forbidden pleasure. (Goosebumps.)

I open a bottle of Montepulciano and pour a glass for each of us. We start talking about our lives. She talks about the movies and Shah Rukh Khan. I talk about high finance and myself.

She is seated on the far end of my long sofa, her endless legs stretched out on the leather upholstery. I settle into the adjacent armchair trying not to look too much at her abnormally proportional ankles.

'So tell me how you and Gouri met, Einstein.'

I tell her. She sits enraptured as I talk about Gouri and love and relationships and life itself. Wow, she says, there are sides to your personality that I had no idea existed. As she says this she runs her fingers through her hair and then flicks it away. As she does this she stretches upwards, arching her back, looking up at the ceiling. The sight of her perfect porcelain neck takes my breath away.

Her next words are shocking if not surprising. 'Pity you are already in a relationship, Einstein. Otherwise ...'

'Otherwise?'

She giggles. I top up her glass. I like where this conversation is going. I gently increase the volume on the Dean Martin playing on my home theatre. (Exactly like Sinatra. But much much cheaper on iTunes.)

I nonchalantly speak up. 'If indeed we were in a relationship, Anu, we wouldn't be sitting on separate sofas.'

Her eyes peer at me over the edge of her wine glass. Did I just notice her pupils dilating?

'So how would we be sitting then, Einstein? Show me. For fun.'

I get up and go sit on the sofa. She slides down and places her feet on my lap. We both giggle. I place my wine glass on the floor. And then caress her left foot with my hands. And I begin to rub it gently.

A barely audible gasp passes through her lips. I pretend not to have heard it. But focus on her foot. Slowly she reclines and reclines and finally she is fully horizontal. Her eyes shut, her mouth mumbling silent moans.

(Wine is continuously being topped up. FYI.)

My fingers move up to the synovial hinge joint (according to Wikipedia). I continue to rub, press and squeeze gently. Perhaps a little sensuously. Anushka can only moan. Now my hands stray farther up to her smooth, perfectly waxed shins. Now I can almost inhale perfume. Something floral but not overpowering.

And at that moment Sharmila walks into my cabin looking very hassled and FUCK.

### 6.42 p.m.

Tried completing that Anushka scene several times. But each time somehow Sharmila's face is coming into my mind. FUUUUUCCCCCCCCKKKKKK. Instantly my penis retracts like the CD tray on my desktop.

She is worried about our pull on campus for summer interns. And wants me to do something. Maybe a presentation or something. I told her I will handle this after the statue unveiling.

## 9 November 2009

### 1.12 a.m.

FUUUUUUUUCCCCCCCCKKKKK  FUUUUUUUCCCCCCKKKKK
FUCKING STUPID EMILIO SPANISH BASTARD FUCCCCCCKKKKK
FUCCCCCCCCCKKKKKKKK FUCCCKCKCKCK STUPID FUCKER
CAN'T EVEN GOOGLE PROPERLY. MARATHA HERO SIVAJI
MARATHA HERO!
EVERYTHING IS FUCKED.

### 6.38 p.m.

As usual while everyone else is running away or laughing at an embarrassing situation it is up to Robin Varghese to once again spontaneously think on his feet and save the company.

Kedarji, as expected, arrived at 5.45 for his 4.30 p.m. appointment. The entire team assembled outside the reception as I made a small welcome address. And then I asked Kedarji to make a short keynote address. He spoke for forty-five minutes, Diary. And forty of those minutes he was looking directly at Sharmila. Even I was beginning to feel a little violated after some time.

And then he pulled a string and the curtain came off the statue.

Immediately the room began to spin around my head. Kedarji looked at the statue puzzled. Sharmila had her face in her hands. And Raghu and Rajeev immediately added value to the situation by giggling like slutty schoolgirls. Bastards.

Once again Sugandh, no doubt the most resourceful person in the office after myself, quickly ushered the still-confused minister and Joyyontoh into the boardroom for snacks. Which gave me a few minutes to regain my composure, walk to my cabin, close the door, and brutally assault a potted plant.

Diary, the prototype sculpture, of course, was top-notch. The amount of detail Emilio had managed to cram into such a small piece was remarkable. The only problem was . . .

One second.

That plant will never grow again.

Diary, Emilio had sent us a sculpture not of Sivaji the Maratha. Of course not. That would lead to unnecessarily high levels of customer service no? Instead the bastard has sent us a beautiful representation of SIVAJI GANESAN THE TAMIL ACTOR.

BLOODY I KNOW YOU ARE ARTIST AND CREATIVE FELLOW AND PROBABLY DID NOT GET PROPER EDUCATION AND ALL. BUT AT LEAST YOU SHOULD READ THE BLOODY SPANISH WIKIPEDIA BEFORE MAKING SCULPTURE? THIS IS WHY CHINA IS MAKING EVERYTHING AND YOU FUCKERS WILL ONCE AGAIN BECOME SLAVES OF THE GERMANS.

FED UP.

Tell me, Diary, how did these European countries become rich and successful? No seriously. How can these be First World when they are full of people like Valentina the Diarrhoea-brained and Emilio the Dumbfuck?

As soon as I entered the conference room Kedarji asked me about the design of the statue. Thankfully Emilio had chosen a photo of Sivaji Ganesan from some old historical film. So he was still dressed in ancient ethnic and pointy shoes. Kedarji said that the face looked very different and also the statue seemed to make Sivaji look very fat. When in fact Sivaji (Marathi) was lean and quite fit. (Yes. Because Kedarji has original photo. Idiot.)

Thankfully at this moment Sugandh intervened and said that this was a style of Sivaji sculpture that was popular in south India. Kedarji was amazed. He asked if Sivaji was famous in the south also.

Sugandh did not even blink. He said that Sivaji was world famous of course. But in the south he was particularly popular in and around Coimbatore district. Kedarji looked very impressed. Joyyontoh just stood there with his mouth open in amazement.

The rest of the evening transpired without incident. While evening snacks were being served a slide show of photos from the career of the minister flashed on the big screen interspersed with Lederman India photos.

Just before leaving Kedarji took one photo of himself with the statue. I accompanied him till the car and just as he got in I gently reminded him of our contract. He smiled and said, 'Sab ho jayega, Mr Varjees.'

Fucker.

Joyyontoh also nodded his head vigorously.

I am now exhausted, Diary. I have done everything I can do to get the project started. I have no strategies left. Whatever happens, happens.

I have asked Sharmila to delay Emilio's payments as much as possible. This is not Europe where people say, 'You fool me once shame on you, you fool me twice shame on me.' In India, 'You fool me once I fuck you madharchod.'

(Sometimes when I get very very agitated I use north Indian abuse. Much more satisfying. But Gouri says it is classless and I should stick to English abuse. Yes, and those gym tights are classy?)

### 8.23 p.m.

I could get used to the statue. It has a certain . . . personality. I was walking past it while leaving office today. And it has this majestic presence in our lobby. This fellow looks like he could have defeated the Mughals.

## 13 November 2009

### 9.01 p.m.

Diary, for the last three–four days I've been thinking: What does the summer intern of the 21st century truly want? What are they truly looking for? When they sign up for two-month projects with some of India's top corporates such a McKinsey, Goldman Sachs what are they hoping to achieve?

Diary, there are many misconceptions about young business school students these days.

For instance many people think that they want money and nothing else. Utter nonsense. Just look at my case. Can I, if I wanted to, just walk into another company that would pay me five times as much?

Without a doubt.

But there is more to life than money. Which other company would let me run the entire India operations at the tender age of just twenty-seven? Which other company would allow me to single-handedly ideate, strategize and drive the AVG2010 project?

How many of my batchmates have twenty-four people reporting to him? Nobody! (Except Vikas Marwah. But he runs a BPO in Gurgaon. I am referring to people with proper jobs.)

I think the trick to understanding what motivates potential summer interns is to ask a simple question: What motivates me?

What motivates Robin 'Einstein' Varghese?

First of all: Excellence. Pure and simple. If Einstein is going to be associated with something it has to be the best.

I work for what many people consider the finest small-size investment bank in the world when looked at holistically in terms of assets, profits, business, employee retention and stock price stability. Thanks to our traditional strength in markets like Ireland, Greece, Italy and Spain, Lederman combines the quality and ambition of a Goldman Sachs with the humanity of a Canara Bank.

But my quest for excellence does not stop there. I went to the best business school in the country. I go to the best gym in Delhi. I wear

65

the best clothes. I eat the best food. I stay in the best hotels when I travel on work. I live in one of the best neighbourhoods in Gurgaon. And I am in a relationship with a very decent woman.

Excellence. Everywhere.

Secondly I am motivated by not just what I do, but how I do it. I don't come to Lederman to swipe my ID card, play solitaire, pick up salary, and go home. For me this company is like a family. It treats me with love and respect. And I operate with complete freedom. This means that even when my mistakes happen, we deal with it like adults.

What happened last year when, in a hurry, I got the date and amount mixed up while preparing monthly vouchers, and paid the coffee machine vendor Three Crore Ninety-Two Thousand and Eight Rupees?

Any other company would have overreacted tremendously and created a huge scene. Not this company. Not Lederman. We just don't work that way. Indeed I did not even have to inform John in Tokyo about the minor hassle. Instead, because I am empowered, I decided to take care of it entirely by myself. The invoice was cancelled immediately. Today that vendor not only supplies our coffee but also our stationary supplies, cleaning services and taxi bookings. And Praveen Kumar in accounts, who reacted with speed and discretion, is now one of our youngest finance directors globally.

Which brings me to my third motivator: Speed. Diary, Lederman may have many faults. But taking time to get things done is not one of them. Look at how quickly we turned out that Sivaji statue. Kedarji has even asked us to send him that photo of him standing next to the statue. He wants to send it to his mother. He likes the statue that much.

And how long did it take us to deliver the statue? Two weeks. Show me Morgan Stanley or Deutsche Bank commissioning a work of art in less than three months.

Nothing in the world irritates me more than sitting around waiting for things to happen.

What you do.

How you do it.

How quickly you do it.

In a nutshell this is what defines Robin 'Einstein' Varghese and the MBA of the 21st century. We want to do great work, we want to do it our way, we want to do it now.

Fucking Eureka, Diary.

And this is how I am going to hit campuses all over India like a whirlwind. Ideas are forming in my mind.

Meanwhile, I had a spectacular session of BodyPump at the gym today.

Jesal can do 100 push-ups in one minute. Just like that. For no reason. Because she enjoys it.

Insane woman.

Finally spotted the Colonel at the gym. But left quickly before he spotted me.

**11.12 p.m.**

Just woke up Sharmila and told her to place orders for 400 T-shirts.

Get ready internship applicants in Ahmedabad!

Einstein is a man. With a plan.

## 15 November 2009

### 7.32 p.m.

Fucking hate MBA students. Fuckers. Complete fuckers. National disgrace.

At Ahmedabad airport. Frustrated. Going back to Delhi.

Later.

### 11.23 p.m.

Things started out so promisingly, Diary. But then life is like that. Everything starts out nicely. It looks like everything is going according to plan. And then suddenly, BOOM, you're standing in the middle of Magical Waves water park in Gurgaon dressed in provocative women's underwear and singing old Prem Nazir songs.

But why bring up the past? Especially when there are fresh embarrassments to be had in Ahmedabad.

The response from campus to our 'Minutus, Prius, Velocius' pre-placement presentation poster had been superb. (That means Smaller, Better, Faster in Latin. Classy!)

As soon as Sharmila confirmed that the presentation and Q&A would be followed by pizza lunch and free limited edition Lederman T-shirts, the placement office reverted with an astonishing figure: Eighty students had signed up to participate in the Lederman PPP.

I'd shortlisted only thirty-four people for interviews. This clearly meant more people were eager to be a part of the Lederman India journey. Or so I thought. Fuckers.

The presentation started very well. I received a huge round of applause when they came to know that I was an alumnus. Then I started my presentation with a question: Why should you work for a company?

I asked the crowd for suggestions. Seven people volunteered replies as follows:

1. Salary
2. Foreign exposure
3. Opportunity to work in an international work environment

4. Dollar salaries
5. Exposure to working with very large companies
6. Develop the ability to work in international markets
7. Growth (What the fuck is growth, you chooth bastard? Like kidney stone? Fucker.)

I immediately made a mental note not to hire a single one of these seven fuckers. Greedy people like them destroyed great companies like Lehman and Enron.

Inside I wanted to slap them across the face. But outside I thanked them for their inputs and for bringing up pertinent points.

And then I told them why they should join Lederman. I put up my vision on a slide:

---

**The Lederman India Summer Internship Programme**

---

BECAUSE.
• We are smaller
• We do it better
• We do it faster
• Come. Do it with us.

---

The thunderous applause that followed, unfortunately, was the best part of the evening. Things went rapidly downhill after that.

After expanding on the ideals of minutus, prius and velocius, I put the onus on the students. How many, I asked, were glad they'd been shortlisted by Lederman? And how many wanted to apply now? Just to prove how we do things better and faster at Lederman, I told them I was prepared to accept résumés and expand the shortlist right away.

The students picked up the onus I had put on them, placed it on the floor, and urinated on it. After that they kicked it in my face.

Not one fellow wanted to be real-time shortlisted by me. Not one. Knowing that lightening the situation might help bring shy ones forward, I giggled and cracked jokes for some time and then stopped after twenty minutes of zero response.

Remember when Gouri told me she was going to get a tattoo in Goa? And I got all kinds of expectations and positive thoughts about our future? And then she got a small Ganesha on her shin? This was 100 times worse.

I was so, so, so disappointed.

Crushed, I asked them how I could possibly attract more of them. What could Lederman do to get them to apply?

If there were crickets in that room you could have heard their hearts beat.

I told them that the faster they gave me feedback the faster we could have lunch.

Within fifteen minutes I had the following:

1. Lederman was too new to be chosen over established brands
2. The reputation of the company and its leadership had been defamed by another unnamed alumnus who works for a boutique consulting firm (Rahul Gupta of The Braithfuck Group)
3. Other Indian investment banks offered higher stipend than Lederman
4. Lederman did not have a policy of making offers to summer interns
5. We did not make it clear how many people we wanted. Apparently they prefer to focus on companies that they have a chance of getting through. What if we wanted only one person?
6. Lederman apparently does not have any 'high-profile alumni who people are aware of on campus'.

And then I immediately suspended the meeting for lunch. Afterwards you should have seen the greedy monsters descend upon the cardboard boxes full of T-shirts. (Plain round-neck shirts in Lederman's signature red.)

Afterwards I hung around outside the hall to answer those inevitable one-to-one questions that students always have. (Indian cultural problem. People are so scared of asking things in public. I am 100 per cent sure in China you are free to ask anybody anything without any fear or embarrassment. That is their secret.)

One fellow came and asked me if Lederman was open to hiring

people from the new Rural Business Management course. I said yes in order to not break his below-average CAT-scoring heart. But made a mental note to eliminate all such CVs.

And then another fellow came and asked me if the shirts were free-size. It took all my willpower to not head-butt him.

I had set aside two hours to be spent on campus to shortlist CVs in real time and handle queries.

Instead I spent two hours sitting in Ahmedabad airport eating a wide variety of terrible baked goods including a chilli paneer croissant that looked, smelled and tasted like fertilizer.

Diary, I had had huge expectations from the Minutus, Prius, Velocius campaign. I know it was planned in a hurry. But I had genuinely felt we had a winning idea here.

Little did I know how much the standard of MBAs has fallen these days. I had no idea they had become so materialistic about everything. Where is the dignity and the pride and the integrity?

Terribly upset, Diary.

I have asked Sharmila to put the rest of the T-shirts in the storeroom. I am killing this campaign. We had had so much planned beyond T-shirts.

What a waste of time.

# 16 November 2009

## 12.03 p.m.

Bad to worse.

John in Tokyo is upset at our overhead expenses. He called me this morning and asked me why I didn't stagger the statue and T-shirt campaign across two or three months. As it is, he said, India revenues are looking terribly weak. I reminded him about the business relevance of both projects. The statue was critical for AVG2010. And Minutus, Prius, Velocius was meant to tell the next generation of Lederman India staff about the independence and speed that made us so awesome.

Apparently local hiring campaigns need compulsory HO clearance. John now wants me to send SmallerBetterFaster to some woman in HO corpo comm. And it is going to take three to six months to clear.

Fuck I care any more.

He asked me how it went at Ahmedabad. I told him that it was an unprecedented success and that we should be prepared for some really strong interns this year. He asked me how many extra CVs we got because of the presentation. I said thirty to forty and growing.

Fucker treats me like a child sometimes.

## 1.14 p.m.

Too tired to type. Just assume I am very angry, Diary.

John has mailed Sharmila with a cc to me. He wants to see a copy of all the extra CVs we got. He wants to see if the additional expense was justified.

Like Sourav Ghosh used to say: Chipkali key laude key baal key something something.

## 18 November 2009

### 11.42 a.m.

Usually, Diary, you know how I dislike talking about my anatomy to anybody else. It just makes me feel very uncomfortable. Very vulnerable. Sometimes when I see episodes of Friends I wonder ... how do these people talk about their naked bodies like this to each other? Or even about their sex lives?

I am sure there is some exaggeration in these TV shows. But still. How are their cultures like this? I feel uncomfortable even if Gouri opens my underwear drawer.

Anyway. The reason I am saying this is so that you don't feel awkward about what I am going to tell you now.

So I just went to the restroom fifteen minutes ago. Diary, it was undoubtedly the best visit to the toilet that I have ever made in my entire life. If there is a Guinness Book of Records entry for most satisfying trip to the toilet I swear I would immediately send an application.

It was absolutely perfect. From beginning to end. Absolutely perfect. Like any Spielberg movie before and including *Saving Private Ryan*.

First of all when I went to the bathroom it had just been cleaned by the housekeeping fellow. He exited just as I entered. It was like walking into a botanical garden full of fresh flowers.

Secondly there was nobody else inside. Not one person. It was completely empty. And every single toilet cubicle was wide open. At a single glance I was able to confirm that I would have the bathroom entirely to myself.

You don't need to go to the loo, Diary. (Which is usually a blessing. But not when the trip is as magical as mine today.) Therefore you will never understand the sheer delight in finding a virgin restroom just waiting for your exploitation.

So I chose a cubicle at random and entered. Despite the floral aromas all around me—hibiscus?—I was still somewhat apprehensive.

There are so many things that can cause problems even inside a freshly cleaned toilet cubicle.

My fears were completely unnecessary.

The toilet paper roll was thick and fat and dry and soft and quite possibly new. The hand-held water gun hanging next to the commode was shiny, flexible and the trigger was perfectly spring-loaded. I tested it with a few quick shots into the bowl. The water was neither too hot. Nor too cold. And it shot forward at perfectly the right velocity. Last week at the gym I used the water pistol without checking first. It shot boiling hot water at 1000 kilometres per hour. I had tears in my eyes the whole evening, Diary.

No such issues here. The pistol worked perfectly.

Now only three things remained to be checked: the lever, the seat and last but not at all least, the bowl itself.

All three, Diary, were in pristine working condition. This was amazing. Normally this only happens in five-star hotels just when you've checked in. For a few moments I just stood there to enjoy the presentation.

Then I dropped my pants and sat down.

Diary, sometimes when I go home on vacation I am forced to go for some family function or the other. You know how much I hate this. Funeral or first holy communion or marriage or something like that. And sometimes I end up getting stuck with a group of retired schoolteachers or bank employees and all. Who then sit and bore the fuck out of me all through the reception. Once in a while these fuckers will start talking about their bowel movements. They will share tips on what to eat, how to eat, how to lie down, how to sit . . . everything except how to die quietly in their sleep instead of going for receptions and irritating people.

Many times I have listened to their toilet conversations and wanted to kill myself.

But, Diary. I think they have a point. Maybe you need to get a little older and a little mature to appreciate this. Today I realized how a satisfying trip to the toilet can be a truly life-changing experience.

So I sat down. And then, without a single moment's delay . . . it just happened. And it happened in utter silence. Not that I had to be afraid. There was nobody else in the bathroom. I could have performed film songs loudly—I can and I have—and nobody would have noticed.

And then just like that I was done. This is not normal. Normally I always feel like waiting for another five or ten minutes. Because I somehow feel incomplete.

Not today. Today I knew immediately that my job was done. Mission accomplished. I flushed, washed up, got up and dressed up again. And the toilet looked exactly like how I had first encountered it.

What magic is this?

I was moved, Diary. Thoroughly moved. So I just put the lid of the commode down. Sat down on top of it. And decided to just relish the moment. Why can't this happen more often, I thought to myself. In life why can't you once in a while have a perfect day at work, a perfect day at home, a perfect day at the gym with Jesal, a perfect meeting in the office where nobody asks any questions . . .

Then I fell asleep. And woke up one hour later. When I came back Sugandh asked me where I had gone. I told him that I had gone to make a secret phone call to someone in MURPS.

But I actually wanted to tell him about the loo trip, Diary. I really did. Don't judge me. It is a human tendency to want to share good experiences with other people. And I am sure if I was living in a more progressive country like Japan or the Netherlands I could have casually walked up to a colleague and talked to him about my bowel movements.

But alas we are a conservative country. And if you talk about all this they will think you are a sex criminal or something. Pity.

So I had no option but to share this with you. A secret between a man and his Diary.

I really hope I have days like this again.

Back to work now. I am writing those sixty extra résumés we need to send to Tokyo. Easier to make them up rather than discuss the messy truth.

## 12.32 p.m.

Tried going again. But there were two guys in the loo just standing there and chatting. Fuckers. So I washed my face and came back.

## 19 November 2009

**8.23 p.m.**

Gouri came home today. For exactly fifteen minutes. She came in. Told me she was in a hurry because she is taking Colonel Kaldog to see some movie at Alliance Francaise (????). Then she handed me a plastic bag. Told me it was a surprise.

She hugged me very unromantically. And then ran away. Disappointing.

Inside the bag there was one Nike shoebox. And one envelope full of papers. I was utterly taken aback. Gouri hasn't gifted me anything since my last birthday. (Hugo Boss cufflinks. Very nice. Very expensive. But I wanted a PS3.)

I opened the box. There was one shoe inside. One shoe, Diary. One shoe. First I thought it was some kind of joke. But for that Gouri needs a sense of humour no? Unlikely. Then I thought maybe it was some sort of game. Where she has hidden the other shoe somewhere. And when I find that I find another clue. And then another clue. And eventually I find Gouri in her flat nearly naked.

So I opened the envelope.

Pandaaram adangan. The fucking woman has enrolled me in the Mumbai marathon in February. She got some VIP invitation through her office. And signed me up also. I will only get the other shoe if I complete the full marathon, the half-marathon or the 15-kilometre 'Champion's Run'.

Very good marketing. Gift somebody running shoes AFTER they have finished running. Nike must have hired all their marketing fellows from the institute in Bangalore. Useless.

I called Gouri. But she kept cutting. And then she sent me an SMS:

'ROBIN ISN'T IT AWESOME???!! NOW COLONEL UNCLE WILL BE TOTALLY IMPRESSED! Love you. Movie going on.'

Oh hahaha! Oh yes yes it is awesome! Oh hahahaha. FUCKING COLONEL MOTHERFUCKER.

Steam was coming out of my ears, Diary. Steam. I was THIS close

**77**

to throwing the shoe out of the window. But then I called up one of the analysts and told him to make a sector profile for private satellite launching by tomorrow. I could hear the life go out of the poor fellow on the phone.

Was somewhat satisfying.

Diary, I refuse to run 15 kilometres. I refuse. 100 per cent.

Yes, I love Gouri very much. But just for the sake of love I am not going to go all the way to Mumbai and run under the sun for one hour or whatever time it takes to run 15 kilometres.

WHAT IS WRONG WITH PEOPLE THESE DAYS???!!!! No seriously, Diary. What is wrong with people? What is the need for Mumbai to have a marathon? As if it has solved every other problem and now has so much free time that it has to organize marathon also. FUCKERS YOU FIRST GO AND CLEAR THE SLUMS AND REPAIR YOUR DIRTY TRAINS MAN! And then you organize marathons.

You know what it is? They want to become like London and New York and Chicago and all. And act as if they are some First World foreign city. Idiots. You take a taxi from the airport in the morning and you will reach South Mumbai in December. Because one-third of the roads are shit, the next one-third is covered in shit and the remaining one-third is flooded because it is raining somewhere in Orissa.

And now Gouri wants me to run in the middle of this mess for 15 kilometres so that her uncle will start liking me. Stupid woman . . .

GO AND MARRY MILKHA SINGH NO???!!!!!

The envelope also has a training schedule in it. If I start immediately I MIGHT be able to train in time for the marathon.

Highly unlikely, Diary. Much better to just give up on Gouri. And marry someone who has no relatives in the Indian Army. Maybe some Kashmiri terrorist.

Very very very very angry. And frustrated. Why is love so hard?

**9.45 p.m.**

No peace of mind, Diary. Trying to get some work done. But no chance. Managed to write one or two fake résumés before getting exhausted.

Too many things going on in my mind. Kedarji and the quotation. John and the résumés. Gouri and the marathon. Lederman and the CEO position.

Too many things. The thing is how do you start and stop worrying. When I think of Kedar I am reminded of John. When I think of John I am reminded of Gouri. When I think of Gouri I am reminded of my job. And this reminds me of Kedar again. A never-ending cycle of worry. Never ending.

**10.11 p.m.**

Just sent an SMS to Jesal. Just like that. Casual. Between friends.

**12.34 a.m.**

Off to sleep now. Spent more than two hours having casual, friendly conversations with Jesal. The girl just gets me.

If I tell Gouri that something is bothering me at work or something she will immediately give one Gettysburg Address about professionalism or some such bullshit.

Jesal? Pin-drop silence. She just lets me offload all my troubles without suggesting anything.

Sometimes that is all a man needs. Someone to listen to him. Someone to let him speak. Someone who will not give a lecture. Someone who does not have uncles. Someone who will not just fucking sign him up for a marathon without showing the basic courtesy of calling him and asking him first.

Anyway no need to point fingers or call names.

Just feeling much better now.

Goodnight Diary.

## 23 November 2009

### 12.01 p.m.

Still no word from the ministry. What the heck is going on?

### 3.14 p.m.

John loves the quality of the résumés. He says that even though I had launched the campaign and spent money on it without going through the proper channels—fucking bureaucrat—he was happy with the end results. He said we should go ahead and roll it out across all major campuses as part of our summer hiring process.

Diary, what more proof do you want about the lack of quality in Lederman's current top management? It took me less than twenty-four hours to realize that Lederman's SmallerBetterFaster plan was simply not suited for India's business school environment. And this idiot wants us to roll it out nationally.

Fuck him. My plan is to never visit a business school again. Those arrogant fellows can go and find their own internships if they want. I don't want to staff my company with people who come in with a sense of entitlement from day one.

A sense of entitlement is earned. Not given.

**24 November 2009**

**3.43 p.m.**

FUUUUUUUUUUUUUUUUCCCCCCCCCCCCKKKKKKKKKKK
FUCK    FUCK    FUCK    FUCK    FUCK    FUCK    FUCK
FUUUUUUUCCCCCCCCCCCCKKKKKKKKKKKK FUCK FUCK FUCK
FUCK.

    Basically, fucked.

# BOOK TWO

# THE LAW
# TAKES ITS
# OWN COURSE

## 3 January 2010

**7.32 a.m.**

Waiting for Joyyontoh's car to come.

Everything is ready in my bag: slides, backup printouts, external hard drives, external speakers, copies of the signed MURPS contract with important sections highlighted, backup mobile phone with backup SIM, Joel's résumé and in-depth credentials deck, plenty of stationery for taking notes, and lunch.

Joyyontoh assured me that there were adequate lunch facilities inside. But I am not taking any chances. There will be some septic tandoori chicken for lunch made by some unhygienic north Indian fellow and then finished. Hepatitis for dessert. So I got Manoharan from Quilon Café to make some omelette sandwiches early morning.

Okay I think he has come. I can see an Ambassador coming through the gate. Talk to you later.

Off to jail.

## 4 January 2010

### 11.42 a.m.

It has been a tremendously traumatic few weeks since November. But I think today's meeting made everything seem worthwhile. For all the uncertainty since last October, things are now finally beginning to make sense.

Anyway damn busy today. I have a call from Joel in ten minutes.

Then I have to go running after work. Jesal is currently helping me tone my hamstring muscles. During our last run she took my hand and passed it over her hamstrings to show me how they felt after some training. It was like running my hand over Italian marble. What flawlessness . . .

With her support and hands-on demonstrations I should easily be able to prepare for this run.

Shall touch base tonight after dinner.

### 10.05 p.m.

Feel both tired and exhilarated at the same time. As if final exams have got over when I was in school, and now I want to sleep for two weeks continuously, but also stay up and watch TV for two weeks continuously.

As you know in November it looked as if all my plans had completely fallen apart. NOT ONE OUNCE of work got done after Kedarji got tied up with the Tarrapin case. For two days he desperately tried to act as if he was innocent. Then when it became certain that they were going to put him in Tihar he suddenly got chest pain and got admitted to AIIMS. (Apparently these ministers do this not to avoid jail, as you may think, but to give the Tihar people enough time to find a nice cell and furnish it according to the minister's wishes. There is a proper process they follow with a questionnaire for demands and dietary requirements and all.)

After two weeks of intensive 'observation' they packed him off to Tihar. When the news came out and Kedarji got sentenced to Tihar for 7.5 years I was 100 per cent sure that my career was finished.

When the only guy who really wants to give you the lifesaving contract goes to prison then, as Johnson chettan used to say, the snake in the fence is now inside the lungi.

But then Joyyontoh immediately phoned me up and told me not to worry. I cried on the phone. Like a little girl. Joyyontoh started laughing. He told me that I should not take all these judgments by the high court and Supreme Court so seriously. He said that when you are in politics these things happen. He said that ministers will keep coming and going to jail.

He said that if every time a minister went to jail a ministry had to stop work, then this country would have gone to the dogs years ago. He said there were 'well-established protocols and procedures to deal with temporarily and permanently incarcerated ministers' in every ministry. In fact, he said, this was one of the major but unknown achievements of the H.D. Deve Gowda administration. These days within minutes of a judgment being passed the minister activates the 'Gowda Protocol', and the ministry immediately prepares to operate from Tihar.

Kedarji moved into Tihar Central Jail in Delhi on 1 December. Three days later the signed contract came from the MURPS. Which was amazing.

Now I know what you're thinking, Diary: How can you collaborate on delivering value to a client when the client is in the nation's highest security prison?

I was thinking the exact same thing. Once again Joyyontoh was my saviour. Within just twenty-four hours of getting the signed contract he sent me a detailed brochure for all the business meeting and conference facilities that are currently available to sitting ministers inside Tihar. ('Regular' prisoners need to pay a nominal fee for the facilities. But they have to book months in advance.)

So yesterday morning Joyyontoh picked me up in his car and we went to the State Bank of India branch on the Andhra Samajam Road in Dhaula Kuan. We went inside with all our equipment. Joyyontoh walked up to the Customer Service Desk and handed a card to an SBI staff member.

There is no such thing as a Customer Service Desk in SBI. This is a fake. The man looked at his card. Cross-checked it against a register and then told us to follow him. He took us into the bank's safe room, opened another door inside, and then led us down a very long corridor. We must have walked for at least fifteen minutes. The SBI fellow apologized profusely for the delay. But he said that if the same government came to power in the next elections they were going to install a small monorail system to make business meetings in Tihar more convenient.

We finally emerged into a small room with windows where we were passed through security and our bags were fully emptied and checked. After this the SBI staffer returned to his 'desk'.

We were now fully inside the Tihar complex. I was, of course, very impressed. When you drive through Dhaula Kuan you have no idea that there is a tunnel like this connecting to the jail.

We walked into the Tihar Jail Business Centre (TJBC) where a receptionist took down our details and dietary preferences. I mentioned this to Joyyontoh. Who told me that the entire TJBC staff are trained by the Mandarin Oriental group of hotels as a favour to the home ministry.

After signing some non-disclosure agreements we were taken to a conference room. We waited outside while a meeting inside got over. Joyyontoh sat down on a chair outside, pulled out a Bengali newspaper. And started reading.

After ten minutes the door opened and the Prime Minister walked out.

Diary, I will give you five minutes to deal with that.

Yes. The Prime Minister. Walked out. He ignored me, nodded at Joyyontoh, chatted briefly with the receptionist and then walked off. Behind him emerged all the members of the cabinet. Including Kedarji. As soon as he saw me he hugged me lovingly and invited me inside the room.

He pulled out his camera and showed me the wallpaper. It was a picture of the 'Lederman Sivaji'. I told him it was wonderful. Meanwhile a whole group of uniformed attendants quickly cleaned up the room for our meeting. Diary, these fellows were not like regular government peons who take three photocopies the whole day in the gap between tea break and Bharat Bandh. These guys were like five-star waiters.

Two fellows packed a massive plasma TV into a box. Another fellow packed a Bose home theatre into another box. Each box was clearly labelled 'TJBC: Cabinet Meetings Only'. In fifteen minutes the room had been completely cleaned. The three of us sat around the massive conference table. In front of us they kept writing pads, pens and pencils all marked with the SBI logo. (For secrecy.)

Then, just before our designated time, one waiter-fellow came and kept a platter of snacks and assorted beverages. Diet and non-diet versions of all major drinks were available.

Kedarji ordered mini idli–sambhar and filter coffee for me. And bhelpuri for himself. I keep telling him I am not Tamilian. But he never remembers. But in any case the food is excellent.

So we sat down and I began to set up the tech for our teleconference. Kedarji seemed very excited. I had been hyping up this meeting with Joel Harrison in our London office for weeks. Joel used to be an investment banker for many years before joining Lederman's special projects team. He is one of the key figures behind the financial success of the Vancouver Winter Olympics and the profitability of the 9/11 visitor centre in New York. Joel is just a genius with things like merchandise and licensing revenue.

But, more importantly, talking to him is like talking to Pierce Brosnan's James Bond. He sounds so absolutely, perfectly English. So English. So posh. So refined. Gouri once overheard him talking to me on speakerphone. And she said that Joel would get laid instantly just on the basis of his voice.

I asked her if his voice was enough or did he have to speak sexily while simultaneously running a marathon also. She just laughed without getting the nuance in my comment.

The moment Joel's voice came streaming over the speaker Kedarji was sold. Joyyontoh looked extremely impressed and wrote on my letter pad: 'Very articulate like Jhumpa Lahiri.'

The rest of the meeting was a walk in the park. Kedarji agreed to everything Joel said. And Joel said everything we had planned to. We are now drawing up a six-month road map for the MURPS that will have merchandise up and ready for sale by July. Well in time for the Allied Victory Games.

Meanwhile I can focus on correcting the press and media optics. (HUGE HEADACHE.)

Minutes after Joel said bye Kedarji asked me what kind of person Joel was. I told him I had never met him. But he had a reputation for being one of Lederman's finest people. Future global CEO material even.

He wanted to know if we could get Joel to relocate to Delhi for the duration of the project. I told him this would be possible but quite expensive. Partners like Joel charged several thousand dollars per day.

Kedarji threw his head up and laughed. He told us that the Prime Minister had informed the cabinet that NO EXPENSE WHATSOEVER should be spared in order to make the Allied Victory Games a success.

Kedarji said that the home ministry was placing an order for 16 crore worth of metal detectors. By comparison one Joel Harrison was peanuts. He told me to arrange for the paperwork immediately. I enthusiastically agreed.

Diary, this could be huge. Getting Joel to work exclusively on a project can easily double the contract value of the project. Of course at that moment in time I did not show my enthusiasm.

After the meeting one waiter asked us if we wanted any documents destroyed. Kedarji said, 'My CBI charge sheet!' And we all laughed and laughed.

Then we took the tunnel back to the SBI branch. And then I came to office.

Spent all day on the paperwork. And then this evening I went for a 7-kilometre run with Jesal in the gym. She is a machine, Diary. She easily does 7 kilometres in thirty-two minutes. IN THIRTY-TWO MINUTES. Unbelievable. So today I decided to set myself a really tough target: 7 kilometres in forty minutes. So far I have done 6 in forty. And that was tough, but not impossible.

So I went to the gym, got on to a treadmill and began to run. I was running just behind Jesal who was on a cross-trainer. Now when most people are on a cross-trainer they look like they are in the process of giving birth. Not Jesal. She manages to make even this look like a ballet movement.

After a few minutes I looked up and she spotted me and winked. Instantly my heart detached itself from all connective tissues and fell right through my body. And I began to sweat even more.

After 4.5 kilometres I was desperately thirsty. So I paused the machine, got off and went to get a drink.

By the time I came back Jesal had vanished. I got on to my treadmill and pressed 'continue'. I began running again. For five minutes. And then I realized something strange was happening. The treadmill was slowly tilting upwards. This was a new complication. I was clearly on the wrong treadmill. I reached forward to press the stop button when Jesal reappeared. I nonchalantly shifted my fingertip on the speed increase button and pressed it.

She looked really impressed. She said that even she, with all her experience, hadn't dared try hill-training on the treadmill. And now a novice like me was running uphill!

I told her that frankly I had begun to get bored of running on flat surfaces. It was just too repetitive. Also in the real world you never ran a long distance on a flat surface. Hill-training, I told her looking casual even though I could clearly feel one of my lungs failing, was the only challenge I was prepared to take seriously.

I could sense that she was looking at me in a whole new light. Then she asked how much time I had left. We both looked at the machine readout. It said I had 7.8 kilometres left to go uphill, followed by 2 kilometres flat and then a 2-kilometre sprint finish. Both of us were stunned.

By now most of my major organs were beginning to shut down one by one. And I was certain I would pass out in another five minutes or so. I told Jesal to carry on with her workout and not wait for me. She said she was done for the day, but would be happy to motivate me through the rest of my run. I laughed for a few seconds, trying to take deep breaths, and then told her not to waste her time. Einstein's middle name was self-motivation. I would never give up till I was done.

ALLELUIA PRAISE THE LORD! She said bye and left.

I waited for a few seconds to make sure she had left and then reached for the stop button. Just as pandaaram adangan Jesal came back with a gym trainer. Immediately I pressed another button. Which made the slope increase a little bit. By this point I had no bodily sensation below my waist. She said the trainer, a friend, had offered to make sure I completed my run properly. And then she left.

This motherfucker then stood there and started saying things like: 'Come on, Robin! Pump! Push it! Push it easy! Come on! You can do it! Just 11 kilometres more! Come on!'

I have never wanted to punch a man in the face more. Here I am dying of exhaustion and the fucker thinks he is Shah Rukh Khan in *Chak De India* climax. Bastard.

I reduced the speed a little. He increased it a little. I reduced the slope a little, he increased it a little. Not yet, not yet, keep going. Push those legs, Robin! Push those legs! Can you feel it?

I told him that if he touched my treadmill one more time I would complain to the management that he had acted inappropriately with me in the steam room. He chuckled for a few seconds and then stopped when he saw the deadly serious look on my face.

I hit stop. Waited for the treadmill to land. Then I told him that as far as he was concerned I had completed the complete session. He said okay.

But in total, across both treadmills, I had managed to run 6.6 kilometres and burn around 560 calories. A new personal best.

It had proved to be a traumatic but effective day at the gym.

Right now, to be frank, I am doing it for Jesal. She has high hopes for my timing. And I cannot let her down.

Fucking Colonel is still here. Gouri says that he has decided to stay in India indefinitely. I have a fucking feeling the old fuck wants to hang around here till he convinces her that marrying me is a bad idea.

I can sense some conspiracy. Robin 'Einstein' Varghese did not get this far in life without a nose for fuckers trying to fuck him over.

Fed up of the Kalbags.

Thankfully workwise and Jesal-wise things are looking up.

Exhausted. I have to go lie down.

## 5 January 2010

**4.29 p.m.**

Kedarji's request has exploded through Lederman like a nuclear bomb. In a good way. John is bubbling with excitement.

Finally, FINALLY, it looks like the Lederman India office has a mandate with the size and scope that will make the other offices shut up and just stare.

(Note: Diary, apparently 'mandate' is what Lederman calls a 'project'. I don't know why. Once I said 'project' during a meeting with John in Tokyo and he got damn upset. Then he gave me a fifteen-minute speech about the difference between bankers and consultants. He told me that I still had a little consultant stuck inside me. And if I had to become a proper leader at Lederman I had to pull this consultant out. I told him I would work on it. Idiot.)

For the last two or three quarters India has been the worst performing Lederman office in the region. Now as interim-CEO I should put my hand up and take responsibility for this. I have to be a man and own up to our problems.

But to be fair this is not at all my fault. First of all we only properly opened up an office twenty-four months ago. Before that, for one whole year, John and the other fellows from Tokyo just kept doing feasibility study after feasibility study about the Indian market. While the Indian economy was booming and money was flooding the market the idiots wasted time doing country studies and surveys. I kept on telling them: Bloody fools you invest now and worry about the country later. Tomorrow when all the Indian airlines and retail companies become multi-billion-dollar companies Lederman will be sitting here with our heads up our asses.

But that is the problem with outsiders. They don't get how the Indian market works. You won't believe this, Diary, but John actually hired a company in October 2007 to do a study of India's political stability before they finally established our investment fund.

After three months they gave us a 300-page report that essentially said India would be very stable in the future unless there was civil war, communal riots, war with China or Pakistan, or terror attacks.

Fuckers should go on *Mastermind India* with all that insight and wisdom.

So first of all we wasted a lot of time. Secondly I think we made a lot of hiring mistakes. Again simply because John wouldn't trust my gut instinct. Immediately after interviewing Rajeev I told John that I got a bad vibe from the guy.

Rajeev simply has no class. Whatsoever. Last year for the Christmas party he came in a light pink suit, Diary. Apparently this is his 'party suit'. Yes, but only if it is a party of the All India Prostitution Promoters Council.

I don't think I have ever seen him actually wear anything that is his size. Either his suits are too tight. Or too loose.

How do you trust a person who wears the same cufflinks on two consecutive working days? During the interview John asked him what he would bring to the company that was unique to him, and Rajeev said he had plenty of USB drives full of confidential client information about all kinds of important people in Delhi. John burst out laughing along with Rajeev.

I joined in but inside I was completely scandalized. Who even jokes about things like that? What kind of professional are you if you're happy to parade all your confidential information and office goings-on in public. Shameful, Diary, shameful.

(One of Sugandh's main duties is to keep an eye on everything Rajeev does in office. Especially on things like USB drives.)

I opposed Rajeev's hiring vehemently. But John said that hiring someone from BancoGeneve would indicate to the Indian market that Lederman was serious.

On the other hand Raghu's hiring seemed a great idea at the time. He seemed like a nice, hard-working type. Smart, but not too smart. He was forty-five years old but still had only managed to become vice-president at ICICI Ventures. Not at all CEO material. And nowhere near the calibre of a person to make me feel insecure.

However, as you are aware, Raghu has since proved to be a wolf in sheep's clothing. He looks like a harmless south Indian accountant on the outside. But inside he has the heart and soul of Auto Shankar.

But my biggest problem with John was that he insisted I stay as interim-CEO till he was convinced I was ready for the full-time job.

Personally I think John is just jealous that the board of directors assigned the India office to me without consulting him. Fucker has no idea how I saved Lederman in 2007. No idea.

(Thankfully he at least gave me greater freedom to hire the rest of the India team. With other senior people like Raghu and Rajeev in office I knew that I needed more allies. Sugandh was more than happy to shift immediately to Delhi as general manager—knowledge management.)

Because of this lack of leadership and poor senior hirings, Lederman India has simply not been as aggressive as we should be. We've been slow to respond to potential mandates. And when we get mandates Raghu and Rajeev handle them so unprofessionally.

It is unbelievable.

Once Rajeev included some middle management guy at the client's office (SigmaSix Green Tech) in an internal Lederman email chain by mistake. For weeks we kept exchanging emails making fun of SigmaSix's business model. (Diary, if SigmaSix ever makes a single rupee of profit in the next fifteen years I will change into a skintight see-through salwar kameez, wear full 'Punjabi aunty make-up' and go for a 10-kilometre run through Gurgaon.)

And then just two hours before we signed a deal to raise money for SigmaSix this bastard fellow sends me an email saying he has had great fun reading the joke emails and was now going to show a printout to his CEO.

God only knows how I had to think on my feet and arrange for Sharmila to hire the fucker's wife as an external subject matter expert for Lederman on a Rs 5 lakh consulting fee.

For all these reasons we've lagged behind every single Lederman office in Asia except Pakistan. (Thank you Al Qaeda!)

John keeps asking me to step up, but there is only so much an interim-CEO can do.

But all that can change with the Allied Victory Games. Just getting Joel Harrison down to work on it can easily double our billings on the mandate. Per se it is not a large mandate. Along with Joel's daily charges we should make a few million.

The real point of it all is to make inroads into the government. It doesn't matter if you are a bank or a consulting company or bloody dry cleaning shop. There is plenty of work for everybody.

Joyyontoh explained all this to me during the New Year party. He told me that the government hired so many companies to give it advice because of democracy.

Confused? So was I.

And then he explained. Look at China. Now in China if the government decides to do something it just does it. High-speed train? Done! Man in space? 3 ... 2 ... 1 ... Launched! Invade Tibet? Run lama run!

Now if things go well everybody in China is happy. But if things go badly? One of two things happen. Either the government acts as if nothing happened and covers up the whole thing. Or it says sorry, somebody gets fired or executed, and life returns to normal. Nothing happens to the government itself.

But in a democracy like India somebody has to be responsible for everything. So suppose the government wants to sell a PSU or build a bridge. It can go ahead and just do it. But if things get fucked then the government will have to face questions from the public and the media.

I reminded Joyyontoh that the government also has to face tough questions from the opposition. He laughed loudly for one full minute, asked Sugandh to bring him another whisky and soda, and then told me not to talk like some stupid political science student from Delhi University.

So instead of just doing something the government will ask a bank or a consulting firm or some 'neutral third party' to give advice. The third party, of course, will tell the government exactly what it wants to say. The government will then simply 'implement the plan recommended by prestigious international company with proven track record'.

If things go wrong a minister can stand up in Parliament and say that he had been given bad advice by a consultant. Now the only way to rectify the mistake is to conduct a new study, prepare a new report and make some course corrections. Boom! Even more business for 'neutral third party' specialists.

But now I was worried. Didn't this really slow down the government's ability to make decisions? Exactly, said Joyyontoh.

The entire point of democracy, Joyyontoh explained, is to make it as hard as possible for the government to do anything. Why would you want a room full of old, sexist, racist, narrow-minded, uneducated frauds randomly taking decisions and reforming things? You don't.

(I was spellbound.)

Instead you want to slow these fuckers down as much as possible so that whatever they finally end up doing is either utterly pointless, like the budget, or extremely important, like war. This is why, he explained, bankers and consultants and NGOs are so important. We are the conscience of a democracy. Between a government that seeks power without accountability and a public that seeks comfort without direct effort, the consultants, bankers and NGOs maintain the critical balance.

You, he said, pointing at me, are the true heart and soul of our democracy.

I would have stood up and clapped for several minutes if Joyyontoh hadn't gently tilted to one side and fallen to the floor on top of Raghu's three-year-old daughter.

Diary, I was spellbound by Joyyontoh's insights into the politics of this country.

From a business perspective this can only mean one thing: For Lederman AVG2010 is just the beginning.

If we play our cards right, if Kedarji helps us with connections, if Joyyontoh continues to mentor us, and if Raghu and Rajeev never ever email anybody in the government, Lederman might just be able to develop a solid public sector practice that could be worth millions.

And then Japanese Asshole will make me proper CEO, and then all my dreams will come true.

GOOD GOD. How long have I been typing?

Jesal will come in another fifteen minutes. Today is going to be my first proper ninety-minute run.

Phew. Tense. If it wasn't for her constant support and encouragement I would have never been able to make it so far. She is a real friend. A real, understanding friend.

Also feeling more optimistic about the job than I have in months. There seems to be a greater purpose about everything.

## 7 January 2010

### 9.23 p.m.

Just came back from Tihar after a meeting with Kedarji. I went in panicking. But came out in a considerable state of calm. But now I have even more work.

This morning while going through the MURPS contract I suddenly realized that there was no provision in the original contract for raising any additional fees except expenses.

John told me clearly that he wants to charge a lot of money to get Joel to come down to work for us. This is because Joel is currently spearheading a massive Lederman push into the Formula 1 segment. A lot of teams have no money. And a lot of stupid Russian mafia have too much money. Lederman is trying to create an interface between both clients. Millions of dollars are involved. Pulling Joel away for something much more low profile like AVG2010 is not easy.

So John wants Kedarji to compensate lavishly.

And then this morning I suddenly panicked.

DEIVAME NOW I WILL HAVE TO GET THREE QUOTATIONS FOR THIS ALSO AND WAIT FOR ANOTHER THREE MONTHS???

I ran to the SBI branch and literally raced down the tunnel for a meeting with Kedarji at jail business centre. Unfortunately the entire centre was booked for an Empowered Group of Ministers meeting on judicial reform. Thankfully the receptionist was able to book a private table for the both of us in the jail's twenty-four-hour cafe, The Tossed Salad.

(One of the best cafes in Delhi apparently. The menu looked awesome. Kedarji ordered an 'Anticipatory Bhel' while I ordered a 'Quattrocheese Pizza'.)

Kedarji laughed off my worries. He told me that I had to stop panicking and that I had to learn to trust the government machinery more. Now that one contract has been signed, getting more contracts is going to be very easy. All I had to do was submit another three quotations. Approval for a contract extension would come within one week.

Then Kedarji told me that I had to immediately figure out a way to deal with the bad media swirling around because of his jail sentence. He was confident of being released in another month or so. But already the BBC was beginning to ask if nodal oversight of the Games could be trusted with a man who is in jail. Kedarji wanted me to figure out a comprehensive response that would kill these rumours and give the foreign media, foreign sportspeople, Indian government and, if possible, the Indian public complete confidence in the MURPS's abilities.

As of now, he said, the AVG2010 was exactly behind schedule as planned. But it would soon be time for the MURPS to switch into Games mode.

Both of us simply cannot wait to launch into these Games with gusto. Joyyontoh, the minister told me, is quietly preparing the entire MURPS for this task of national importance.

But first, he said, I had to clean up our PR problem. Immediately.

I promised to do what I could.

Before leaving he invited me for the Sanjay Gandhi Memorial Tihar Inmate's Annual New Year Party on the 22nd. I asked him why the party was being held so late in January. He said this was to give the VIPs enough time to deal with public activities and Republic Day commitments.

A driver will come to pick me up after office. Kedarji said it in a way that I could not refuse.

Just reached office now.

Now I have to sit and think about this PR problem. What to do?

Tired.

**9 January 2010**

**12.15 p.m.**

S.O.B. TIME!

After months. Maybe years, I have just had one of those sparks of brilliance that energized my career in my younger days.

(Diary, this is one of the burdens of leadership. The higher you go in a company the less potential you have to innovate and invent. This is because your entire time is used up in doing stupid things like getting quotations, commissioning statues and keeping an eye on criminal co-workers. In fact, I think, the best way to kill somebody's usefulness is to make him country manager or CEO. Instead companies should make some idiot fresher the CEO, so that the actual smart people can get work done.

Like government.

I think this is an exciting concept for a book. 'The Idiocy Theory'.)

But this morning, while running in the gym, I suddenly realized how I could handle Kedarji's PR problem.

This is my master plan.

What is the world media, especially the British Behenchod Corporation, thinking right now about Kedarji? Let me analyse this using one of my favourite Dufresne frameworks: Myth or Fact.

Myth: Kedarji is a criminal who cannot be trusted with overseeing the AVG2010 activities.

Fact: Kedarji may be in jail. But this in no way indicates that he is a criminal. In the Indian context such an assumption is a flagrant misrepresentation of facts. The BBC needs to get its facts right.

Myth: Since Kedarji is in jail the MURPS is a rudderless organization lacking leadership or vision.

Fact: A minister is critical to a ministry's functioning. But let us not forget that the ministry is also staffed by a number of experienced managers and bureaucrats with several thousand man-years of experience in managing large projects. For instance the MURPS was single-handedly responsible for the Bandra-Worli Sea Link Accelerated Five-Year Completion Programme from 1987 to 2003.

Myth: Even if Kedarji comes out of jail now, there is little time to salvage the AVG2010. The Games are beyond redemption.

Fact: Delays are inevitable when it comes to sporting events such as the Allied Victory Games. As they are when it comes to events like the Olympics. Countries all over the world struggle with delivery deadlines before always making the events happen. India will do exactly this. Please have greater faith in us.

This will be the thrust of my strategy. To prove Kedarji's innocence, to prove the MURPS's abilities, and to prove India's ability to deliver on time.

And what is my strategy?

In what I think will be a radical new strategy for any Indian government ministry the MURPS will commit to a brand new initiative I am calling 'Need to Know'.

First of all let me give you some background. Now usually when some companies say that such and such information is on a 'Need to Know' basis this means it will only be shared with people who absolutely need to know it. So, for example, John says that remuneration details for Raghu and Rajeev are only shared on a Need to Know basis. Therefore he refuses to share them with me. This is despite my clear right to this information on the basis of my position as interim-CEO.

Thankfully John is an idiot who refuses to change the default password (L3d3rman) on his email inbox and VPN data folder. Sugandh sends me a nice monthly report on all such Need to Know information that the fucker refuses to share and acts pricey about.

But back to my plan. So now tell me, Diary, as far as the MURPS's activities regarding AVG2010 are concerned who has the Need to Know?

EXACTLY! The entire country. Transparency is the cornerstone of a proper democracy. And I am going to restore that cornerstone to the Allied Victory Games.

The NTK programme is a radical new way of involving the public and the media. Once the plan is in place the media and the public will be freely allowed to visit the ministry and watch the Nodal

Oversight Committee functioning. But I am going to go one step further. And really push this concept into the 21st century.

ET VOILA DIARY: www.UCUNTK2010.org!

Puzzled? Let me explain:

You[U]+Country[C]+Universe[U]+Need to Know[NTK]+2010 = UCUNTK2010.

A brand new world-class e-governance website that is devoted to complete and utter transparency of all Allied Victory Games coordination activities. Every quotation, every purchase order, every complaint, every response and every single document that the MURPS generates in order to deal with the Games will immediately be uploaded to the website for public scrutiny. So that you (I mean each citizen), the country and the entire universe of media people, sporting organizations and other governments can all see how openly and freely we are functioning.

Not impressed? There is more.

The website will also have a real-time status update of preparations at every single major sporting venue, the Games Village and all other ancillary departments such as security, broadcasting, accreditation, doping and testing, etc. Every minute of every day anybody in the world will be able to log on to the UCUNTK system and verify the status of our readiness.

Not impressed? You hungry, hungry Diary. There is more.

The crowning glory of the UCUNTK system will be an unprecedented implementation of technology in a ministry. For the first time ever a network of webcams situated in every office and every room of the MURPS will broadcast a continuous stream of video all embedded on the UCUNTK website.

As far as I know nobody anywhere in the country, perhaps in the world, has come close to doing anything like this.

The message to the world is simple: We have nothing to hide. All our cards are on the table. Trusting us is now your prerogative. Now fuck off you bastards while we get work done.

I am over the moon, Diary. This is exactly the kind of PR coup that the ministry, the minister and the nation needs. This is a good solid, sober idea.

Going to call Joyyontoh right away. Have to start working on this while I am still fired up on enthusiasm.

### 1.23 p.m.

Finally got through to Joyyontoh. I've never seen the fucker actually do any work except order tea. But his phone is engaged constantly.

He said he would only be able to comment on the idea if I sent it to him in writing. Bloody killjoy!

(Killjoy would actually be a pretty good Bengali name. Killjoy Sengupta.)

And he wants it to be written in some standard policy proposal format.

Sigh. Talk to you later. Joyyontoh will send the format in PDF and then I will have to type for hours and hours.

### 1.33 p.m.

I don't know what to say. Really. The PDF is a scan of photographs of the policy proposal format. Useless.

Maybe China should invade us. Or at least invade the government offices in Delhi.

Idiots.

## 12 January 2010

**9.12 a.m.**

Off to the MURPS for a meeting with Joyyontoh on the UCUNTK concept. He sounded enthusiastic on the phone.

**11.20 a.m.**

Joyyontoh is a genius. A political mastermind. UCUNTK is good to go. With some minor modifications.

Usually I don't like to see my proposals tampered with. Especially on the minor details. That just pisses me off so much. So when Joyyontoh sat down with me with a fountain pen and began to mark changes on my proposal I took a deep breath.

But I was wrong. His changes will not only turn the PR game in our favour. But also make foreigners look like idiots. This is not two or three birds with one stone. This is like a branch of Kentucky Fried Chicken with one stone.

Sheer genius.

No time to chat. Have to work like a madman. And then somehow find time to go for my first ever proper 15-kilometre run.

Gouri has just sent me a book called *Born To Run* to keep me motivated. I haven't read the book. But I checked on Wikipedia. It is about this South American tribe of insane runners. Some of these guys run for four or five days at a time.

WHY? Okay fine, you are a poor country and don't have taxis? Import autorickshaws no? Bloody tribals are running because they have no option in life. And you are celebrating this like some major achievement.

I don't know how this is motivating.

Instead send me a Bose headphones or something no?

**2.54 p.m.**

FUCCCCCCCCCCCCCCCCCKCKKKKCKKK.

I don't have time right now to add more abuse here. I will do that later.

But Gouri has invited me to lunch with the Kalbags on the weekend. Dinner also potentially possible it seems. The Colonel will be there.

On the upside this is a good chance to dust his dhokla with cyanide or something.

Damn.

Back to work, Diary.

**17 January 2010**

**4.34 p.m.**

HA HA HA HA HA HA HA HA HA HA HA. AYYO. HA HA HA HA HA HA HA HA. PAAVAM BBC FUCKER WAS NOT EXPECTING THAT! HA HA HA HA HA. POOR FUCKER THOUGHT HE COULD JUST WALK INTO THE MURPS WITH HIS NOTEBOOK AND FOUNTAIN PEN AND CONDESCENDING ATTITUDE AS IF HE IS LALU ALEX IN SOME OLD MALAYALAM FILM AND MAKE US LOOK LIKE IDIOTS.

NOW WHO LOOKS LIKE AN IDIOT, NAYYINTE MONE JOURNALIST?

Diary, today's great success was all down to some excellent coordination, cooperation and brainstorming on the part of both yours truly and the remarkable Joyyontoh.

Once again I must admit that I was too hasty in thinking that Joyyontoh was just another IAS officer who wants to see ration card and birth certificate attested by village officer before doing anything.

He is little bit like that.

But he also has tremendous insight into the way this country functions. Every time I sit and listen to him it is like sitting through a wonderful political science lecture. (Of course the student also has to be enthusiastic. If you make Rajeev or Raghu sit with Joyyontoh they will basically use his contact to get a second LPG gas cylinder.)

So as you may recall last week I sent him the UCUNTK proposal and asked him for his inputs. He said he broadly thought that the 'transparency offensive' was a very smart, world-class move. But I had forgotten to take two things into consideration.

First of all we had to make sure that everybody in the government would cooperate with our ideas. The other ministries should agree to let their documents be uploaded and their projects to be tracked on the UCUNTK portal. Apparently this is very, very complex and there are protocol issues involved.

Secondly, he said, there was not enough Indian culture, history and heritage in my proposal.

Sounds odd right? But everything will become clear soon. Trust me.

Joyyontoh said that he would take care of both problems. Meanwhile he asked me to draft a press invitation for an important press conference at the MURPS conference room. Joyyontoh said that usually inter-ministerial approvals took many months. But in this case he would put it on the fast track. So we scheduled the press conference for this morning.

The next afternoon imagine my surprise when the Prime Minister's Office put out an announcement saying that:

The Prime Minister has asked the Ministry of Urban Regeneration and Public Sculpture to immediately put into place a new transparency scheme for the Allied Victory Games 2010.

The three-part scheme will involve placing all Games documents in the public domain, real-time status reports on Games projects and a new multimedia scheme to enhance transparency in functioning of the MURPS. The Prime Minster has personally discussed the initiative with all concerned ministries. All parties have whole-heartedly supported this exciting new experiment in accountable governance and public investment.

In order to operationalize the scheme and ensure compliance the Prime Minister has decided to release an additional Rs 35 lakh to each ministry from the Allied Victory Games Contingency Fund.

Subsequent to this consensus the Prime Minister has asked MURPS to finalize and announce details of the new 'Project for Inter-Ministerial Promotion of Allied Victory Games (Empowered) 2010' as soon as possible.

I saw this on the TV in my cabin in the office. And to be frank I had mixed feelings, Diary. The Prime Minister had completely taken credit for my idea. PIMPAG(E)2010 had always been my baby from the beginning. Now no one will ever know how Einstein and Lederman were instrumental in making it happen.

On the other hand I was once again amazed at Joyyontoh's secret abilities. Somehow he had managed to get the Prime Minister to not only buy into the idea of PIMPAG(E) but to also make it sound like it was his idea. No doubt this helped to speed acceptance across ministries.

Two hours later the MURPS released the press invitation I had crafted, inviting the world media to the ministry for the unveiling of the project.

So far so good. But I was still apprehensive about the press conference. Joyyontoh invited me to attend, of course, but he would do all the speaking. I had grave doubts about this, Diary. Ordering tea is one thing. Facing questions from some of the world's top journalists is quite another matter. I repeatedly asked Joyyontoh if he wanted to go through some mock questions or presentation.

Right up till this morning he refused. Even fifteen minutes before he took the stage I asked him if he wanted me to share any of my well-honed presentation tips.

Nothing. Stubborn fucker.

So when the press conference started I was still very, very nervous. The BBC fellow came and sat right in the front row. And you could see from the look on his face that he wanted to really grill Joyyontoh.

Exactly on time Joyyontoh welcomed everybody and quickly outlined the three-step programme. He told them that a new website would be launched within two weeks.

You should have seen the faces of the assembled journalists when they heard about the real-time updates and twenty-four-hour video feeds. Some of them immediately started informing their editors about the big news.

And then Joyyontoh invited questions.

The next five minutes were pure theatre, Diary.

Immediately the BBC guy asked him how the MURPS had any credibility to run a transparency project given that the minister was in jail. Joyyontoh told him that Kedarji's case was under appeal and that he may very well be back at work in two weeks.

But once someone goes to jail he has no credibility left, said the BBC guy.

Joyyontoh looked at him for a second. And then asked him if he meant to say that Mahatma Gandhi had no credibility left just because the British had sent him to jail many times?

The room was so silent you could hear the sound of the tapes winding inside the video cameras. The ministry's official photographer, Balakrishnan (from Kodungalloor, lives near Anita aunty's house) came forward, took a photo of the BBC journalist. And then went away.

Okay fine, said the journalist, but the second question remained. Without a minister at the helm how could the MURPS function? If Kedarji was not released soon, who would execute projects? Wasn't the ministry right now a rudderless organization?

(I had predicted these questions perfectly, Diary. Perfectly.)

This time Joyyontoh merely chuckled to himself politely. And then he said that the BBC needed to place a little more trust in India's democratic mechanisms. Kedarji is just a minister and not a king, said Joyyontoh. We have institutions in place and operating procedures for ministries. Unless the BBC wished to share some insights on how to run a constitutional republic that we were not aware of.

The BBC fellow got upset. 'This is not about Britain. This is about the Indian government, sir!' he said.

'Are you sure, Mark?' asked Joyyontoh in his most polished St. Stephen's dramatics English.

One reporter for some Rajasthan newspaper clapped a little.

The BBC fellow then said that he had one last question: Was there enough time now to get all the projects completed? Several stadiums were still months behind schedule.

Joyyontoh nodded his head solemnly in agreement. Yes, he admitted, we have several projects behind schedule. This is unfortunate. But this should not be surprising, he said. Sporting events have a history of being delayed right up till the opening ceremonies. Governments have their plans. But ground realities are challenging. Delhi is a difficult city to build in. But he asked the media to have faith in the government.

Then Joyyontoh asked the BBC fellow if he had ever attended a Punjabi wedding. The BBC fellow said he had attended many. Joyyontoh told him that just like in a Punjabi wedding we would get the Allied Victory Games delivered on time. Things might look completely chaotic right till the last moment. But in the end everything would fall into place, and everyone would be very happy.

This time the whole audience clapped and chuckled politely.

After this there was time for just one more question. So Joyyontoh extended it to an Indian journalist from Star News who asked if there was any truth in the rumour that Shah Rukh Khan and Salman Khan had a difference of opinion in the choreography currently being planned for the opening ceremony.

Thank god our domestic media shows courtesy and knows how to focus on the simple things and asks useless questions.

After this we broke for tea and snacks.

I walked over to Joyyontoh and congratulated him on his performance. He merely smiled at me like Swami Vivekananda in that photo outside Kedarji's office where he stands with his arms crossed looking into the distance.

WHAT. A. TRIUMPH. Diary.

Right after the press conference you could sense the positivity and excitement in the room. Except for the BBC guy everyone seemed upbeat and happy.

I had to rush back to office to finalize some details on Joel's contract. And also I need to figure out some stuff about our summer interns. Fuckers will all turn up in two months and John wants to see our training and project plans for them.

Also—the very thought of this is making my stomach churn—I have to have lunch with the Kalbags tomorrow.

Gouri said she will come over tonight to get me mentally prepared. It is that kind of family.

**9.32 p.m.**

Diary, Gouri just left.

I am willing to share what transpired between us from 7.45 p.m.

to 8.30 p.m. What happened after that will remain a secret between me and Gouri. No, Diary, no. No point in asking. Einstein is not the kind of man to 'kiss the neck and shoulder areas and tell'.

Who knows what would have happened if she wasn't so nervous about the lunch?

Gouri has given me a full background on the family. Basically the idea is to impress her family with my professional achievements. Also, I am not to say anything about my family right now. That would come later when things become more serious. Right now, she said, they were only keen to get to know me well.

The problem, of course, was the Colonel. But she said that the best thing was to avoid engaging with him at all.

I could sense that she was terribly nervous. So I reassured her, Diary. I sat next to her, put my hands around her, inhaled the smell of her hair deeply, and then spoke to her. I told her that I would do everything possible in my power to make sure the lunch goes well. If nothing else I would do this to make up for the pain I have caused her for so many months.

She calmed down a little bit. So I took her face in my hands and . . .

And then Einstein rocked her world.

She left looking somewhat more happier.

I have no doubt in my mind, Diary, that this lunch will go better than Gouri's wildest imagination.

**18 January 2010**

**7.21 p.m.**

WORST LUNCH IN THE HISTORY OF MANKIND. WORST.

I don't want to talk about it. But Gouri will. I have cleared my SMS inbox in preparation.

**20 January 2010**

**3.03 p.m.**

So far this is the status of things:

1. PIMPAG(E) website and real-time status update system is currently being designed by a team at the National Informatics Centre in Hyderabad. Fingers crossed.
2. Another team from NIC is currently figuring out camera placement locations inside the MURPS office. Fingers crossed.
3. Everything is set for Joel's contract except the two fake quotations. I have asked Sugandh to do the needful.

As expected the BBC was the only media outlet to run a somewhat negative story about PIMPAG(E).

Their words:

While the ministry is showing uncommon alacrity in unveiling an unprecedented new scheme to bring greater transparency to the Allied Victory Games, it remains to be seen how sincere these efforts are. The Allied Victory Games are perilously close to becoming a national embarrassment. Allegations of corruption and shoddy work are rife in the corridors of power in New Delhi. Is this initiative by the fringe MURPS too little too late?

Or just another headache that will plague the organizers?

My words:

YOU KNOW WHAT IS A NATIONAL EMBARRASSMENT? PRINCE CHARLES'S FACE, YOU BASTARD. WHAT HAPPENED TO HIM? AND ONCE HE BECOMES KING YOU WILL BE THE ONLY COUNTRY IN THE WORLD WHERE CHILDREN CRY WHEN THEY SEE YOUR MONEY OR STAMPS. YOU KNOW WHAT IS SHODDY WORK? MILLENNIUM DOME! WHAT IS THAT NONSENSE? WHO BUILDS AN EMPTY DOME TO CELEBRATE ANYTHING? NEXT WHAT? A SPECIAL CHRISTMAS CAR PORCH?

Stop giving lectures to other people, man. Just because you beat the Germans in two wars you think you can tell everyone how to run their country. First you win just one penalty shoot-out in an international football match and then you talk.

I think I know whose words I enjoy more.

**5.05 p.m.**

Some idiot called me up from the MURPS accounts section with some doubt. Unbelievable, Diary.

He asked me if it was compulsory, as per the PIMPAG(E) programme, to upload every single piece of AVG2010-related work on the website. I said this was 100 per cent sacrosanct and non-negotiable. If it can't be uploaded then the project should not be undertaken. Any fraud and the public and the media will lose all faith in us.

So he asked me what he was supposed to do with the work order that was being sent to NIC for designing the website. He said since there was no website right now, he could not upload it anywhere. And if he can't upload it anywhere he can't release the work order to NIC. And if they don't get the order they can't make the website.

I told him to wait for one second. Then I put the phone down, closed the door to my room and assaulted one of my potted plants for two minutes. Then I picked up the phone, told him to relax and file the work order in a temporary folder somewhere. Once the website is up we could upload all of them in bulk.

He seemed satisfied.

DIARY HOW ARE THESE PEOPLE WORKING IN OUR GOVERNMENT? HOW IS INDIA NOT COLLAPSING INTO A MESS?

Instead of bombing Pakistan we should be bombing our ministries.

Unbelievable.

**6.23 p.m.**

SMS from Gouri: 'Why are you making things so hard for both of us?'

That potted plant is so fucked today.

## 11.42 a.m.

Harish, Fundango CEO, came to meet me today.

Now it sounds very high class and posh. Two CEOs meeting each other, exchanging notes, discussing strategy. Maybe they go to play golf. Compare their frequent flier miles. Go on luxury holidays together. Their children become best of friends and go to the same boarding school in Ooty or Geneva.

Unfortunately Harish is clearly some kind of smuggler/kidney harvester/criminal-type fellow. He is the sort of guy I would only let into my office if all the female employees have already gone home.

You should see the amount of oil in his hair. One day America will invade his head just for the oil.

Slimy fellow.

But the bastard always gives us fake quotations on his letterhead whenever we need. Even for this Joel quote. Sugandh went to his office. And in fifteen minutes he came back with a quote for expert international consulting services.

So I can't throw him out also.

Harish came, sat in my office, had some tea and then spent one and a half hours trying to basically figure out how much salary I was making. This never happened before in Mumbai or London.

Only Delhi people will shamelessly try to find out how much money I make. When I refused to share that information he moved on to the next headache: He reminded me of my promise to get him some government project in return for his services. Once again I reiterated my promise to help. But told him that it would take some time. Maybe after the Allied Victory Games were finished I'd arrange for something in the MURPS.

He looked very pleased. He told me that Fundango was ready to help Lederman with any mandate of any kind in whatever way possible. All I had to do was ask.

I laughed politely, shook his hands vigorously and then escorted him outside. And then I immediately washed my hands.

Painful guy. Instantly reminds me of that Bansal real estate fellow who used to live in Wadala.

**3.19 p.m.**

Where the heck is my Cross pen? I swear it was on my desk when Harish came to meet me.

Did I drop it in the restroom? Fuck. Gouri gave it to me when I moved back from London. Fuck.

I haven't even met Joyyontoh recently. Can't be him.

**3.24 p.m.**

Not in the restroom. Bloody.

**22 January 2010**

**6:05 p.m.**

WOOHOO JAILHOUSE ROCK! PARTY TIME!
  Off to Tihar.

## 23 January 2010

**11.42 a.m.**

Good news, Diary!

A rudimentary online PIMPAG(E) database is up and running at http://murps.nic.in/yashovardhan/finalfinaltestfinal_oneortwo mistakes.asp

(Joyyontoh has promised to get www.pimpag-e2010.nic.in set up in another week or so.)

Initially it looked like NIC would take weeks to get it ready. But then somebody remembered that they had an unused online web-enabled database system lying around from last year.

It had been made for the old Universal Citizen's Database project that got scrapped. Joyyontoh made a few phone calls and the UCD guys were more than happy to let us have it.

The sample database is not bad. Gets the job done. Joyyontoh tells me that testing should take another week. And we should have something to show the public by mid-February.

Also, Joel may fly to India as early as the first week of February. Which is pushing it a little bit in terms of merchandising strategy. But Joel is god. Joel will know exactly what to do.

I mean I have never worked with a more organized guy. He has already taken care of visa, accommodation in Delhi, and has even got approval to bring his own executive assistant to help him settle quickly into 'Indigo Hemingway'.

(That is the code name of this mandate. Indigo means it is based out of India. And Hemingway is the name someone in corporate accounts in Tokyo has chosen. I don't know why. In fact nobody knows why the Japanese office chooses such names. The Kingfisher mandate was called 'Indigo Polystyrene'. Must be all that raw fish in their diet.)

Now all that he needs to see before flying over is the signed contract from the MURPS. The moment that comes Joel flies in from London. When Joel flies billing starts. When billing starts money comes. When money comes John is happy. When John is happy Einstein becomes CEO.

When Einstein becomes CEO Raghu and Rajeev get terminated. Perfect plan.

### 7.12 p.m.

Was hoping to go tomorrow evening for a longish run with Jesal. But now Sharmila wants to sit late with me to finalize the summer intern plan. I don't even know why we're putting so much thought into this. The fuckers who are coming have no interest in Lederman. Half of them accepted our offer so that they don't have to sell sanitary napkins to tractor drivers in rural Haryana.

But you know how idealistic Sharmila is. I can understand the people in legal or finance being worried about morality and all. But people in HR?

Comedy.

Anyway will call Jesal up and postpone.

### 7.15 p.m.

In fact I should meet her at the gym and postpone. Anyway it is on the way home. Might as well say hi.

### 7.19 p.m.

You know what? Might as well just go for dinner. If she is free.

## 24 January 2010

### 11.42 a.m.

Utter useless panic in the morning. Cleo called up from corporate HR in Tokyo to know why I haven't sent the appraisal forms yet for last year. I told her that we were too busy with actual work that made revenue for the company rather than waste time with irrelevant documentation.

Then five minutes later John called me up.

For the last forty-five minutes everyone in the office has been sitting and filling in their self-appraisal forms. After this I need to review all the forms, add my comments and send them to Tokyo by Wednesday.

Fucking nonsense. They won't make me CEO. But they will make me do all the work of a CEO. Fed up. Anyway the one benefit of being interim-CEO is that I don't have to fill one of those stupid forms myself.

Small blessings.

### 1.46 p.m.

Have ordered lunch from Subway. It will now take anywhere from thirty minutes to three and a half hours for delivery. But till then I should tell you about last night.

From the office I went directly to Fighting Fit to pick up Jesal. I waited at the reception till she finished her Pilates class, took a shower, changed and came out.

That is when, Diary, I realized something. I've actually never seen her dressed in anything but gym clothes. In gym clothes, as you know, she is a 75 per cent carbon copy of Anushka Sharma in *Rab Ne Bana Di Jodi*. Almost ditto. Jesal has a slightly sharper nose and much more high-pitched voice, but otherwise in terms of overall look and feel she is Anushka.

But today, when she was leaving the gym, she was wearing a tight black full-sleeve formal shirt tucked into her skinny blue jeans and sensible high heels. ENTE DEIVAME ENTHORU HOT!

You know sometimes when you are standing in a line outside a theatre, or when you're boarding a crowded plane you suddenly spot a woman right in front of you? You are standing so close that you can literally smell the shampoo in her hair (jasmine? jojoba?) and see the tiny hairs on the back of her neck? And suddenly you are overcome by a need to kiss this woman?

And you think to yourself what would happen if you did? Would she scream? Would she call for help? Or maybe, just maybe, she might melt in your hands, lean backwards, open her mouth and just succumb to your sexual energy? And then she will reach up and put her palm behind your head and draw you even further into the kiss because, frankly, she has never been kissed like this before. And then your hand drops to the small of her back and you draw her towards you, your bodies meeting in the middle ...

But of course at this moment Gouri will ask you why you are so quiet and what you are looking at. Thus destroying the only sex you are getting ever since that bloody uncle has come to Delhi. So you suddenly look around and make up some lie about how the colour of that woman's shirt reminds you of a bottle of Issey Miyake perfume you saw in the airport that you were planning to buy as a surprise for someone. And then Gouri nudges you and smiles sweetly and you hug her while making a mental note to recreate that imaginary kiss later when you have more privacy.

If I could, Diary, I would have walked up to Jesal and ...

(Goosebumps everywhere right now.)

Of course I effortlessly hid my desires, and Jesal had no idea that these thoughts were going through my mind as I got up with my laptop bag in front of me and said hello. She looked absolutely thrilled to see me. I told her I had come to postpone our run but also to ask if she wanted to join me for a quick snack.

Jesal thought about it for a while, and then suddenly looked really excited. She said she was ready to come, provided I would accompany her on a brief shopping trip before we ate.

Fifteen minutes later we were at the Connaught Place Shoppers Stop. I was slightly afraid that Gouri might catch us together inside.

Shoppers Stop is her absolutely favourite place to actually buy something. She will go to Benetton and Mango and all. But then for three hours after that she will cry about how fat she is. No such issues at Shoppers Stop.

Jesal ran inside and directly went to the women's clothing section. I followed at a respectful distance behind her. She walked straight past Indian formals. (I was intrigued.) Then she walked past Indian casuals. (Hello!) Then she walked past Western casuals. (What the . . .) And then raced past Western formals. (My pulse started to pick up.) She ignored footwear and accessories completely. (I was beginning to get that feeling.) She zipped past handbags, T-shirts, and one Shoppers Stop employee randomly shooting some perfume at innocent passers-by. (THUD THUD THUD THUD)

And, just as I predicted, she stopped right at the lingerie section. (INSTANT HEART FAILURE AND ASTHMA) I immediately took a step back and began to study a handbag with great concentration. Jesal could see I was a little embarrassed. She giggled, told me to go for a walk if I was embarrassed and meet me outside at the exit in fifteen minutes.

Ten minutes later she came down with a tiny Shoppers Stop bag in her hand. Diary, a thousand images flashed through my mind: images of lingerie, images of Jesal, images of Jesal in lingerie, images of Anushka in Jesal's lingerie, images of Jesal and Anushka in lingerie, images of Jesal helping Anushka put on lingerie . . .

Next thing I know we are eating some form of salad-type thing at the Imperial Hotel's coffee shop. It was nearly impossible to have a conversation with Jesal without my mind falling into that lingerie-thought-loop again.

Between salad and our shared dessert (tiramisu) Jesal suddenly asked me if I had to run back home after dinner. A piece of bread completely missed my throat and went straight into my lungs. A few seconds of suffocation later, I told her I was in no hurry whatsoever and had nothing to do. She asked me if I minded dropping in at her house for a few minutes after dinner.

I told her I was prepared to drop in for as long as she wanted.

She said she had a huge surprise for me.

Diary, you must have heard that A.R. Rahman song called 'Urvashi Urvashi'. In the beginning of that song there is a bass beat. My heart was beating exactly like that.

After dinner we took a cab directly to her house near Gol Market. It is not a very glamorous house. Still it was small and reasonably furnished. She told me to sit on the sofa and watch TV while she prepared my surprise.

Lingerie in a small packet. Special surprise. That look of excitement. Dinner. Questions about my work schedule.

Diary, there was little doubt about what was about to happen.

A thousand moral and ethical problems ran through my mind. First of all had I done anything to intentionally seduce Jesal? As far as I know I had done nothing at all. These things can happen unintentionally also. And how can I control spontaneous seduction?

I am helpless, Diary.

Secondly, was I exploiting Jesal in any way? Was she in a vulnerable or damaged state of mind where she is trying to use sex as a remedy? Perhaps she has broken up with a boyfriend and is trying to take out her frustration?

I made a mental note to talk to her about this at a later date. Bringing up something like that with her right now would be just too traumatic and cruel.

Thirdly entering into a sexual relationship with my girlfriend's cousin was just not correct in our culture. However, there are other countries in the world where this would be perfectly normal. In fact they even encourage you to experiment with other people. So that you can be certain when you finally decide to settle down with someone that he or she is the right person for you. And that it is not a fling.

It is only in our petty, narrow-minded culture that such things are discouraged. This is why in India so many people are unhappy in their marriage. Because they have no experience or exposure to either their own spouse or to other people of the opposite sex. This is why Kaiser chettan in Kodungalloor did not know till three years after marriage that Rashmi chechi had only one kidney. And you know very well how he is nowadays. Very sad.

Diary, I do not want to marry Gouri only to discover tomorrow that she has organ shortage. Or that she was not, in fact, my ideal soulmate. The more I sat there and thought about it, the more it became clear to me. Whatever would happen with Jesal would only help to strengthen my decision to marry Gouri. It was a test, and I had to pass it. For Gouri's sake.

I cannot afford to step back now.

I sat there and tried to think of non-sex-type thoughts so as to prolong . . . the process. I thought of the most repulsive person I know right now. Harish, the CEO of Fundango. It was an excellent move. I could literally feel my penis withdrawing into my body.

Suddenly Jesal shouted from inside her bedroom: 'CLOSE YOUR EYES ROBIN! THE SURPRISE IS COMING!'

OH MY GOD DIARY OH MY GOD OH MY GOD OH MY GOD OH MY GOD OH MY GOD OH MY GOD OH MY GOD!!!!!!!!!

I closed my eyes and simultaneously thought of both Jesal and Harish in the most sexy lingerie possible. To maintain balance.

I could hear her footsteps on the floor. Firm, slow, shy yet determined. I could hear her walk towards me. Soon she was right in front of me. I could now smell Jesal's unique fragrance: Head & Shoulders (menthol). My heart thumped like a diesel engine.

Breathing had stopped long ago itself.

She put her hands over my eyes. 'You are not looking no?'

As she touched my face I trembled. Suddenly my stomach felt like it was being dissolved in acid. My mind was telling my hands to reach out and grab her. My hands were telling my mind to maintain some dignity and self-control. My mind then told my hands that they were unnecessarily dragging out the inevitable and being cautious. My hands, still on the sofa, said that they would never make the first move on a woman. My mind may be a third-rate bastard. But my hands have class.

I could hear a rustling in front of me. In my mind's eye I knew immediately what was happening. She had walked into the room in a little spaghetti strapped silk nightie. And now she had shrugged them off her shoulders. Her nightie was now on the floor, a pool of light and shadow around her feet.

Then the rustling stopped.

'Okay Robin. Open your eyes now!'

Diary . . . I opened my eyes.

And immediately in front of me I saw a shoe. A Nike shoe. She was holding it right up to my face. My immediate thought was: 'What the fuck does a Nike shoe have to do with mad, all-night, animal sex?'

And then I smiled. Jesal surely had some wild idea that involved standing on one leg, or gently slapping with a shoe . . . Whatever it is I was ready!

And then suddenly something occurred to me. I had seen this same type of shoe before. But where? Where? Where?

OH FUCK YAAR!

This was the Bombay Marathon shoe.

'I AM GOING TO RUN THE MARATHON WITH YOU ROBIN! TO GIVE YOU MORAL SUPPORT! THIS IS SO EXCITING ROBIN!!!!'

She withdrew the fucking shoe from my face and then showed me all her marathon application forms and papers. There was a plastic bag on the floor.

Instantly I switched from 'Sexually Betrayed and Devastated' to 'Outwardly tremendously excited but inwardly suicidal and enraged!' This was exactly how I felt when at Pranchi's wedding they told me to sit for dinner last because I was a part of the groom's family. So the whole afternoon I had to go around serving useless buggers meen curry and pork. And by the time we sat down to eat only chicken and fish gravy was there. It was terrible.

I told her I was so taken aback that I did not know what to say. (Of course I knew what to say: a mixture of Malayalam, Hindi and Punjabi abuse. And then suicide.)

I told her that this was one of the nicest things anyone had ever done for me in a really long time. And that I was utterly moved. She looked at me. And then came and hugged me. Of course by now my sexual organs had already withdrawn completely into my body and were now probably stuck in between my kidneys forever.

She hugged me tightly and told me that from the look on my face she knew how much this meant to me.

After all this drama, hugging me so tightly was just human rights abuse, Diary. 100 per cent human rights abuse. Either you give mixed signals and then present yourself in lingerie. Or you give 100 per cent unambiguous signals no? And then on top of that you come and hug me as if you are trying to show what I am missing. I responded to her hug by gently putting my hands around her.

Her body, Diary . . . It felt like it was carved out of the most supple, smooth teak wood. Every curve flowing into the next curve smoothly. Occasionally I could feel a bone. But not in a bony way. In an athletic, toned way. If she had been born in Switzerland instead of Surat, Jesal would be one of those mysterious, angry Victoria's Secret models who come on FTV.

Also the height. What a perfect height. When she hugged me, her ears were perfectly in alignment with my mouth. Her hair, fine and soft and perfumed, caressed my cheek.

And then she said that the whole thing had been her boyfriend's idea. He knew somebody who could arrange a VIP invitation for the 15-kilometre event at short notice. And he thought that Jesal running along with me would provide me with the perfect motivation to complete my run in good time.

I told her that her boyfriend had been very kind. And also WHAT CRIMINAL THIRD-RATE BASTARD SON OF A BITCH MOTHERFUCKER SCUM OF THE EARTH TAX EVADING TRAITOR CRIMINAL was this boyfriend? Why had she not mentioned him before?

Apparently between all her motivation and coaching she had never found an opportunity. She had met 'Subbu' in the gym one day. They were using adjacent elliptical training machines. Jesal had never used that particular machine before and was struggling to find the setting for 'Fat Burner' mode.

(WHY THE FUCK DOES JESAL WANT TO GO INTO FAT BURNER MODE? WHY? WHAT IS WRONG WITH THESE PEOPLE? THEN WHAT MODE SHOULD I GO INTO? STOMACH AMPUTATION MODE?)

Subbu stopped his training, and asked her if he could help. He set up her machine and asked if he could buy her a smoothie from the Diet Bar after her workout. One thing led to another and now they've been going out 'seriously' for six weeks. Jesal says she has a good feeling about him.

I told her that she was very lucky to find such a smart and thoughtful guy. And probably once she did some background checking to make sure he was not a sex criminal, because this is Delhi after all and you never know, I wished her all the best for the relationship.

She just laughed and said that not all men always had sex on their minds. I told her I was just joking except that sometimes you never know till it is too late. She kept on laughing. Stupid, stupid, poor trusting Jesal.

I told her that she should introduce me to Subbu some day. Perhaps in the gym. She promised.

After that we discussed our final set of training plans and our travel schedules for the trip to Bombay for the marathon.

And then I went home.

You may think, Diary, that I was somehow very very upset about the terrible fraud that Jesal pulled off. I was, for a little bit. But then there was also a positive outcome.

I really understood the value of a person like Gouri.

Now, Diary, I am not saying that Gouri is perfect. She is not. Nobody is. Like any other human being she has her own set of faults. She worries too much about her family. She keeps comparing me to other people. She enrols people for marathons without waiting for their opinion. She has terrible taste in gym clothes. Sometimes when we are in restaurants with other people she will order complicated things for me just to show them that I am sophisticated. Once she ordered something Korean that smelled like the gobar gas plant in Rani Aunty's house in Mavelikkara. She thinks I am not sophisticated.

But she would never, never, ever, ever treat me like Jesal did today. She would never lead me on like that and then leave me feeling like a manipulated idiot. Gouri will either say 'Yes, let us make out now' or 'No! We will make out now only after a decision is reached between Papa and Colonel Uncle.'

This is why I love her.

Jesal means nothing to me any more. As far as I am concerned from now onwards she is a close friend. And unless something develops that is how I would like to keep things.

I want a woman I can trust. Just a sexy, smooth, supple, fragrant body is not enough by itself.

## 25 January 2010

### 11.42 a.m.

HA HA HA HA HA HA HA HA HA HA HA. AHA HA HA HA HA HA HA HA ... HA HA HA HA HA HA HA HA ...

Ayyo ente Diary. I have been laughing non-stop for the last two hours going through Rajeev's and Raghu's self-appraisal forms. HA HA HA HA. There is more fiction in their forms than in that *Anna Karenina* book that I got for poetry writing in engineering college and ammamma fit under the water pump to stabilize it.

Apparently Rajeev is a 'game-changing addition to the Lederman Delhi office'. And Raghu is 'the central strategic lynchpin and defacto chief mentor for all junior staff'.

Dey dey dey dey dey dey. Too much. Too much.

Clearly they think that I will just sign off on this rubbish and forward it to Tokyo. So that they can get their increments and promotions.

Fuck off, Rajeev. And Raghu. Hey. Fuck you too.

Now I am going to sit and add my own comments to their appraisal forms. And unlike them I am going to keep it 100 per cent authentic.

This is going to be fun.

### 1.46 p.m.

WOO HOO! Joyyontoh called to say that a courier has just been sent from the MURPS. And then he cut the phone. Drama queen.

MUST BE THE JOEL CONTRACT! AWESOME!

### 3.23 p.m.

Just got a courtesy call from Tihar Balasubramaniam. Interesting fellow. But I didn't think he would actually follow up on our conversation at the Sanjay Gandhi Memorial Tihar Inmate's Annual New Party.

I haven't told you about that no? Later. I am too busy ripping a new anus for both Rajeev and Raghu.

**5.09 p.m.**

Finally. I have finished my comments on Raghu's and Rajeev's forms and uploaded them to the central HR system for John to review. There is going to be some awkwardness in the office for the next few days. As soon as I upload their appraisal forms a copy of my comments is downloaded to the HR folders in Raghu's and Rajeev's Intranet space. Those guys are going to be pretty shocked when they come to office tomorrow and log on. Try and change that game you strategic fuck-pins.

Forget CEO. When John sees my comments those bastards will be lucky if they are retained as summer interns in the peon department. Thoroughly satisfied.

Left John a quick email to pick up my comments whenever he had the time. No point in delaying the delight no?

Wink. Nudge. Wink.

P.S. Joel's contract has been signed, approved and delivered. Mission accomplished. Einstein delivers again!

**6.21 p.m.**

Long long hard day. But now I want to sit and tell you about the most amazing New Year party I have ever been to ...

One second. Fuck. John is calling from Tokyo. Does he ever sleep? Later.

**6.23 p.m.**

Fucked.

Fucked fucked fucked.

**11.32 p.m.**

Still in office. Waiting for Sugandh to come.

Five fucking hours ago John called me and basically destroyed my complete strategy. He said he didn't want to review my comments before Raghu and Rajeev had submitted their comments on my self-appraisal.

What the ...

I told him to clarify. After all I was always under the impression that the branch office CEOs did not have to fill in forms. They had their appraisals carried out, if required, in the form of a one-on-one conversation with their regional head. In my case that would be John.

John said that I was correct. But not in the case of interim-CEOs. So I asked him what interim-CEOs had to do. Yes, Diary, I inserted a little bit of sarcasm into my voice. Just to let John know how displeased I was.

John said that India was a special case because we did not have a CEO. So to make things fair for all three senior staff members he has decided to make each of them review the other two. In other words I had to fill in a self-appraisal form myself. And then get Raghu and Rajeev to review it. And then John would review all our individual forms.

Infinite number of fucks.

So John told me that he was going to wait for all three forms to come in before reviewing them. He asked me if I had already filled in my form. I said no. He said that if I had ambitions of becoming a CEO I needed to start getting the small things right at least. He said he wanted to see all three forms by end of day tomorrow. And then he went back to sleep, or dress like a girl, or eat in a toilet-themed restaurant or whatever it is those Japanese people do for amusement.

Of course now I was completely screwed. I immediately called up Sugandh and told him to rush to office. Before I sat down to fill in my appraisal form, I had to remove my original comments from Raghu's and Rajeev's forms.

Look, Diary. People like to think that they are honest and just and meritorious. But in reality people are unfair, dishonest, biased, conceited motherfuckers. Even if Rajeev and Raghu know that my self-appraisal is good they will screw me over. In revenge for my harsh yet accurate comments on their appraisal.

There was now only way to save my appraisal. First I had to

somehow delete my original comments from the HR server. Then I had to put fresh comments on both those idiots' appraisals. Reupload them. And then send them my own self-appraisal and hope they don't act like complete assholes.

There was one problem. Once you upload comments on to the HR server you can't delete or remove them. Only a server admin can do that on the express orders of somebody senior from corporate. HR's excuse for this stupid rule is that this makes people think seriously before uploading reviews and comments. And prevents the system from being manipulated.

Very good. Thank you very much you Mahatma Gandhis in HR. I hope you get at least the Ramon Magsaysay Award for human rights. You dicks.

But what the hell do you do in a legitimate situation like this where I have to prevent a gross injustice being done by Rajeev and Raghu? This is the problem with HR departments. They want you to work like adults. But then threaten you like children. I am fed up of having to deal with these idiots, Diary. One day when I start my own company I will make sure I will not have an HR department whatsoever.

Wait. No. I will hire an HR department. Then I will fire all of them and make them all take each other's exit interviews and then I will laugh at them and tell them all to fuck off.

Of course once again I have no option but to ask Sugandh to help me. He is not supposed to have server admin rights to our HR server. But Sugandh is Sugandh. He always has a way. Thank god, Diary, that I convinced him to move with me from London.

He was very reluctant. After the FSA investigation scandal in London they had hired him to work for the company on a pretty good salary package. And they even managed to get him a Tier 1 visa. He told me that it had been his lifelong dream to work abroad. And now that he finally had an opportunity I was asking him to move back to India.

Then when John asked me to hire somebody for IT in Delhi I called him up again. Again he said no. Finally, after several negotiations about salary and designation he agreed. Provided that he always had an open option to go back to London if he wanted. I actually managed to get this for him in writing in his offer letter.

You will ask why I did this, Diary. Why did I go to all this trouble for a guy who has less formal education in computers than a Big Bazaar cashier? Well, the one thing I learnt in London three years ago was this: You cannot fight alone. You can be talented, hard-working and a superb strategician. But you can still be defeated in the battlefield of the modern office if you don't have resources in the form of trustworthy assistants.

Sugandh is the ideal right-hand man. He is discreet, resourceful, loyal, hard-working and always has my interest topmost on his list of priorities. But most importantly he is a man of his word. This is why I was prepared to make any sacrifice to get him to move from London.

Unfortunately tonight he has gone to see some award-winning film at the India Habitat Centre with some new girlfriend. (Even I don't go to IHC. Fraud.) He has promised to reach office in another . . . ten minutes or so.

### 11.45 p.m.

Sugandh is saying he will take another thirty minutes now.

Useless fellow. Never lands up anywhere on time for anything. His punctuality is terrible. I don't see why the company didn't just recruit someone locally who values their job more.

Anyway. No option but to wait.

### 3.18 a.m.

Soooooooo sleeeeeeepppppppyyyyy.

But also sooooooo relievedddddddd.

Sugandh came, and I told him of the problem. He thought about it for a while and said that there was only a small chance that we could still rectify my comments. It was only possible if Raghu and Rajeev hadn't still accessed the HR server. If they had, they already knew and there was nothing we could do. If they had not, then Sugandh said he knew what to do.

He would log in as admin into Raghu's and Rajeev's desktops, log in into their Intranet space and then access the HR server. There he would replace their forms with my new ones with 'kinder' comments. (PUKE PUKE PUKE)

After that he would access the HR server logs and edit them. So that our minor modifications don't show up. Also this would prevent the system from sending both of those imbeciles a second notification email. But of course all this depended on both of them not having checked their files already.

Diary, you know how these slimy people like Raghu and Rajeev are. Send them an urgent email saying 'client is waiting for information' or 'if you do not close this mandate in two days I will personally come and castrate you with a glue stick' and they will not reply for three months. But send them an email about salary or appraisal or reimbursement and you will get a response even before my 'sent mail' sound—'Boom Shaka-Lak'—has come on the computer.

Terrible sense of priorities.

So I was holding my breath while Sugandh logged into Raghu's computer first. MOTHER OF GOD PRAISE THE LORD ALLELUIAH! He had still not accessed the form. Sugandh immediately removed the form, changed the logs and logged out. Raghu's password is 'JaiMataDiJandewalan'.

And then, while Sugandh was accessing Rajeev's computer, a thought suddenly occurred to me. Had both of them started work on my review? What if a set of comments about R-E-V was lying on their desktop somewhere? So while my Man Friday logged into Rajeev's machine I browsed through Raghu's.

As far as I could see there was nothing. Nothing in document history, MS Word history, recycle bin or trash. And he hadn't logged into the HR server for weeks. I searched for all kinds of things: 'Robin review, Varghese review, Robin appraisal, Super boss,' etc. etc. Zilch.

Rajeev's machine also looked uninteresting until, at the very last second before Sugandh quickly logged off, I noticed that the folder on his desktop called 'HR Documents' was 3.4 GB in size.

Interesting. No, Diary? Maybe his REV comments were hidden away somewhere inside.

So while Sugandh waited, and he was very unhappy about this, I took a pen drive and made a copy of this complete folder. Sugandh said that this was not part of our original deal. And that he was uncomfortable doing such immoral things in India when he'd rather be in London doing serious IT work.

BLOODY FOOL! WHAT SERIOUS IT WORK???!!! BEFORE I GOT YOU A JOB IN LEDERMAN YOU WERE AN ILLEGAL IMMIGRANT SITTING IN A HOTEL HELPING PEOPLE PRINT BOARDING PASSES! WHEN JASON IN LONDON ASKED YOU IN THE INTERVIEW IF YOU KNEW HOW TO FORMAT A SERVER YOU SAID 'WHITE SHIRT, BLACK TROUSERS, BOW TIE IF IT IS A HIGH-CLASS HOTEL AND A SMALL WHITE TOWEL'. AND YOU ARE GIVING ME LECTURE? FUCKER.

I took the pen drive and came back home one and a half hours ago. There are thousands of files in it. But nothing seems to pertain to me. In fact most of them are files belonging to his stint at BancoGeneve. Folders called Provident Fund, Salary Slips, Insurance, Retirement Plan. Useless shit like that.

Anyway I will go through these files in detail sometime later. Too tired right now. It has been late night after late night after late night these days. First that lunch with Gouri's family. (Diary entry pending.) Then Tihar New Year party (Diary entry pending). And now this appraisal nonsense.

Off to bed.

We have a lot to catch up on.

**26 January 2010**

**9.02 a.m.**

Happy Republic Day, Diary.

On the one hand I feel quite patriotic this morning. Especially when I see the parade on TV. At least once a year we manage to get more than ten Indians to stand in a line and move together.

On the other hand traffic is going to be horrible to get to office because of security.

**2.32 p.m.**

Massively busy day today, Diary. No time to chat. Joel's contract has been sent to HO. Internship plans have to be sent to Tokyo for sign off. Appraisal forms done. (Those guys seem to have no idea about our midnight operation. Fingers crossed.)

You carry on. I will talk to you later then.

## 27 January 2010

### 11.01 a.m.

Had a long telephone call with Gouri just now. She wants to plan another surprise party with her family. So that I can make up for the minor misunderstandings that happened the last time I went to her house. She wants me to plan something on the weekend so that I can spend the day with her family outdoors somewhere. And then go to a nice restaurant for my 'treat'.

I told her that I will think about date, venue and feasibility based on my schedule and then get back in touch with her. She said that she had already invited her family 'on my behalf' for entertainment followed by dinner next Friday. Of course I was enraged. How can she just take me for granted like that? But then she quickly said she loves me and cut the phone before I could retaliate.

Women are such sly, evil creatures, Diary.

Honestly speaking I am prepared to do anything to avoid next Friday. Like inject myself with typhoid bacteria (virus?) or cut off a small piece of my body or something. But then 100 per cent Gouri will come to hospital with her family and Domino's Pizza and try to create bonding.

Might as well go along with her plan.

### 3.41 p.m.

Joel Harrison will arrive on the 7th of February. I called up to inform Joyyontoh. Who said it was always a pleasure to once again have people with the finest British education in the ministry. Apparently Lord Mountbatten used to once handle the MURPS back when it used to be the directorate of architecture.

### 5.16 p.m.

In order to seem enthusiastic about the dinner plan I sent Gouri an SMS: 'How many people should I book tickets and table for sweety?'

She replied: 'Eleven people excluding you Robbie.'

I took the phone and threw it straight out of the door and across the cubicles where it hit one of the printers and then bounced off into the conference rooms. (BlackBerrys are solid.)

ELEVEN PEOPLE! ELEVEN! THEN DO ONE THING NO? CALL ONE VIDEO CAMERA FELLOW, ONE STILL PHOTOGRAPHER, COME IN A SARI AND THEN LET US GET MARRIED NO? ANYWAY YOUR ENTIRE FAMILY IS ALREADY THERE? WHY WASTE THE OPPORTUNITY???

STUPID.

Gouri plus Giggs plus parents are four. Colonel plus his wife is two. Total of six. Who the heck are the other five people? There are no more Kalbags in Delhi that I am aware of.

Don't think. Just obey. That is the trick to a good love life.

### 7.13 p.m.

Called up FresCo at Ambience mall and booked a table for twelve people. Ideally on Friday night there should be a lot of traffic and Gouri's family should get stuck for at least one and a half hours. Small joys.

Initially I was thinking I will book a table at Grey Peter's Grill and laugh like a madman inside while they ordered from the exclusive vegetarian menu of three items. But then that will just piss off Gouri too much. I may complain about her always to you, Diary. But I do still love her very much indeed.

It is only the rest of the family I can't stand.

So let me tell you about the 'Lunch From Hell'.

As you know Gouri's father runs an industrial supplies business with the head office in Delhi and a branch in Mumbai. I don't know exactly what they sell. Gouri never talks about it because she thinks it is extremely unsophisticated.

(I don't know. Maybe he deals in toilet commodes or something. Which is actually tremendously dignified if you think about it. What if nobody used commodes? The whole bloody world would be like Tamil Nadu.)

Gouri's mom is a housewife. Paula Aunty used to be a schoolteacher for a few years before marriage. Believe it or not, Diary, she used to teach English in school.

HAHAHAHAHAHAHAHAHAHAHAHAHAHA.

Reminds me of Srinivasan Uncle who teaches Hindi in a school in Abu Dhabi. Three or four years ago several parents complained to have him removed. Some of the kids had come to India for an international Hindi debating competition in Delhi. Apparently everyone laughed at them because each and every one of them spoke high-class Hindi with a horrible Malayali accent. Throughout the event they were known as the 'Abu Dhabi A.K. Antonys'.

I have briefly met both her parents before. They had come to the Institute for our convocation. And then again for her dad's 60th birthday party event.

This was last year. In September I think. The party had a theme: 'Paneer'. In everything: samosa, kebab, dhokla, mini-puff, sandwich and even dosa. It was horrible. They arranged it at some shady marriage hall in Gurgaon next to a hospital. So I asked them how the patients coped with all the noise during weddings. One of the catering staff told me about the hospital's arrangement. Whenever there is a wedding and there is too much noise the hospital puts all the emergency patients in one of the ambulances and takes them for a long drive till the party gets over.

For this they charge Rs 2500 per patient from the marriage hall people. Free markets, Diary. Capitalism. Shocking. But true. Welcome to north India. This is what I have to deal with on a daily basis.

Anyway. At that time Gouri still had not informed them about us. So we had to act as if we were very close friends and nothing more. The funny thing, Diary, is that this was actually much more enjoyable than acting like a couple in a relationship.

If you are a couple in love then Indian parents are damn scared that some hanky-panky is going on. Boy and girl are in the car alone? Definitely making out. They are alone at home? Sex and sex and even more sex is happening. They have gone to the supermarket together? They are secretly groping in the health-food section.

Don't blame me, Diary. Blame the dirty mind of the Indian

parent. Bloody fools think that their daughters are just dying to jump into bed with their boyfriends. HA HA HA HA. Ayyo.

On the other hand if you are a 100 per cent confirmed friend of a girl you can do whatever you want in front of her parents. Jump on top of her. Hug her. Dance with her. Go for films. Go swimming together. Tie one rakhi once in a while wearing a kurta and then Pongal-O-Pongal! You can do synchronized swimming with her naked and her parents will clap and encourage.

Stupid narrow-minded idiots. So I really enjoyed her dad's birthday party a lot. Full on 'friendship' happened.

But I had never met her brother till our lunch. During both our convocation and that party Giggs was in the UK. I was under the impression he worked or studied there or something. The truth is much more bizarre.

Now I always assumed that Giggs was some kind of shortened Gujarati name. Short for Gignesh or Gourikanth or something.

I had no fucking clue, Diary, that Giggs is a complete nut job.

So I went to her house exactly on time. Gouri had me completely trained for the meeting. I was supposed to talk to her father about my job, to her mother about my family and to Giggs about guy things like sports or something. I was not to speak to the Colonel or his wife unless I was specifically asked something. (Why? He is the Pope? Fucker.)

I dressed smartly in my black shirt, black jeans and shoes. Gouri opened the door with a huge smile on her face. Diary, she looked devastating. She had changed into one of her kurta-skin-tight-pyjama combinations. Mind blowing. Her hair was all combed and blow-dried and she was wearing just a hint of some kind of lip gloss. I immediately fell in love with her all over again.

And then Giggs came to the door.

HA HA HA HA HA HA HA HA HA HA HA HA HA HA HA HA HA. HA HA HA HA HA HA HA HA HA.

Diary, how can the same set of parents produce both the astoundingly gorgeous Gouri and the abstract art form that is Giggs?

Giggs was slightly taller than Gouri and almost painfully thin. He had a terrible stubble on his face that was full of hairless patches. And then there was his hair. He had it combed and gelled into some kind of bizarre pyramid thing on top of his head.

And he was dressed completely in red. Huge red T-shirt, bright red shorts, red socks and a pair of red sports shoes. I have seen people wear red in Kerala also. During election time Marxist idiots come to ask for votes wearing a red shirt. But even they have the common sense to wear a white dhoti for contrast.

What the fuck is this? A Gujju Maoist type?

Giggs shook my hand and said 'Hello mate!' with an accent I have never heard before. Then I went in and one by one shook hands or did namaste with everybody. We went and sat in the living room around a massive coffee table made of marble. Each leg was in the shape of an elephant. Huge elephants.

Diary, Gouri's house is actually very nice. It was not at all what I was expecting. To be frank, Diary, I had no idea she came from such a prosperous family. There was one huge TV in the living room and a smaller one in the dining room. And almost everything I could see was made of bronze or marble. And in a very classy way.

After a few minutes Colonel Kalbag came and sat in an armchair opposite me. He just sat there and looked at me. I said, 'Hello Colonel.' He did not say anything. I should have tried 'Hello Insane Old Man-dog'. I did not.

Gouri vanished into the kitchen. Her father, who seems like a reasonably harmless type, sat down on the sofa next to me and asked me how things were at office. Gouri had told them that I was working with the MURPS. And he seemed very impressed.

(Update: Colonel is still just sitting there and looking at me. In silence.)

Of course I immediately knew that they wanted to hear an oral biodata. So I gave him a quick but exhaustive outline of my educational and professional qualifications. He kept on humming in a very satisfied way throughout my presentation.

(Update: No sounds still from the Crazy Kakkoos Colonel.)

Then I asked him to tell me a little about himself and the family.

Diary, I know what you're thinking. But hasn't Gouri already told you everything about her family? Of course she has. But then why am I asking him again?

Oh Diary, will you never learn? These are fundamental people skills. I am fed up of having to remind you over and over again. See most people like talking about themselves. It is a basic human tendency.

If they don't that means there is something fundamentally wrong with them. Which is why I always ask this question to people in an interview. Tell me something about yourself. If you sense any discomfort immediately dismiss their application. Only the most useless people have nothing nice to say about themselves.

Most people enjoy the question. It makes them feel less nervous. They feel more comfortable and casual and open up. Also, human beings like answering open-ended questions they know the answers to. This makes them feel intelligent and socially well adjusted. Can you tell me something about yourself? Who is your role model? Where do you see yourself in five or ten years? Would you mind if I pick up this small marble statue of Lord Krishna and beat your psycho uncle to death with it?

Etcetera etcetera.

And if you listen carefully you can even pick up subtle hints to their personality. All these are basic techniques if you want to be a good interim-CEO, Diary.

Gouri's father must have spoken non-stop for some fifteen minutes. Meanwhile Gouri, her mother and the Colonel's wife came and placed several hundreds of kilos of snacks, drinks and sweets on the table. There were at least five types of dhoklas in three or four colours. I've never seen food in so many colours in my life, Diary.

It was becoming impossible to pay attention to her dad without constantly wanting to look at the food. Of course nothing was non-vegetarian. But some of these things were completely new to me.

And then suddenly Gouri's mother said that there was plenty of time to talk later. And that we should eat something first. Gouri got up to pass around the plates. But Aunty told her she would do it herself. She came and served me food with the broadest smile possible in the world.

Which is when I noticed. Aunty was wearing a backless blouse with her sari. Normally I notice these things immediately. Perhaps the tension of meeting her parents had got to me. But now I noticed it fully.

Now between the food and the backless blouse it was becoming impossible to keep track of what Uncle was saying. But soon I settled into a rhythm. I would look into his eyes for a few moments. Then I would look down my plate while simultaneously scanning all the other food. And then I would look into his eyes again. And then I would sip from my glass while popping a glance at Aunty's blouse over the rim.

Then suddenly Comrade Giggs reappeared and sat down next to Uncle. Red colour everywhere.

And then I realized that Uncle had stopped speaking.

(Update: Nope. Not a single word yet from the Colonel. Perhaps, I thought, he has died of some cardiac arrest or stroke. In which case it was best to let him be till I eat and leave.)

I asked Giggs why he wore red always. Gouri, Aunty and Uncle chuckled a little. Giggs looked dead serious. In fact he hadn't smiled even once since I arrived. Strange boy.

Uncle said that Giggs only wore the colour red always because he was a huge Manchester United fan. Giggs said that he was currently the founding president of the Gurgaon Manchester United Fans Association. I told him this was very impressive.

He said that his ultimate goal in life was to become the president of the All India Manchester United Fans Association. Aunty said that this was very hard and took years of preparation and determination.

I asked Giggs if he saw every single Manchester United match on TV. Gouri burst out laughing, shaking her head as if to say, 'You have no idea what you are getting into, Robbie sweety.'

Uncle asked Giggs to show me his room. So both of us got up and went.

Diary, Giggs's room is the single reddest thing on the surface of this planet. Perhaps even in the universe. One wall was covered only in various T-shirts. I could see small child-sized shirts to big man-sized shirts. Giggs said this was every shirt he had ever owned over the years. On another wall there was an assortment of posters and flags. The third wall had a massive hand painting of what looked broadly like a man giving birth to a massive jackfruit in the middle of a dirty purple mattress. Giggs, looking very proud, said that he had painted it himself. And it was a copy of the famous photo of Ryan Giggs taken in Munich in 1998 after some nonsense tournament. He said it took him three months to draw and he failed an exam because of it. And he said it with the same tone of voice in which someone would say that they had just saved a bucket full of babies from falling into a nuclear reactor and now wanted a cash prize. Bloody idiot.

On the fourth and final wall there were two TV screens. One was marked 'TV' and the other 'Devilscope'. Devilscope was playing a recording of some old football match. Everyone was wearing very short shorts and had long stupid hair. Giggs explained that Devilscope played a twenty-four-hour stream of Manchester United recordings, clips, highlights and news. He had the TV hooked up, illegally, to some UK-based channel that only broadcasted Manchester United programming.

By this time I am already struggling to not slap him across the face ten or fifteen times before referring him to a professional.

After this he asked me if I wanted to see his ticket collection.

Of course, I told him. But inside I was insanely jealous of those LTTE-type people who have cyanide capsules inside a tooth and can just commit suicide by biting on a molar. I was 100 per cent sure by now that there was something fundamentally wrong with him.

He removed a photo album from a cupboard and showed me dozens of original tickets for matches at the Manchester United stadium. Did he get fans in the UK to send him old tickets? He chuckled. Of course not, he said. Each year he spent two months in the UK watching Manchester United games.

This is why he couldn't attend Gouri's convocation or Uncle's birthday party. He was in Manchester watching the team play.

My eyeballs almost popped out. I told him that he must be really passionate. He said that Manchester United was more important to him than anything in the world. Even money or his family.

MY GOD DIARY WHAT IS WRONG WITH YOUNG PEOPLE THESE DAYS? DO THEY HAVE NO RESPECT FOR MONEY OR FAMILY OR REGULAR MENTAL HEALTH? WHY IS THIS LITTLE FUCK ALLOWED TO SPEND HIS TIME OBSESSED WITH SOME FOOTBALL TEAM IN SOME USELESS CITY IN THE UNITED KINGDOM?

At this time lunch was served. Thank god.

I sat down at the table with everyone including the Colonel and his wife. Both still silent. Aunty insisted that I sit in between Uncle and her. So that both of them could talk to me and make sure I ate. Gouri had a huge smile plastered across her face. Clearly things were going well. Of course this came as no surprise to me. What that Einstein was to physics this Einstein is to people skills.

Aunty insisted on serving me. She stood right over my shoulder loading up my plate with food. Which is when I realized that every time she served me . . . she was leaning into me quite considerably. As in she was . . .

Diary, basically her breasts kept nudging me in the back of my head over and over. Of course I acted as if nothing at all was happening. Then she sat down, placed one hand on my lap and asked me how the food was.

Ice-cold surprise shot through my body. Every muscle tightened. What the heck is going on? Does Gouri not see this? Of course not. She just seemed utterly satisfied. The Colonel and his wife ate quietly. Uncle talked about how his grandfather worked in Libya during the Second World War. And Giggs was eating with one hand. And using his mobile phone with the other.

Giggs told Aunty to stop bugging me and let me eat peacefully. She got slightly pissed off. She told him to shut up and be polite to visitors.

But wait. What did she call him? She didn't call him Giggs. She called him something else. I asked her what she called Giggs.

Giggs got very, very upset. Apparently he had told them many, many times to never use that name, especially in front of strangers. Aunty grabbed my shoulder and said that Robin was no stranger but like a member of the family. Then she looked at me and said that Gouri's brother had adopted the name Giggs when he was in school. It is the name of some Manchester United player.

Actually, she said, his name is Radheyshyam Brahmakumari Kalbag. A much better name, she said looking at the mad little fucker, than Giggs. She again repeated it just to irritate her son a little more.

Radheyshyam Brahmakumari Kalbag.

Diary, I tried very hard. I tried very, very hard. But sometimes there is only so much self-control someone can have. I burst out into what started as a laugh, but then quickly became an explosion of food and coughing and choking. Half of the pav bhaji in my mouth came bursting out of my nose and on to all the dishes kept on the table as I laughed.

I immediately tried to cover my mouth with my hand to prevent further spillage. But by then masala had entered my nose, my throat and perhaps even my lungs. I coughed violently depositing the rest of the pav bhaji all over the front of Aunty's sari.

I immediately gasped for air and in the process swallowed a massive piece of bun. I began choking almost immediately. The Colonel's wife, seeing me gasping for air, made a small yelping noise and fainted. Straight into her plate.

Meanwhile Uncle came and began to thump the top of my head and back to dislodge the bun. Aunty grabbed a glass of water and helped me drink it. Gouri just sat there frozen. Her face entirely expression free.

Meanwhile my face was beginning to turn purple. Thankfully Uncle held me by the shoulders and shook me vigorously till the blockage cleared and I could breathe again. It was only now that Aunty noticed Mrs Colonel lying face down in khandvi. Even the

Colonel hadn't noticed. (Super. These are the people standing at the border looking at China. No wonder.)

Aunty immediately offered to help me clean up. (I declined wholeheartedly and ran to a bathroom. Mostly marble. Several different types of facewash.) Meanwhile Gouri, Colonel and Uncle tried to revive Mrs Colonel. Giggs just sat there looking like the useless idiot that he is.

Thankfully there was no lasting damage. I politely waited for Mrs Colonel to regain consciousness, before I went home. (It seems that she used to have acute asthma as a child. And the moment she sees anyone gasping for breath she passes out from fear.)

And then I said bye to Gouri and ran back home. The afternoon had started so well. But it had clearly ended in a disaster. Now you know why Gouri was so upset afterwards.

Now she is hoping I will salvage the situation over dinner on Friday.

All this is very unfair. As if it is my mistake that her brother is such a cartoon character with the name of some B-grade villain in some horrible Akshay Kumar film.

But what to do. These are the prices we all have to pay for love.

Except you.

Sometimes I envy you, Diary.

Such a peaceful life. Just sit there every day. Quietly. Without ambition or disappointment. Without expectations or betrayal. Just existing.

I envy you.

## 29 January 2010

### 4.44 p.m.

Just got off a conference call with John, Joel and Sandy. (Sandy heads special projects in London for Lederman. Sounds like a posh foreigner no? Fucker is a desi who went to London ten to fifteen years ago and then eventually became a British citizen. Plays rugby on weekends. Multinational chooth bastard.)

You know what is more irritating than stupid foreigners talking about India? Indians talking about India. You know what is more irritating than that? Foreign Indians talking about India. Fuckers think we are living in some Satyajit Ray movie with children running around in shorts, women looking out of the window for weeks at a time and everybody else dying.

Thank you, traitorous bastards, but we have moved on. Nowadays all that only happens in places like UP, Bihar and Orissa.

John was the usual ignorant firang. He asked Joel to not let the 'primitive ways in which the Indian government worked' to put him off. HA HA HA HA. JAPAN IS TELLING US ABOUT PRIMITIVE GOVERNMENT. Fuckers change prime ministers like I change that hanging deodorant thing inside the commode.

John was just being ignorant. Sandy was being a madharchod. He told Joel not to drive because the roads in Delhi were full of 'cows and elephants'. Yes. Because Joel is coming to Delhi via a time travel machine.

Joel asked me if there was any problem in bringing his two laptops (work and personal) through Indian customs. Before I could answer Sandy jumped in and said that there was no problem because 'you can always pay them off with a hundred quid'.

Quid it seems. As if the fucker was born in Buckingham Palace, went to Eton, 'read classics' at Oxford and now plays polo for a living. BASTARD YOU WERE BORN IN BHATINDA AND WENT TO BITS PILANI.

However, full credit to Joel. He called me up later on this phone, and apologized for Sandy. And then we had a nice quick chat about all the arrangements. We have prepared an office both for Joel and for the assistant he is bringing from London. He will stay at the Lederman guest house in Defence Colony. Also Joyyontoh has arranged for a full-fledged series of orientation meetings before Joel starts work.

How exciting, Diary! This way I can just focus on all the important day-to-day public relations activities of the MURPS while Joel focuses on the revenue-generating part of the project.

However, something did happen that I got a little concerned about. Towards the end of the conference call John cracked a little joke. He jokingly told me not to get too used to having Joel around or Joel might just stay back to run the India office. I jokingly replied that if Joel did that he would be in violation of the terms of his business visit visa and would be amenable to a fine and time in prison. Sandy immediately started saying something about bribing the Indian police when John stopped him.

The joking stopped immediately.

But John's comment is still on my mind. Could that be a threat to me, Diary? You think John will try to pull a fast one on me once Joel is done with the project? Getting visa and all is not a problem these days. You bribe one or two people here and there, speak in some English accent, sign some MOU about investment and visa will happen.

Throughout this whole Joel process I had not even once thought of this long-term threat.

Hmm. I must be vigilant.

Five or six years ago I would have got completely hyper just thinking of John's joke. But today I am older, wiser and more mature. Not everything is a life-threatening crisis.

**4.56 p.m.**

FUCK DIARY THIS JOEL BASTARD IS GOING TO COME AND SHINE AND MAKE MONEY AND IMPRESS JOHN AND EVERYBODY ELSE AND THEN PEOPLE WILL THINK WHY DO

WE NEED SOME INEXPERIENCED INDIAN FELLOW AS THE
NEW CEO WHEN WE CAN GET THIS HI-FI BRITISH FELLOW
WITH HIS ACCENT AS THE CEO OF THE INDIAN OFFICE AND
THEN THEY WILL DEMOTE ME TO JUST BEING A SENIOR
PARTNER OR SOMETHING AND THEN I WILL GET INSULTED
AND THEN I WILL HAVE TO QUIT BECAUSE OF THIS AND
THEN I WILL HAVE TO FIND ANOTHER JOB BUT THEN
EVERYONE WILL SAY I AM UN-HIREABLE BECAUSE I AM
OVERQUALIFIED AND I USED TO BE INTERIM-CEO AND NOW
HOW CAN THEY HIRE ME AS A PARTNER IN THE GOLDMAN
SACHS INDIA OFFICE AND THEN THIS WILL KEEP ON
HAPPENING OVER AND OVER AGAIN AND I WILL GET FED UP
AND FINALLY END UP JOINING ICICI BANK OR SOMETHING
WHERE THEY WILL ALWAYS CALL ME THE UNDERACHIEVER
AND ALMOST-CEO AND THEN WHAT IS THE POINT OF LIVING
LIKE THAT DIARY? AYYO I AM GETTING SOMEWHAT PANICKY
NOW.

**5.03 p.m.**

Too much tension. So I ended up drinking seven cups of coffee. Now
I want to go to that Haven of Solitude, but for the last fifteen
minutes somebody or the other has been in the bathroom.

**5.32 p.m.**

Diary, that trip to the loo has helped me in many more ways than
just quality alone time.

Let me explain.

So after waiting ten to fifteen minutes I was finally able to secure
the HoS (Haven of Solitude) all to myself. I went in leisurely, found
a cubicle in pristine condition, sat down, took out my phone and
began to relax.

After I got highly agitated during my summer internship
recruitment trips last December Sugandh downloaded some really
nice games on my phone so that I can play them between interviews
and control my blood pressure.

So I started playing a football game on silent. (It gets very very loud inside the cubicles. Which is ridiculous no, Diary? If anything you would assume that people would make toilets with extreme sound absorption capabilities. Instead they make these places where within five seconds everybody on the floor will know that you had chilli paneer for lunch.)

After five or six minutes I heard two people walk in. Then they started talking. It was Raghu and Rajeev. And they were talking about the appraisal forms. Rajeev said how he was really happy that both of them were getting a chance to speak their mind about my leadership. Raghu made some crude joke about how you should never make a Malayali the CEO of anything or pretty soon everybody in the company will be a Malayali.

YES BECAUSE WE ARE LIKE EBOLA VIRUS NO? Fucker.

Then he asked Rajeev what their strategy was going to be. Rajeev said that since all of us were going to review each other's performances there was only so much they could officially put on record about me. Also, he said, it would be a bad idea to let 'Robin say something stupid about us to John'.

Raghu agreed.

Rajeev suggested that they leave generic, useless comments in my appraisal. And because I wanted to become CEO so desperately I wouldn't dare piss the both of them either and put my own review in jeopardy. So the three of us would give each other random not too good, not too bad reviews.

Rajeev said that the plan would be to later call up John privately and share their thoughts about my fitness to lead. Also, since Joel was coming from London, Rajeev suggested that they bitch about me to Joel as well. By getting John and Joel on their side they would get rid of me first. After that, Raghu said, it would be up to the company to pick one of them.

Then they suddenly went quiet while someone else came in to use the loo. They both quickly did a big drama of washing their hands and all till that person left.

After that Raghu asked Rajeev if he had any 'dirt' on me. Rajeev said he'd checked extensively before joining Lederman. But found nothing in his database. Raghu sounded disappointed.

Don't worry, said Rajeev. Robin was an easy guy to fuck over.

And at that exact moment my phone began to ring. Of course thanks to the fucked-up acoustics in the bathroom everybody in the bathroom and perhaps most people on the floor heard seventeen glorious seconds of the theme to The A-team (original TV show).

It was Tihar Balasubramaniam. Of course. Idiot. He hasn't stopped calling since the party at the jail. Fed up.

My immediate reaction was to cut the phone and stay silent. So that both Raghu and Rajeev wouldn't know who it was.

But then I had a better idea. I picked up the call, zipped up my pants, and slowly walked out of the cubicle. I nodded at both Raghu and Rajeev with a smile on my face, winked at both of them, washed my hands and then walked out. All the while talking to Tihar Bala on the phone.

Diary, you should have seen the look on their faces.

Subbu simply called to ask me if there was any way he could help me with anything concerning the AVG2010 Games. Any project, any contract, any press release. Anything at all. Poor fellow sounded desperate. I told him I had nothing right now. But I promised to help with something well before the Allied Victory Games started. He thanked me at least 5000 times before cutting the phone.

Funny guy.

Diary, after coming to my cabin I sat there and pretended to work. I was actually waiting to see how Rajeev and Raghu looked when they came back into the office.

They both came separately. And I could immediately make out that they were trying to look casual. Raghu kept trying to look into my room out of the corner of his eye.

I am sitting here with a permanently evil, knowing smile on my face. I am sure it is driving Raghu mad.

Then just a few moments ago Rajeev dropped by and asked me if I was working late. I told him something urgent had come up today and 'I had one or two new problems to solve immediately and I had full intentions of eliminating these problems as soon as possible.'

He asked me if there was any way he could help with these problems. I told him there was no need to 'get his hands dirty or search through any of his databases. I could take care of things myself.'

Inside my head I could hear the sound track of Rajinikanth's *Padayappa*. Outside there was no noise except the sound of Rajeev's career slowly dying. He left immediately.

What a day of triumph, Diary. Everything, so far, is going according to plan. My arch-nemesises in the office now live in fear. My projects at the MURPS proceed well. John is happy. And if all goes according to plan I should be able to impress Gouri's family in a much better way day after tomorrow.

Touch wood.

**6.21 p.m.**

What is this 'dirt' that Rajeev has? And what is this database? Must ask Sugandh to do some reconnaissance for me.

**9.43 p.m.**

Hello Diary. Power cut.

Till the light went I was watching *Lord of the Rings*. Not bad. But I no longer know who is hero and who is villain. And there are semi-heroes also. The movie is full of short people with long hair, long people with short hair, long people with long hair and also trees that talk. Confusing. But there are good action scenes. And I hope the ending is good.

But there is still two hours of power in the laptop. So I thought I'll catch up on some old business. Finally write about the Sanjay Gandhi Memorial Tihar Inmate's Annual New Year Party that we have all been waiting for?

I know this sounds odd. But I was actually extremely excited about the New Year party at Tihar. Especially after Joyyontoh assured me that it was exactly like any high-class party at any good four-star hotel. (There is no swimming pool in Tihar.) And on top of that he told me that many popular VIPs were expected. So it would be a good opportunity for some solid business and political networking.

As usual I arrived at the SBI branch at Dhaula Kuan and the Customer Services fellow escorted me through the tunnel. (The tunnel had been fully decorated with flowers and 'Happy New Year' signs. It was very festive.) At the exit a hostess checked my name against an invitation list and then led me through a new set of corridors into a courtyard. By the time I reached the party, around 8.30 p.m., the venue was already packed with people.

Immediately one waiter approached me with a platter. There was one glass of champagne on it. Just as I was about to reach and pick up the glass I was intercepted by . . . you will not believe this, Diary . . . but Sri Sri Saishankar. He slipped in between the waiter and me, snatched the glass from the platter, turned back and smiled at me, and walked away stumbling.

It was an overwhelming moment for me, Diary. Saishankar is a big hero for Gouri and her family. I think Sugandh is also a devotee. Back in Defresne in Mumbai one of my colleagues who had a major alcohol problem had got cured by going for Saishankar's TechnoYoga programme for two months.

And here the great man himself was snatching a glass of champagne from my hand during a party. Too much! Immediately I knew this was an opportunity to make some casual small talk with him.

The thing is, Diary, there is a technique to doing this. Celebrities, at the end of the day, just want to have a good time like everyone else. They don't want to be hassled by fans or common people pestering them for attention, or giving them career advice or begging them for autographs. They just want to be treated like normal people. Therefore the trick in striking a conversation with them is to talk about mundane things.

So I turned to Saishankar and asked him if he 'preferred to drink champagne or was he also open to trying out some Prosecco'. Saishankar looked at me for two seconds without saying anything. And then walked away to a small group of people near a fountain (temporary) that included two or three foreigners.

Words may not have been exchanged between us, Diary. But there was an unmistakable feeling that something almost spiritual had transpired between us. Saishankar is powerful.

Kedarji immediately pounced on me after that. First of all he told me that both Joyyontoh and I were doing a fantastic job with the MURPS and AVG2010 in his absence. He was thoroughly excited to know that Joel would be joining us within days. If things went according to plan, he said, he should be released on bail shortly and be back in office by the time Joel came. I asked him how this was possible. He said that CBI should be making a procedural error in his case in the next twenty-four to forty-eight hours.

From the look on my face he knew I did not approve of this miscarriage of justice. He slapped me on my back and told me to cheer up. The arrangement was that as soon as AVG2010 ended the CBI would immediately find some 'new evidence' and put him back in Tihar. After which the case would take off from where it had left off. The Games were a matter of international pride, he said, and such compromises had to be made. I reminded him, politely, as we walked to the bar, that justice delayed was justice denied. Kedarji told me that one more morally upright word from my mouth and he would hand over all the contracts to The Braithwaite Group.

The bar inside was called 'Behind'. That is it. Just 'Behind'. What kind of a stupid name for a hospitality outlet is Behind Bar? That too for something that is located inside such a high-profile prison. Stupid branding. While the bartender mixed a screwdriver for me I noticed Rahul Gupta standing in one corner engaged in a very serious conversation with some senior members of the Planning Commission. He was giving some speech about something. And they just listened to him and nodded every few seconds. Also remember how Rahul Gupta used to look like in the Institute no? Scrawny, clean-shaven fellow with a face like a scrotum.

He has changed. Now he has one of those NRI beards that all the minicab drivers have in London. A thin beard on both sides, just a line of hair along his jaw, that meets a thin french beard in the centre. That scrotum look has gone. This is a new rapist look.

Fucker.

You can imagine my irritation. That too in an environment where there were no potted plants or analysts to provide any immediate relief. Here it takes me months to finally get some peanuts thrown my way from the MURPS. And there this incompetent asshole is giving gyan to the Planning Commission.

A million hostile, violent thoughts were going through my mind, Diary, when Kedarji tapped me on the shoulder and asked me to say hello to somebody.

Diary, I turned around and looked straight into the face of Anushka Sharma. KARTHAAAAVE!

Everything in the world came to an immediate halt. Everything. My heart, mouth, brain, all sound in the universe, everything. The bar, Kedarji, everything vanished. My entire universe, in that instant, was Anushka Sharma. Diary, in real life she is seven million times hotter than on screen, on YouTube or on small printouts.

There is literally not a single imperfect thing about her. Not one. Usually even the hottest women have some flaws. Look at Gouri's friend Megha. Megha was perfect and at one point even seemed open to a romantic relationship with both me and Gouri at the same time before she suddenly decided to become faithful to some fucker boyfriend. The girl was a goddess sculpted out of wood. Except for her bizarre jungle hair. All curly and tough and not at all feminine.

Jenny, if you remember, was the quintessential Asian seductress. Small, delicious, fragrant and flawless except . . . except for her feet. I've never seen such disproportional feet on a human being. Jenny has HUGE feet, Diary. Huge, monster feet. If I were to ever indulge in sexual activity with Jenny, hypothetically speaking, I would never want to see her feet during the process. Otherwise instant penis withdrawal.

But my Anushka. Her hair was perfectly cut to shoulder length. Not a strand was out of place. Her eyebrows sculpted but not so much that she looks like a transsexual. Her eyes sparkled. How do her eyes look so bright and lively and twinkle-ful? Her skin . . . oh Diary, her skin . . . soft and smooth and blemish free. And her bone structure. Diary, her cheekbones are high and wide and sharp and alluring like Burj Al Arab. Her chin is made of marble. Some people may say that her nose is not sharp enough. Those people are idiots. For me her nose is perfect.

And all this perfection is mounted on top of an endless neck made of expensive porcelain. Her neck is skinny enough to see the light play in the pits and crests of her throat. But not so skinny that you think she has just recovered from typhoid or pneumonia. That neck seamlessly melds into a chest of bountiful beauty. You know, when you look at her chest, that it is a proper, full north Indian chest.

At which point she shook my hand and asked me if I was a guest or an inmate of the jail. I clarified immediately, and then, in order to keep the conversation flowing, asked her if she was a guest or an inmate herself.

The moment the words came out of my mouth I knew I had made a buffoon of myself. I wanted to immediately turn around and run out of the prison with my dignity in tatters. (Which you cannot of course, technically speaking.) But once again, praise the lord, a person misunderstood my minor verbal error for sense of humour. She threw her head back, letting her hair spill back dramatically, and laughed heartily. After two or three laughs she brought her hand up to her mouth to regain composure. Of course you already know what I am going to say next: Her fingers are the gold standard upon which all female fingers should be made.

Kedarji told her that I was helping him with the Allied Victory Games and was his most faithful assistant. She smiled. I nodded. Then he told her that I was also instrumental in designing the party's return gifts. Again she smiled. Again I nodded, but without any clue. Then I told her that I was a huge fan of her work and it would be nice if she could let me come over to see her at work during a shooting. Anushka said that this would not be a problem at all.

Then she asked me to give her a missed call. After that she saved my number and promised to arrange for me to visit the next time she was shooting something in Delhi.

What does this mean, Diary? THIS MEANS I HAVE THE TELEPHONE NUMBER OF ANUSHKA SHARMA ON MY PHONE AND WHAT ELSE CAN POSSIBLY BE BETTER IN A MAN'S LIFE THAN THAT DIARY YOU ONLY TELL ME??!!!

Outwardly, of course, I was acting all cool and calm and collected. But inside it was like a new Mohanlal film had been released right in the middle of Thrissur Pooram. I could hear my heart beat in my head!

Then she smiled the most beautiful smile possible in the history of mankind and asked us to excuse her so that she could go and talk to some other people.

Anushka, I told her in my mind, I will excuse you as much as you want day and night, and against a wall, and in the back seat of your car and draped over the back of a steady sofa, and right now in the Tihar Conference Room if you want.

That, of course, was the highlight of the evening. None of the other famous people there could even match that goddess. However, Kedarji still insisted that I at least shake hands with a long list of important people:

1. Seven major Bollywood actors
2. One Bengali actor. Never seen him before. Maybe some award-winner.
3. At least two dozen CEOs from top Indian companies
4. Three or four CEOs of international companies
5. Joy Allukas

Somehow almost all of them seemed to know Rahul Gupta very well. He was hugging and laughing with all of them. Bastard.

Then after a while Kedarji left me alone as he said he had a small surprise.

I was just standing there, with a drink in my hand, trying to make eye contact with Anushka across the courtyard when this strange man in a white shirt and white dhoti pounced on top of me. (Not literally.)

Immediately I was afraid. As you know, Diary, 'Always be wary of any Malayali who tries to be friendly with you for no apparent reason because most probably they are trying to steal your passport, sell you insurance or raise money for Kerala Congress' has been a personal motto of mine for many years. And it has never failed me yet. Immediately I leaned against a lamp post so that my wallet in my back pocket was safely out of reach.

I was mistaken, Diary. This fellow was something else entirely.

He introduced himself as Tihar Balasubramaniam. And told me that he was a social worker in New Delhi. He told me that he was impressed with my work at the MURPS and the Allied Victory Games. Then he asked me if there was anything he could do to help me with my assignments with Kedarji.

I was in no mood to talk business during the party. But still I did not want to be rude to him. He seemed like a nice, eager fellow. And besides you know what New Delhi is like, Diary. Today's social worker will become tomorrow's home minister. Why make enemies?

So I asked him what services he could offer that we could use. Immediately he stopped smiling and looked around suspiciously. Then he dragged me into one of the rooms being used by the catering company. And then when he was sure no one was listening he began to explain.

Balasubramaniam said that he was ready to do anything. Fake quotations, duplicate documents, money transfer, newspaper story placement, TV news leak, car accident for any business enemy, etc. etc. I was utterly taken aback. This man was offering criminal services to me INSIDE A BLOODY JAIL WITH POLICEMEN AND JUDGES STANDING WITHIN HEARING DISTANCE.

I didn't know what to say when . . .

**11.56 p.m.**

Sorry. I ran out of battery. Power just came back.

Ah. So I was standing in the kitchen cornered by this criminal madman when Kedarji came running in and pulled me out. He abused Balasubramaniam severely and told him to stop irritating people at the party. Kedarji warned him that he would never invite him for a function inside the jail again.

Balasubramaniam completely lost it. He began falling at Kedarji's feet begging to be forgiven. Strange man. Kedarji told him to stop making a scene and to just make sure not to irritate anybody again.

Balasubramaniam promised.

Then we rushed outside just in time to see the Prime Minister stand up in front of everybody with a microphone. (How did he enter? I would have noticed the commotion. Maybe there is another secret entrance to Tihar from the Prime Minister's residence. Convenient.)

First of all he wished everybody happy new year. He said it was a privilege to once again kick-off the Tihar New Year party with so many close friends and colleagues. He said this was a rare opportunity to mix and mingle with so many important people in an informal environment. Then his face became serious. He said that many people may find it ironic that so many VIPs are enjoying themselves inside what is supposed to be one of the country's major prison facilities.

But, he continued, this was really a beautiful vindication of the power of our democratic system. The visitors and inmates gathered here were a reminder that irrespective of how rich or powerful you may be, in a democracy nobody was above the law. Everybody would eventually be apprehended and brought to justice.

And then he just stood there with a face like rock, looking extremely serious. Suddenly that face broke. First into a blank look. And then slowly into a smile. And then he began to laugh. And then the entire audience began to laugh and clap, and in the middle of all the whistling and cheering, waiters came out with fresh glasses of champagne and we immediately moved to the 'Mr and Mrs Tihar' competition.

Then just before dinner Kedarji took the mike and asked for attention. He said that he would like to make the traditional presentation of this year's New Year gift to the Prime Minister. According to custom each year the seniormost politician jailed in Tihar at the time of the party was supposed to arrange for special mementos. The first piece was always presented to the PM.

As Kedarji was the seniormost he had personally chosen and commissioned this year's memento. He then handed a gift-wrapped present to the Prime Minister. Who then unwrapped it and held it out to the audience.

Diary, I was not at all prepared for what I saw next.

The Prime Minister was holding up a small wooden replica of the bloody Sivaji statue. It was a perfect copy. I was dumbstruck. The audience loved it. Kedarji waved at me from the stage. I waved back at him. He looked absolutely thrilled. The Prime Minister also seemed very happy.

To be frank I had mixed emotions, Diary. On the one hand I was happy that my investment in getting that statue made was worthwhile. It had clearly helped us to impress Kedarji win the project. But on the other hand I HATE THAT FUCKING INACCURATE STATUE.

But that apart the evening went along really nicely. Several times Kedarji came over to tell me how much everybody loved my design of the Sivaji statue. I told him not to make a big deal out of it. He said he was planning to ask the jail administrators to make a large version inside the compound out of concrete or even bronze.

I came back home by around midnight. Now I have this ugly as hell wooden statue of Sivaji Ganesan standing on the dining table. I want to throw it out. But in case the minister comes home for anything the fucker will definitely want to see it.

I have an entire stack of business cards with me after the party. Didn't really get to network with anybody at any great length. But it is a good start nonetheless. Exactly the kind of thing I can highlight to John. There is absolutely no chance someone like Joel from abroad or any of these Raghu or Rajeev fuckers now have the contacts I have in New Delhi. The more I think about it the more I am convinced that getting into the Tihar network makes brilliant career sense.

But most of all I am overjoyed at having broken ice with Anushka. I am not saying that the both of us will ever be anything but vague acquaintances.

But what if? What if it starts with the occasional phone call or trip to location? What if we go from becoming acquaintances to friends? What if she realizes that I am the non-film-industry friend that she can depend on as an emotional and physical anchor? What if I can become the Hugh Grant to her Julia Roberts (*Notting Hill*)? What if she decides that what she seeks in a man is not the wealth of a Shah Rukh Khan or the body of a Jayan or the masculinity of a Suresh Gobi, but the sensitivity, realism, reliability, dependability, honesty, integrity and sexual imagination of a Robin Varghese?

What if? And if that happens surely Gouri will understand when I have to make tough decisions. I love her, of course. She is a princess among women. But this is Anushka Sharma. Look at her, Gouri. Just look at her. And now please leave without making a scene.

Ha ha! Diary, I am just joking of course.

## 30 January 2010

### 10.42 a.m.

Off to the ministry. We're going to do a dry run of the new PIMPAG(E) website and database system. Also some of the cameras at the MURPS will go live today. HUGE day in terms of our media credibility.

And then in the evening I need to go for another gym session. Jesal suggests two more sessions before the race. One today, one day after tomorrow, and then the race next week.

Busy day. But at least everything is proceeding in an orderly fashion.

Bye.

### 3.02 p.m.

Back from the ministry. Give me five minutes to demolish this new potted plant and fuck one of these analysts.

### 4.12 p.m.

I am back, Diary.

What a terrible day. What a truly terrible terrible day. If I could I would go to China and somehow convince them to invade India as soon as possible. And if that is not possible at least bomb the MURPS.

What a bunch of dim-witted, stupid, idiotic, brainless motherfucking bureaucratic assholes.

Joyyontoh was not there today. He has gone for a Private Secretaries Conference on Industrial Safety in Bhopal.

So I had to test PIMPAG(E) with a fellow from the MURPS's IT department called Ashmath. We opened a browser on my laptop and went to the address. It seemed to look okay. Even if it was the ugliest fucking website I have seen in my life. The entire background was in purple with yellow text. On top there was the MURPS logo that blinked every ten seconds.

I took a deep breath, counted to twenty, and then asked Ashmath if we were ready to search for documents on the database. He made a phone call to somebody at NIC and then confirmed. They had switched on all the databases.

I entered a search term and hit enter. The site crashed immediately. I looked at Ashmath. He calmly clicked around the screen two or three hundred times, hit spacebar followed by some random keys and then restarted the computer.

It crashed again. He restarted the computer again. It crashed again. After watching this Nobel Prize winning scientific activity for fifteen minutes I asked him to call up NIC again and ask them what the fuck was going on.

While he called, a peon came and asked me if I wanted any tea. I asked him for some coffee. Like Subhas Chandra Bose that peon has never been seen again.

Meanwhile Ashmath spent twenty minutes on the phone in heated discussions with NIC. Then he cut the phone and told me about the problem.

Apparently all the documents have the names of concerning authors or approvers in a 'name' field. And this field needs both first name and last name details. So that the public can search for documents by individuals. Unfortunately while uploading the documents to the database every document involving Joyyontoh was uploaded with a first name and no last name. Because unlike normal human beings he has no second name at all.

Unfortunately every time you do a search for anything on the site the software searches each field, sees the null entries in Joyyontoh's documents and immediately crashes.

I asked Ashmath why this had not been tested before. He told me that because of lack of time he only had the time to check design and layout.

FUCKER BASICALLY ALL YOU HAVE DONE IS LOOK AT THIS HIDEOUS, VOMIT-COLOURED LAYOUT AND APPROVED IT YOU ARTLESS, TASTELESS, NATIONAL DISGRACE.

I wanted to take his head in my hands and drive it into the

computer monitor. But I did not. Instead I asked him how we could solve the problem. With a look of tremendous satisfaction on his face he told me that the NIC guys had solved the problem. They would remove the document search field and replace it with a request form. Users could then put in a request, which would get forwarded via email to the NIC guys, who would then forward it via email to the MURPS where someone would look for the document and email it to the NIC who would then forward it to the person who had requested for this information.

I waited silently for twenty seconds to see if this was some bizarre behenchod joke and there was some punchline coming. But there wasn't. Ashmath just sat there with a very satisfied look on his face as if he had just discovered a combined cure for AIDS and cancer and was waiting at Rashtrapati Bhavan for the President to give him the Padma Bhushan.

I told him that this was not an ideal solution. The entire point of the exercise was to show how transparent we were. And to dispel rumours of corruption. Creating an email-based system would just give people the impression that we were trying to hide something. I told him that they had to restore the search box and repair the database immediately.

He called NIC again. They said the fastest way to solve it was to use a second name for Joyyontoh. Ashmath asked me to suggest anything they could use instead of leaving the space blank.

I thought for ten seconds, decided to fuck with factual accuracy, and said 'Banergee' spelt with a G instead of a J. Just to make it harder for people to find by mistake.

Ten minutes later the NIC guys got back to say that everything should be working okay now.

One problem solved.

Next Ashmath opened the status update section.

CHINA, WHY DON'T YOU JUST INVADE US AND SPARE US THE MISERY OF BEING RUN BY SUCH TOWERING FUCKNUTS????!!!!!

Time for KAUN BANEGA CHUTIYAPATHI.

1. Diary, how many projects are displayed on the Allied Victory Games PIMPAG(E) Dashboard?

76.

2. How many projects are behind schedule?

75.

3. Which one is on schedule?

Only PIMPAG(E) itself.

4. Which project is the most behind schedule?

The Allied Victory Games Messaging and Communications Package.

5. How many months is it behind schedule?

Twenty-one months. At this point we were supposed to have finalized a series of overall Games slogans, branding and created several options for the merchandise manufacture team.

6. What messaging do we have right now?

Two options. 'AVG2010: Come join in the kakkoos' or 'Delhi 2010: Fuck hone waala hai!'

7. Which project is least behind schedule?

Opening Ceremony.

8. How bad is the situation with the Opening Ceremony?

According to the schedule we should have finished first rehearsal. However, currently the Opening Ceremony Committee is saying that rehearsals will only happen one week before the ceremony.

9. What if the rehearsals turn out badly?

I have no idea. I will probably just clear out the stadium in Delhi and then mark out a runway in the middle with lights.

10. How does that help?

This way the Chinese Air Force will know where to land and start the invasion.

Congratulations, Diary, you have won.

You have no idea how frustrated I was. I told Ashmath that the module looked nice. But there was no way we could show this to the public. Joyyontoh was urgently required to rectify the situation. If the BBC saw the true state of affairs of the projects India would get humiliated internationally.

Finally I asked Ashmath to show me the webcam installations inside the MURPS. He told me to wait and left the room. Five minutes later he came back with a large blueprint of the office. All across the blueprint he had marked positions where the webcams had been placed. The distribution seemed fairly comprehensive. I asked him to show me the locations before we went live with the webcams. He took me to a position just outside Kedarji's office in the waiting area. He pointed at the wall. On the wall there was a little bracket sticking out. And on the bracket there was absolutely nothing. No camera, no webcam. Nothing.

I looked at Ashmath. He looked back at me again with his Padma Bhushan face. Where are the cameras, I asked him. He said they had put out tenders for thirty-six webcams. And should be sending purchase orders within one week.

Of course by this stage, Diary, I didn't have any anger left in me. I told him to get me a copy of the tender so I could do something to speed up the quotation process.

Finally I congratulated him for this good work and left the MURPS and came back to office. For the last fifteen minutes I've been thinking.

This is one seriously shitty project. I hope I don't get fucked by the MURPS and Kedarji and Joyyontoh and Ashmath and all the other dickheads.

**8.01 p.m.**

Off to the gym. At least there is one place in the world where I am not constantly having to solve problems.

Just me, the machines and my willpower. No depending on other people to meet my goals. That is how life should be. Uncomplicated. Straightforward. Clean.

I love the gym.

**10.34 p.m.**

FUCKING NEVER GOING TO THE GYM AGAIN.

## 1 February 2010

**11.02 a.m.**

In order to speed up things I've decided to bid to supply webcams to the MURPS. I might end up losing money. But I can't handle any more delays. As usual Sugandh will take care of quotes.

**1.43 p.m.**

Superbly sweet SMS from Gouri:
'I know you have plenty to worry about at work right now, Robbie, but I hope you realize how important it is to get this inconvenience with my parents sorted. I love you. I really do, Gouri.'
I am feeling bad now, Diary. Am I letting my work impact how I treat Gouri?
I think so.

**1.44 p.m.**

SMS from Gouri:
'Also will you please, please grow up and treat Colonel Uncle and his wife with some respect? They matter to me.'
Bitch.

**2.13 p.m.**

FUCCCCCCCCKKKKKKKKKKKKKFUCKFUCKFUCKFUCKFUCKFUCKFUCKFUCK
Wonder if anyone here knows anybody at the BBC.
Fuck.

# BOOK THREE

# PIMPAG(E)

## 2 February 2010

**10.12 a.m.**

What complete and utter humiliation. Kedarji just Skyped me from the TJBC. He is livid. As he should be. No word from Joyyontoh yet. But I am sure he is fuming in Bhopal.

A thousand times I told Ashmath and the NIC guys that they WE'RE NOT TO MAKE THE WEBSITE LIVE till we had sorted out issues with the cameras, databases and the sad status of the updates page. In the current form the site simply isn't ready for consumption and international media.

So what did the motherfuckers do? They made it live almost instantly.

DIARY WHY THE FUCK DO PUBLIC SECTOR SERVANTS DO THE ALMOST EXACT OPPOSITE THING OF WHAT YOU ASK THEM TO DO? WHEN YOU ASK THEM TO CLOSE A WEBSITE THEY MAKE IT LIVE. WHEN TOMMY UNCLE TOLD THEM TO CORRECT A SPELLING MISTAKE IN HIS PASSPORT THEY SENT IT BACK WITH THE WRONG GENDER. AND WHEN HE SENT IT BACK TO CORRECT HIS GENDER THEY LOST THE FILE. AND THEN WHEN HE APPLIED AGAIN THEY BLOCKED IT BECAUSE HE HAD APPLIED TOO MANY TIMES AND NOW HAD TO BE CLEARED BY LOCAL POLICE. WHEN HE CALLED LOCAL POLICE FOR VERIFICATION THEY CAME AND NOTICED THAT HIS AIR CONDITIONER WAS DRAWING POWER FROM AN AGRICULTURAL CONNECTION AND INFORMED THE ELECTRICITY BOARD. NOW HE HAS NO ELECTRICITY AND NO PASSPORT. JUST BECAUSE HE STOLE SOME ELECTRICITY HE

WON'T BE ABLE TO GO TO JERUSALEM FOR EASTER NEXT YEAR.

What is the point of living in a country like this?

Anyway almost immediately somebody from the BBC saw the website, used it and then wrote a terrible article yesterday on the BBC website. Diary, it is terrible. And to make it worse it is written by some British Indian fellow who went to Oxford along with the Prime Minister. The article is called: 'Ministry of Blunders: How India's inept MURPS is making a proper mess of the Allied Victory Games'.

TRAITOROUS BACKSTABBING BASTARD.

I spent all of yesterday and will spend most of today fighting fires now. The Prime Minister's Office, John in Tokyo, Joel in London, Kedarji in jail . . . everybody is tremendously upset. Joel called me up this morning to say that I was lucky the BBC hadn't mentioned Lederman in the article. That, he said, would have meant immediate termination.

What is most frustrating is that this whole PIMPAG(E) wasn't even really my idea. I was merely trying to bail the stupid ministry out of the bloody mess it had got itself into. I am not even contracted to help them with this shit. And now I am getting hammered.

The site has been taken offline now. And I've asked Ashmath to put up a banner saying that we're currently in the beta testing mode and will be up within a week.

Meanwhile quotations for the cameras went to the ministry yesterday itself. I have asked the idiots to clear them as soon as possible so that the video stream can be ready to go by the weekend.

My plan is to get all the damage control done before Joel arrives. I don't want to give him the impression that things are out of control, and in any way tempt him to step into running the India office.

I am also preparing a rebuttal to the BBC. But Kedarji wants Joyyontoh to see it once first before sending.

Meanwhile Raghu, Rajeev and I have finished our mutual appraisal forms. Everyone has said good things about each other. But I have asked them not to send anything to John yet. Right now John is in a bad mood about the Ministry of Blunders. This is the worst time to send him an appraisal form. Will wait for one or two more days.

I don't get why John is putting so much attitude. As if the fucker is some Mother Theresa in a suit with funny eyes. There have been terrible scandals in Japan involving Lederman. Six or seven years ago, when John was still a manager I think, they discovered that Lederman's Japanese office had helped Ferdinand Marcos launder billions of dollars through our office in Monaco.

And he is giving me lecture.

Phone ringing. Fed up. Later.

**10.16 a.m.**

Tihar Balasubramaniam again. Again asking if there was any way he could help me.

Acted as if signal was weak and cut the phone.

Mad fellow. Getting on my nerves now.

**11.17 a.m.**

Finally some good news. Kedarji is being released this evening. I am going to Tihar to pick him up. We simply have no time to lose right now. Many, many things need to be done.

This is going to be a long day.

**7.12 p.m.**

Just came back from Kedarji's house. Meeting Gouri for dinner. I really need to see her. It feels like we haven't had any privacy in months. Later.

**11.42 p.m.**

SOOOOOOOOOOO TIIIIIIREEEEDDDDDD . . .

Took Gouri to Ritu Dalmia's place at Khan Market. (That market is really becoming unbearable now. People on motorcycles and all have started coming there. Also, number of foreigners reducing.)

Given how rarely we meet these days I found her absolutely

wonderful tonight. Casual and cool. Pair of jeans, simple Fabindia kurta. The same look that stole my heart when we were at the Institute.

Just looking at her immediately reduces my blood pressure.

We were generally talking about work and the ministry and all when suddenly, between starters and main course, she asked me if I was still serious about getting married. Was all this unpleasantness with her family an attempt to back out. She told me to think for a few minutes and answer.

Thankfully she asked this in her 'let us be adults and discuss something properly' voice. And not in Gouri's patented 'irrespective of what you say I am going to cry after this and make you apologize and feel terrible about yourself for about ten minutes and then you will get fed up apologizing and then you will raise your voice a little and then I will cry a little more and then you will start apologizing all over again and like that bit by bit I will demolish your life force' voice.

So I sat there and thought quietly, Diary. A hundred million thoughts passed through my head. I thought about the Institute, about Dufresne, about Mumbai, about how she supported me during the voicemail crisis, about London, about Tom Pastrami, about coming back, about how she decided to move with me to Delhi so we could be nearby, and I thought about Megha, and Jenny, and Colonel Kalbag and his wife and her stupid brother, and our trip to Mount Abu, the famous 'naked weekend' in Ranikhet, and then I thought about Anushka Sharma and that took a while, and then I thought about us and about living together and about the challenges and about how hard those things would be and how invariably we would fight and how this would bring out the worst in me and her and . . .

I had no doubt in my mind at all. I am not one of those people who believe that 'Somebody out there is meant for you and it is very hard to find them'. What nonsense. That would mean that most of the couples in the world are miserable because they are incompatible. What nonsense. Most of the couples are miserable because sometimes life sucks, Diary. You plan every single thing and still nothing goes according to plan.

At which point you want somebody who will make things as nice as possible. I am not a poet or romantic novelist or anything. But I think that is the point of love and relationships and all. So that on a good day you have somebody to share it with. And on a bad day you have someone to take care of you. Sharing good things is easy, I think. You can celebrate T20 World Cup victory or first rank in an exam with random people. Roadside people. Useless friends who want treats.

But what happens when you lose a job? Or your mandate is the subject of international humiliation? Or somebody dies? Then who do you go to?

When things in my life go bad I go to Gouri. She may not always say what I want to hear. Or do what I want her to do. Sometimes she can be terribly painful and factual and unnecessarily honest.

But would I go to anybody else? No chance, Diary. No chance.

I told her that I was 1000 per cent sure. I know things have not been easy with her parents. And I still think that Colonel Kalbag should ideally be one of those people who die when power comes back suddenly after load shedding and they get electrocuted from the water heater in the bathroom.

But that is not me trying to back off. I love her very much indeed. I may not always show it or say it. But I feel it inside.

I asked her if she felt the same thing for me. And I told her to think.

We ate our main course quietly for five minutes.

Then she said she felt the exact same things. She said that I was a strange man. And that nobody really understood me. But also that I am a nice guy. I just want good things to happen to everybody. And that she really looked forward to spending our lives together.

It was of course the perfect time to give her a ring or something. I had never really proposed to her like Americans do. In India who has time for all that drama. Literally from the first kiss marriage is a certainty.

I initially thought of just popping outside and buying a ring from one of the shops in Khan Market. But then how can you buy something like that without doing proper online research? How much does a diamond cost, Diary? I don't know either. So I postponed that plan.

But after dinner we both bought massive frozen yogurts and went for a walk. She asked me how my training for the marathon was going. I told her about the fiasco at the gym yesterday. She laughed and laughed. And then I also laughed.

With hindsight it was quite funny.

Gouri said that I should not just stop because of this. I should complete my plan. Go for the final day of training. And then off to Mumbai next week for the marathon. I agreed.

After a while she said she was sorry she was asking me to do this running thing just to make Colonel Kalbag happy. I told her it was okay. At least it was an excuse for me to get fitter and healthier.

She thinks I have lost a little bit of weight.

I dropped her at the metro station afterwards and came home.

This has been a wonderful evening, Diary. Best evening I have had with Gouri in months. I know I complain about her all the time. Don't take all that too seriously. She is a wonderful person. I think we make a fantastic team. And sometimes members of even a very good team will fight. I am sure Michael Jordan occasionally had fights with one of his teammates about reimbursements for shoes or something.

These things are natural.

Amidst all the chaos in my professional life it is a blessing to have Gouri around. Otherwise I would have gone mad by now. Now if only I can sort out this family nonsense . . .

Off to bed now, Diary. I have a very early meeting with Kedarji tomorrow. He has promised to focus only on the Allied Victory Games and nothing else till the event is finished. Cannot afford to have him going back to jail or something.

## 3 February 2010

### 2.13 p.m.

A most excellent day of firefighting and mess-clearing.

When he wants to Kedarji can be a tornado of efficiency. Especially when Joyyontoh is also functioning in top form.

I went in this morning and both of them were already at the ministry. I quickly sketched out our immediate problems.

No. 1: Our central strategy was the PIMPAG(E) programme. If we got that right then no one could later point fingers at us and say that the MURPS did not perform as the agency for nodal oversight. Also the press would then have nothing to complain about. We had to deliver PIMPAG(E) on time.

No. 2: We had to respond to the BBC article. Staying silent would merely be an admission of guilt.

No. 3: While it was important to engage the media as quickly as possible we still could not lose focus on the merchandise programme. As soon as Joel landed we had to have everything ready for him to launch into the plan with gusto. No delays whatsoever. We don't want anybody to later say that the MURPS made no attempt to generate any revenues.

There was immediate consensus across the board.

We were about to discuss the next steps for everything when Kedarji got a phone call. He picked up the phone, said hello, waited for a second, then unleashed approximately 120 seconds of pure, undiluted Marathi abuse and then cut the phone. And then he carried on speaking as if nothing happened.

Joyyontoh smiled as if he knew what was going on.

Once again just as I was about to speak my phone rang. It was Tihar Balasubramaniam again offering to help me in any way possible. Kedarji snatched the phone from my hand, unleashed another 120 seconds of world-class abuse in Marathi and hung up.

I asked him why he was so angry with Bala.

Kedarji's story about Tihar Bala is truly hilarious and can only happen in India, Diary. So Bala used to be a Lok Sabha MP for some small political party in Tamil Nadu. Once during an election, as per party orders, he put up a whole series of posters insulting Jayalalithaa in his constituency. Two years later his party merged with the AIADMK and Jayalalithaa specifically asked for Bala to be thrown out.

Of course he immediately went and joined the DMK. Then one day, following party orders, he made a speech in Salem praising the wisdom and leadership of the DMK's Maran political family. Unfortunately this was twenty-four hours before a story critical of Karunanidhi appeared in one of the Maran-owned newspapers.

By the end of the week Bala had been relieved of his second political party membership. With nothing left to look for in Tamil Nadu Bala moved to Delhi and began to look for any political posts: even Rajya Sabha membership. Not one party or politician would touch him given his history.

During that period, Kedarji explained, some friendly inmate at Tihar made the mistake of inviting Bala for a party inside the prison. Bala was star-struck by the assembled dignitaries. Within the jail it was much easier to have a chat with the Prime Minister or home minister than outside.

Ever since then, for the last three years, Bala has been desperately trying to get caught in some scam so that he can be imprisoned in India's highest-profile jail. This is why everyone calls him Tihar Bala. Not because he has gone there. But he has been trying everything possible to get arrested.

Diary, the poor fellow has tried every trick in the book. But unfortunately it is impossible to be a part of large scams if you are from outside the political or bureaucratic systems.

Joyyontoh said that he once even tried spreading a lie that he was involved in the 2008 cash-for-votes scam. After spreading that rumour for weeks the Delhi Police finally raided his house to find that he only had some 60 or 70 lakh in his bank account. There are TV news clips of the police leaving his house laughing loudly.

Now that the run-up to the Allied Victory Games have started he has been desperate to suck up to one of the ministries so that they will hand out some sort of small contract which he can then fraud.

I didn't know whether to laugh or cry at this situation, Diary. Parties inside prison. People dying to get put in jail for career advancement. Bizarre.

Anyway after that we got back to work. Kedarji instructed the purchase department to clear the webcam purchase order by end of day. Joyyontoh has promised to coordinate with the other ministries regarding the online status updates. Either they had to accelerate their work or fudge their status data.

Also, both Kedarji and Joyyontoh have agreed to set up a ministry merchandise committee immediately which will start working with Joel right away. As soon as he lands.

And finally we agreed on the broad terms of our response to the BBC. First of all they had no business using the site when we still had not officially launched it. So they had no right to assume all that data was true. Secondly the terms and conditions on the site clearly state that data is for information purposes only. All reproduction requires prior permission from the NIC and the MURPS. The BBC is in violation of all these terms and conditions.

I will be personally drafting our official response, and putting up a copy on the PIMPAG(E) website.

When I left the office both the minister and his secretary were already hard at work making phone calls and talking to people.

FINALLY DIARY! FINALLY! The MURPS is acting with a sense of urgency.

Relieved.

Talk to you later. Many, many things to do.

### 6.32 p.m.

Response drafted and sent.

Now off to gym as promised to Gouri.

Talk to you later, Diary.

### 8.02 p.m.

The purchase department, in all its wisdom, has decided to award the contract for webcams to ... FUNDANGO! THIS IS DESPITE

FUNDANGO'S QUOTATON CLEARLY BEING A FAKE AND NOT EVEN THE LOWEST.

YOU HAVE NO IDEA HOW IRRITATED I AM RIGHT NOW. NO IDEA. MINISTRY FULL OF MORONS. FUCKERS DON'T EVEN KNOW HOW TO FOLLOW ESTABLISHED FAKE QUOTATION PROCESSES THAT WE HAVE USED SO MANY TIMES BEFORE.

Harish called me while I was coming back from the gym. I have asked him to meet me tomorrow morning itself.

WHY ARE MY PROBLEMS NEVER-ENDING DIARY???

Too many things to do now. So I've postponed the Second Dinner with the Kalbags till after I come back from Mumbai. Gouri again sounded concerned. But I promised her it had nothing to do with me wanting to avoid them.

I suppose she is going to be like this till the very moment I go around the fire or whatever.

## 4 February 2010

**11.42 a.m.**

Where the heck is my table clock? Gouri gifted it to me when she went to Machu Picchu last year. I swear it was on my office table last evening.

HATE losing things.

Harish has agreed to not cause headaches. He will supply the webcams as per quotation. I apologized for the inconvenience and told him that our plan was always to make sure his quotation got rejected.

He said such things happen in large projects like the Allied Victory Games. Before leaving he once again pitched for business. He said that given the bad press the Games are getting it may help to run a small social media campaign to counter the negative sentiments.

I told him I would think about it.

Yes, Harish. I am going to hire a guy who looks like a Meru cab driver and runs a company full of hippies who sit all day poking each other on Facebook to create a positive sentiment for the Allied Victory Games. Yes. I will.

Fuck off.

**1.12 p.m.**

Joel called me up from London to give me some 'unsolicited' advice. THEN WHY ARE YOU GIVING IT BOSS? DO I COME TO YOUR HOUSE AND SAY THAT I AM GOING TO CLIMB INTO YOUR BED AND TAKE AN UNSOLICITED NUMBER TWO?

He thinks that there is too much negativity building up in the media about the Games. The Indian media is focused on delays and scandals and incompetence and the international media is adding fuel to that fire. (Fair enough.) So he wants Kedarji to try something cool. Perhaps a Facebook or Twitter social media campaign to get at least young people excited about the Games. Apparently this is the cheapest way to get some media attention.

I told him I would think about this social media idea strongly and revert.

Joel will arrive in three days.

This is not looking good for me. Already Joel is beginning to stray out of his mandate. And trying to tell me how to do my job. This is the problem with these posh British types. Unbearable superiority complex.

Screwed now. If I don't follow up on his suggestion John will screw my happiness. If I follow up on his suggestion and it works then he will come out looking like a star. The best option would be to follow up his suggestion but screw it up. But then that would screw up the Games and the entire mandate.

Fuck. This is like that thought experiment question Professor Kannabiran asked us in the final exam at the Institute. An out-of-control train is speeding down a track on which people have been tied down by an evil madman. However, you can push a lever and divert the track on another line where the madman has tied just one person. What do you do? You have to make a choice. And whatever you do somebody will die.

(Of course I knew the correct answer in three lines: Don't do anything. If those five idiots couldn't work together to defend themselves from one single madman they are worthless to human society. Save the poor lonely guy.

But then the fucker would have given me an E grade. So I wrote some 17,000-word global bullshit about ethical dilemma, railroad technology and some HR funda and got a B+.)

I suppose I will now have to call the Meru cab driver for social media marketing inputs. Puke.

### 3.24 p.m.

Jesal wants to meet outside the gym to plan our day in Mumbai. And she will 100 per cent bring that bastard along.

This is why I think life is sometimes unfair. Suppose somebody like Rahul Gupta tries to screw you over. And you somehow manage to counter-attack and survive. The least you expect from life is to not see that person's face again.

But in reality you keep running into these painful chutiyas over and over again.

On the other hand what happens if you suddenly find yourself on a plane seated next to some hot architecture student on your exact same wavelength? Fifteen seconds after leaving the plane you lose them inside the airport and never see them again.

Such is life, Diary.

**4.36 p.m.**

Joyyontoh has sent our official response to the BBC. And the BBC has responded in some vague bullshit way. They will edit the story to suggest the website was just on trial. But they will maintain that projects are wildly behind schedule.

Thank you so much.

**4.53 p.m.**

Harish sounded like he was giving birth on the phone. Project proposal due in forty-eight hours. No time to waste.

**6.43 p.m.**

Off to meet Jesal and Dickface.

**10.12 p.m.**

Back home. Leaving for Mumbai tomorrow evening. Terrible time to have to do something like a marathon. But now that I have committed to it might as well get it over with.

Trip to the gym was awkward. But at least I was able to meet both of them, indulge in polite conversation and then leave without once punching that bastard in the face.

What an improvement over the first time I met him.

Diary, four days ago I had gone to the gym for my second last session. Since I have already been running so much, and in order to avoid any further injury, I decided to work out instead with one of those exercise groups. Why unnecessarily put strain on the legs before such a big run?

So I went to the gym, changed, looked through the list of classes and finally decided to go for the Core Combat session. Jesal and I, before we broke up, used to go for Core Combat classes regularly. It is a good workout that focuses on balance, coordination, stamina and upper body strength.

So I went inside, found a nice spot up in the front near the instructor and did some basic stretches to while away time. After five or six minutes the instructor came. He is a really nice guy. Very careful, very restrained, not at all intimidating and almost certainly homosexual. Also, he plays fantastic music during the classes.

As usual he went through the room shaking hands with everybody and saying a quick hello. I spoke to him for a few minutes, he asked me if I was all set for my marathon, and then he moved to the person behind. Who was, I noticed, Jesal. I waved at her and smiled.

And then my heart came to a complete and utter standstill. I felt mildly dizzy and then the entire classroom began to spin in circles.

KARTHAAVE ENTHAANU ITHU?

Standing right next to Jesal was an old arch-nemesis of mine: Yetch. Suddenly it all made sense to me now. Subbu was none other than Karthik Subramaniam. That evil mastermind.

The last time I saw him was right after he'd bitched about me to a group of very senior partners at Dufresne. Thanks to my spontaneity and presence of mind his attempts had been quashed and I had emerged from that crisis with flying colours.

After that I had been transferred to London, then moved to Lederman and lost all contact with the guys at Dufresne. Not that I tried. Most of those guys were jealous, insecure frauds.

And now here he was. Standing right next to me. And right next to the ravishing Jesal. Two questions flashed through my mind:

1. Why is this fucker in Delhi?
2. What the heck makes perfectly nice, sexy girls like Jesal choose to go out with career criminals like Yetch.

And I had one bonus question also:

3. Why is this bloody country fellow now calling himself Subbu? What happened to his original name Yetch? Inferiority complex. I am sure of it.

For the first few minutes in the class I could not focus at all. I did all my stretches and squats and lunges completely out of sync with the instructor. Seeing Yetch again after all these years was making all kinds of emotions go through my mind: surprise, disgust, fury, anger, curiosity, bewilderment, jealousy, injustice, frustration, what-the-fuckery, etc. etc.

Thankfully I was feeling much more calm by the time we reached the important Combat Simulation part of the class. Once again the instructor asked us to pair up into groups of similar gender. Immediately Jesal came up to me and asked me to pair up with Yetch. I immediately acted all surprised and told her that we were old acquaintances.

Yetch also smiled and shook my hand. But the message in his eyes were clear: Robin PLEASE PLEASE don't take Jesal away from me!

Keep her boss. As if she is some Manju Warrier.

I told Jesal I'd be happy to pair up with Subbu/Yetch/Dickface.

According to instructions Yetch held up the big padded cushion while I punched it lightly for one minute. And then we switched places. We were meant to go on like this for some twenty to twenty-five minutes using a set of various light punches and kicks.

My first one or two punches were very light. But then just the sight of seeing that backstabber made me a little aggressive. So I began to punch the cushion harder. Each time that weak vegetarian got thrown back by my power.

Then it was his turn. And there was no mistaking that he was trying to hit me hard as well.

GAME ON DOSA BOY! This was human hostility at its most primeval. This was how real men in the days gone by sorted out their problems. Raw, merciless man-to-man combat.

Round Two: This time I hit the cushion with lightning fast elbow punches and fist backhands. I was giving it to him, via cushion, solidly. Each time I hit the cushion you could hear a solid thud. And if you listened even more closely you could hear Yetch making yelping noises. Like a little dog.

This was just complete, brutal, martial domination, Diary.

Round Three: It was my turn to hold the cushion now. By this time blood was pumping through my ears. I could hear my heart beat over the sound of the session music. This training sequence was going to be light kicks at waist height. Yetch kicked the cushion gently, like a girl studying to become a nun. I chuckled softly and told him to kick like a man. He tried again. Again I chuckled. What happened, I asked him. Maybe consulting had made him too soft? His face turned red. Yetch took a deep breath and kicked again. Pfft, I said. Pfft! What is this nonsense? Has he never kicked before? Or like all consultants maybe he has only read the Wikipedia entry for kicking? Yetch told me to shut my mouth. I told him to shut it himself if he wanted. He took four or five steps back. And then took a running jumping kick at my head.

Of course this was a complete violation of Core Combat regulations. So I smartly moved to one side. Yetch's hilariously contorted body went right past me and into the aunty next to me. His foot caught her perfectly on the side of her mouth.

There was a brief explosion of pink and a cloud of saliva. And then the woman's false teeth went flying through the air. It landed right in front of the instructor. There was a moment or two of stunned silence. And then several people started making noises. Our Core Combat instructor stared at the teeth in front of him speechless. And then started sobbing gently. The old woman collapsed to the floor and began to make mumbling incoherent noises. Yetch just stood there with a dumb expression on his face. While Jesal screamed for help.

I rushed to Jesal, by now covered in a delectable coat of her fragrant sweat, and asked her if she was okay. She said I should be taking care of the instructor or the old woman. Meanwhile she rushed to Yetch's side looking very concerned.

I made a quick choice and went to help our instructor. He just seemed to be in a state of shock. I splashed some water into his face and shook him gently till he seemed more normal. Then I wrapped the false teeth in a gym towel and handed it back to the original owner.

Now that he had regained his composure Yetch began to apologize profusely to the woman. The class quickly disbanded while someone called for a doctor to look at both the instructor and the old woman. Yetch seemed fine, though his feet were too sore for him to stand on. Jesal just stood there looking tremendous.

After the doctor left I approached Jesal and Yetch and apologized profusely. To Jesal I apologized for having embarrassed her like this in front of so many people. I respect women, I told her, and would never think of doing something like that to her or to the old woman. After that, making sure Jesal was still listening, I apologized to Yetch. I told him that I should not have egged him on like that. But I had not known that he was such a novice puncher who still had much to learn about the art and craft of Core Combat. In case he was looking to improve, I said, I would be more than happy to hold his hand and teach him the ropes.

Yetch got very angry and began to argue. He said that if I hadn't moved at the last moment this would never have happened. I told him that if it made him feel any better I was happy to take the blame. This made him even angrier. And then Jesal told him to shut up, not create a scene, and just admit his mistake. Yetch shut up immediately.

Later he received a very embarrassing warning from the gym manager. Who told him that 'this was a fitness centre and not some fish market'. Adipoli. One more such incident, they warned Yetch, and they would refund his fees and ban him from the facility forever.

You should have seen Yetch. Almost fell at the gym manager's feet. Then I stepped in and told the gym manager that Yetch was a very close personal friend and a really nice guy. He would never hurt anyone knowingly. The manager told Yetch to 'learn the basics of gym etiquette from outstanding regular users like Mr Varghese'. Yetch nodded vigorously.

After that I did some mild cardio on the cycle and came back home. By the time I left the gym Jesal and Dickface had vanished.

Which basically made it the greatest day I have ever had in the gym. The moral, physical, emotional and popular victory had been all mine.

Still meeting them again today was quite awkward. Sadly for poor Yetch, his girlfriend is very, very keen that her gym friend and boyfriend get along very well. So he has no option but to play along. Therefore as long as Jesal is around his ball is firmly and permanently in my court.

He has left Dufresne and now works for an equity research firm in Gurgaon. (If consulting is the fraudulent underbelly of MBA careers then equity research is the unshaven pubic area. Horrible.)

Diary, you could literally place buckets under his face and collect the jealousy that was dripping off as I told him that while he was putting together fraudulent reports full of fraudulent data about fraudulent companies that would be bought by fraudulent investors to make fraudulent investments with their fraudulent money, I was interim-CEO of a major financial services firm which recently won mandates to help the Government of India salvage the Allied Victory Games.

And if all went according to plan I would be taking over as CEO soon. Yetch, self-loathing and self-pity oozing from every pore of his underperforming body, said that I had been very lucky with my career choices. I told him that while luck may have been involved, I did not wait for luck to come. Einstein did not operate like that. He asked me if I was still using voicemails in office. (Sly attempt to chip ball over goalie's head because he is standing too far forward.) I told him I did not any more because I had underlings to take care of that for me. (Goalie dives and saves the ball before kicking it upfield. Where it is chested down by a midfielder who back-heels it to a forward who hits a shot from 35 yards that curls into the top right-hand corner goalpost. Score 7–0. Ten minutes left in the first half.)

After that Jesal and I finalized plans. We're travelling separately. But we will meet just before the marathon near Eros Cinema. From there we walk to the starting point for the 15-kilometre run. In case we split up during the race we meet afterwards at Sundance Cafe behind Eros. Then back to the airport and then back to Delhi.

Hectic. But if the run goes well, the effort will be well worth it.

I asked Yetch if he was planning to run the marathon too. Jesal laughed and said that she had asked him several times. But he simply wasn't in shape to try a 15-kilometre run. Besides, I added, we don't want any of the old women in Mumbai to lose their teeth. Jesal laughed loudly. (Final score 18–0 after second half.)

Came home two hours ago.

Not staying up late tonight. Or eating anything heavy. Have to keep the body in optimum shape for the run.

## 5 February 2010

### 9.16 p.m.

Just got back from Bombay. The most embarrassing, terrible, humiliating day of my life. And on top of that I couldn't complete my run either.

MARK MY WORDS DIARY: I WILL NEVER STEP FOOT INSIDE THE CITY OF BOMBAY AGAIN. IT IS A TERRIBLE PLACE FULL OF TERRIBLE PEOPLE.

### 9.34 p.m.

The BBC have started a new blog on their India website called 'Blunderwatch'. It will be used to exclusively keep track of all Allied Victory Games-related delays and scams.

So far they have posts about Kedarji's prison term, the beta PIMPAG(E) website and some general nonsense about how the construction sites are unsafe.

Boss, what is your problem? You worry about safety in your country no? We know how to deal with our people. If we don't want reflective jacket, helmet and boots then what is your problem, man? If you have nothing to do why don't you fuckers go and kill one more Princess?

Thankfully neither Kedarji nor Joyyontoh are panicking about Blunderwatch. Joyyontoh says it is too early to react to these things. We first need enough ammunition to counter-attack.

I completely agree. There is no point in sending letter after letter to the BBC every time they write something nasty about us. The only way to prove them wrong is to actually not commit blunders. And get things done for the Games.

Webcams will arrive this evening and will be installed overnight. Meanwhile Joyyontoh is working on a new status update system for the website in collaboration with the other ministries and Delhi PWD.

PIMPAG(E) must be unveiled as soon as possible. I've reiterated that our deadline for this must be no longer than another seventy-two hours. We must nip this Blunderwatch in the bud.

**11.23 p.m.**

Sugandh just sent me a link from the NDTV website. Apparently tremendous pressures in the party to push out Kedarji because of all the negative publicity he has been getting.

Of course. What else can happen? You cultivate one high-powered contact in the government and the Party immediately wants to get rid of him.

The Party is full of hypocrites. Every single fucker is happy to come to Tihar, dance, eat, take return gifts and go away. But outside they are all Raja Harishchandras.

## 6 February 2010

### 1.13 p.m.

Guess who was waiting at the office for me when I went today.
  Harish?
  No
  Yetch?
  Puke. No.
  Tihar Balasubramaniam?
  Bingo.
  Took forty-five minutes to get rid of him. Though you must give the poor, desperate fellow some credit. He had full information about Blunderwatch, PIMPAG(E) and the website issues.
  But still he needs to stop now. I don't want to touch that politically toxic fellow.

### 3.42 p.m.

Good news. All the cameras are good to go. Ashmath has set up a private online link behind a login and password. And each and every one of the cameras seems to be working beautifully.
  However, I have asked Joyyontoh to wait till the project updating system is finalized before launching the site. No more half-measures, Diary. No more compromises.

### 4.32 p.m.

There is a new update on Blunderwatch. An 1100-word rant about how with so little time left for the Games there is still no indication of a communication, messaging or signage strategy. And little time left for a merchandise plan.
  WHAT IS THE PROBLEM WITH THESE GUYS MAN???!!!!
  Every day they provide a new headache.
  Joel might still prove to be a rival for my CEO action plan. But I am relieved that he is coming. Will give some momentum to the

merchandising. At least that way we can divert attention to some positive stories.

**5.17 p.m.**

Meeting tomorrow at the MURPS. Joyyontoh just called.

## 7 February 2010

**2.12 p.m.**

Deivame. Productive day. Fantastic meeting at the MURPS. The ministry has called for a press conference day after tomorrow. At the event we will unveil the PIMPAG(E) website officially. Kedarji is trying to get the Prime Minister for the unveiling.

Fingers crossed.

**4.52 p.m.**

John called. Not good.

He has decided to postpone finalizing Rajeev's, Raghu's and my appraisals for another few weeks. I asked him why. But he made some random excuses. None of them convincing.

I get the feeling that he is waiting to see how the AVG2010 mandates go. And also to get feedback from Joel. I am sure. Fucker doesn't trust any of our judgements about each other. So he wants some non-brown fellow's opinion as well.

So unfair. In any other situation I would have quit by now. I can understand someone being interim-CEO for a few months. But a whole year? Nonsense.

But right now I can't afford to. As it is Gouri's family has a bad impression of me. Now on top of that if I become unemployed also then finished. Things will get even more complicated. For me it is okay. I don't give a damn if they get upset. But can't do that to Gouri.

(Haven't told her about the marathon fiasco. As far as she and Colonel Kakkoos are concerned I finished the distance in one hour and forty minutes.)

On the other hand becoming CEO proper would make things very much easier. How can anybody say no to a CEO as a prospective groom? Impossible.

**7.12 p.m.**

There is a lot of excitement in the office about Joel. Some of it is understandable. Always good to meet colleagues from foreign offices.

But I don't get why some of the analysts refer to this as some kind of second coming of Jesus Christ.

Anybody else in my position would have been quite insecure. Such people would think: This is my office! People should be impressed by me. Not by some idiotic fellow just because he is from abroad.

Thankfully Einstein has seen enough of the world to not be impressed by such things.

**7.21 p.m.**

I have asked Sugandh to move Joel's workstation into my room. Initially I had given him the vacant room across the office near the conference room.

No, no. Not because I want to constantly keep an eye on him or anything. I know it may look like that.

Joel is new here. And having someone nearby will probably help him settle in nicely. After a few weeks, once he is comfortable, I will move him back.

**9.01 p.m.**

Still in office. Spent a few hours doing some review meetings with some of the analysts and associates. Signed off some pending paperwork and expenses.

I don't want to give Joel Harrison any reason to doubt my leadership. I don't want him to think that I am the sort of typical Indian manager who leaves all the paperwork till the last moment and has no punctuality.

**11.23 p.m.**

Off to the airport to pick up Joel.

**2.09 a.m.**

Joel Harrison is a black guy.
????????

## 8 February 2010

### 6.12 p.m.

No time to chat. We're testing the website to see if everything is working. So far so good. The video streams are reasonably clear. The search function is not crashing at all. And Joyyontoh's new and improved project status update system is pure genius. More details later.

I haven't taken Joel to the ministry yet. Sugandh is helping him settle down in the office first. Kedarji and Joyyontoh are dying to meet him.

There is no hurry. Slowly.

### 11.47 p.m.

Still in office. Was at the MURPS till 10 p.m. Everything looks well set for the press conference. Prime Minister has declined to attend the press conference. However, he has promised to put out a statement through the Prime Minister's Office as soon as the conference is over. Basically the bugger doesn't want to take any risks in case anything goes wrong.

Spineless idiot.

Nothing will go wrong. Nothing can go wrong. I don't think I have prepared better for a presentation. Joyyontoh will make the main presentation. And I have no doubts whatsoever about his presentation abilities. Kedarji will also be there. But we have specifically asked him only to speak in case of an emergency. He will inaugurate the website and then hand over the proceedings to Joyyontoh.

After a long debate we have agreed that this time I will accompany them on the stage as a subject matter expert. My job is to counter-attack any media hostility with hard-core statistics, data, facts, on-the-spot ingenuity and presence of mind (i.e. my core strengths).

Our strategy for tomorrow is simple. We welcome everybody, and then make some random small talk global gyan about the Allied Victory Games, India Shining, Economic Development, Mahatma

Gandhi and all the usual spiel. Then Kedarji inaugurates the PIMPAG(E) website. (Diary, he wanted to inaugurate the website by cutting a ribbon. I told him this makes no sense. But Kedarji was adamant. Apparently this is his first inauguration since becoming minister of the MURPS. So he wants to do it properly. Finally we arrived at a compromise. He has agreed to cut a ribbon wrapped around the mouse. Which he will then hand to Joyyontoh who will launch the website.)

Joyyontoh will then show them a demo while simultaneously taking them through a deck on the salient features of the website. After this we will take fifteen minutes of questions. And then the meeting will disperse for tea. And hopefully, if everything transpires without incident, we will transition to a much more positive and constructive relationship with the media.

That is the plan.

I have gone through every element of the presentation a thousand times. I have tested the website at least a thousand times. The webcams are working. Ashmath has double checked the power backup systems at the ministry. I have even arranged for a backup wired Internet connection in case the primary Wi-Fi connection drops.

I have worried about every single thing that is worth worrying about.

Time to sleep. If I can.

## 9 February 2010

### 8.12 a.m.

I am beginning to get paranoid. But I came to the office at 7.30 a.m. to check everything just one more time. Website is working absolutely fine. The presentation makes perfect sense to me. Joyyontoh's creativity with the status update module is unsurpassed.

I can't believe we aren't actually billing the MURPS for the amount of work I am putting in. Anyway.

Joel, who also came early, was very eager to join the press conference. I told him there would be no place. And besides a new face would just raise suspicions. Best to keep a low profile for now.

He reluctantly agreed.

### 1.23 p.m.

Conference starts in seven minutes. I should be completely nervous right now. But I am not.

Like Michael Phelps and I.M. Vijayan I have now entered a state of zen calm just before the moment of reckoning.

### 5.13 p.m.

CHAOS. UTTER CHAOS. UTTER FUCKING CHAOS. BUT ROBINGENUITY PREVENTS IT FROM BEING A COMPLETE FIASCO.

### 8.01 p.m.

Gouri saw the news reports on TV. She is coming right now to see if I am okay.

### 10.56 p.m.

Ayyo.

What to tell, Diary. What to tell. You have heard of that proverb. Man proposes. God takes a dump on your proposals.

Things started nicely enough. The turnout of media exceeded even our greatest expectations. There were several TV crews and even a couple of foreign journalists in addition to the BBC.

Joyyontoh's opening remarks were excellent. After that he invited Kedarji to inaugurate the website. It was quite obvious that the minister was extremely nervous. You could see his hands shaking from across the room. He stood up, picked up the scissors and then cut clean through not only the red ribbon but also the wire of the mouse.

Of course the inauguration was happening on a MURPS computer that had been originally purchased during the Indus Valley Civilization. So the mouse connected to the computer through some port I have never seen before. I had a mouse in my bag. But the MURPS computer did not have any USB ports.

After fifteen minutes Ashmath came with a mouse in bright pink colour. The journalists chuckled while he connected it to the computer.

The demonstration, thankfully, proceeded without incident. Both the list of updates document and the document search facility were working brilliantly. Joyyontoh's new status update system was excellent.

Each project was divided into eight stages: Pre-feasibility, feasibility, ideation, departmental approval, nodal approval, resource mobilization, planning and execution, delivery. Complete fraud of course. Almost every single project has been stuck in the planning and execution phase for months. But if you look at the graphs quickly without thinking too much it gives the impression that overall we are around 8o per cent ready for the Games.

The journalists looked at the graphs quickly without thinking too much. The BBC journalists seemed stunned.

The video streams were all working perfectly. We showed each stream for a few seconds. They were all good. Except for one in which one of the peons was sitting in a chair and looking straight at the camera. He did nothing except just sit there and dig his nose. It was disgusting but helped to bring a little levity into the press conference.

After this Joyyontoh said that we would be moving into a question-and-answer session. At that very moment one journalist got up and shouted something about the Allied Victory Games being a travesty in a country where farmers are committing suicide and children are dying of hunger. He then bent down, removed one shoe and flung it at Kedarji.

The next few moments will be imprinted in my mind forever. The shoe flew in the air towards the minister. Kedarji just sat there with his mouth open looking stunned. And then, just a nanosecond before it smashed into his face, a hand shot out into space and grabbed the shoe.

Joyyonytoh!

Who then paused for a second to take aim, and flung the shoe back at the journalist. It struck the bastard right between his eyes and then bounced off. You could hear the cracking sound as the heel hit his skull. The fellow then collapsed to the floor. Immediately. Passed out. One peon casually walked up to him and dragged him out of the room.

There was pin-drop silence for a few seconds. And then a few journalists clapped politely.

Joyyontoh apologized for the interruption.

The first question came from one of the Hindi TV channels. Kedarji immediately sat up with enthusiasm. The TV channel guy asked him if he was aware of the situation in the velodrome. I had trained the minister to deal with difficult questions by playing for time. The minister acted as if he didn't hear properly and asked the journalist to repeat the question. He repeated it. Was the minister aware of the scandal in the velodrome? The minister thought for a few seconds. And then asked him to repeat the question again. Meanwhile the minister scribbled something into a piece of paper and passed me a note:

'What is velodrome?'

At which point Joyyontoh intervened. He asked the journalist to stop playing games.

The journalist said that there were rumours of a massive scam in the velodrome construction. According to his sources a substantial portion of the expensive Afzelia wood imported for the construction of the velodrome has been stolen by somebody. The contractors, in complete violation of design norms, are plugging the gaps with cheap local wood. And the track is at least two months behind schedule. Was the nodal agency for oversight aware of this problem? Was this reflected in the so-called status update system? (That chuth's words. Not mine.)

Kedarji just sat there looking like a buffoon. Joyyontoh quickly stepped in and clarified. He said that while the MURPS was overseeing projects on a nodal basis it did not micro-manage them. He promised to check as soon as possible with the Delhi PWD and revert.

But little did we know that the bloody fucknalist had come to the press conference with the express purpose of screwing over the minister. He reached into a bag, pulled out a wooden Sivaji statue and held it up. He then said that he had proof that the pilfered timber from the velodrome had been used to make these statues on Kedarji's orders.

Everyone looked at Kedarji. Who countered superbly with a look of the most complete blankness.

The bastard continued: Not only had the stolen timber been used to make this statue, but the statue had then been distributed as gifts to various VIPs.

Did the minister have anything to say to explain this shameless wastage of public funds and gross display of corruption?

There was pin-drop silence in the room. Nobody said a word. Until Kedarji suddenly broke the awkwardness with a superb counter-attack. How dare you question a minister of the Government of India in such coarse language, he asked. Did the journalist not have a sense of propriety? Did he not have any respect for the office of an elected public servant? How dare he make such allegations publicly? If the journalist has proof why did he not go to the police or the vigilance right away instead of waiting for a press conference?

While saying this Joyyontoh reached for the empty drinking glass on the table. But I immediately held on to his hand.

He asked the journalist to submit his complaint and the proof immediately via the complaint form on the PIMPAG(E) website instead of just spreading baseless rumours.

I just sat there with my head in my hands. Between the shoe-thrower and the statue-fucker I doubted if anybody in the room even remembered any of the good news we had shared with them earlier. Our efforts at great transparency and interactive public interaction had been thoroughly overshadowed by these fools.

Something had to be done. And the opportunity presented itself almost instantly.

One firang journalist got up and asked the next question: Had any progress been made on the messaging and branding initiative? Could the MURPS share the latest status given that this branding was essential for everything from merchandise to ticketing and venue decoration and signages?

Diary, there are moments in a man's life (also woman's life) when adversity, opportunity, ingenuity and invention come together simultaneously and spontaneously. How does this happen? Nobody really knows. How did Einstein (original) suddenly one day think up the theory of general relativity? Where did this spark of brilliance come from? But it comes. And it comes fast and hard. And suddenly the man accomplishes a rare feat of supreme genius.

That is exactly what happened in the conference room. Suddenly, even before the man had finished the question, I had it. I knew what had to be done.

Joyyontoh was going to give one of our prepared generic backup answers when I intervened.

I introduced myself as an independent subject matter expert. And then told the journalist that we had indeed designed a branding campaign for the Allied Victory Games. We were still trying to fine-tune some of the aspects of executing this across various media. And a major unveiling had been planned for later this month.

But yes, we could confirm that the core concept of the campaign was ready.

He asked me to elaborate.

The branding message for the Allied Victory Games 2010, I announced, would be . . .

Delhi 2010: A Smaller, Better, Faster World

Years from now I will not be surprised, Diary, if schoolchildren are taught the text of what I said next as an example of supreme extempore speech. I had not prepared this at all. But it came out of my mouth like silk.

I explained. As we all know the motto of the Olympic Movement is: Faster, Higher, Stronger. We drew our inspiration from the purity of that motto. Just three simple words that signify the endless human striving, the agony and the ecstasy, and the immortality that is sport.

But Delhi 2010 is not just about Olympic ideals. The Allied Victory Games are also about unity and cooperation and ambition. They are about smaller nations stamping their presence on the world stage. Also, and this is sometimes forgotten, the Allied Victory Games hark back to a time when some of the weakest powers in the world got together to fight a vastly more powerful evil. This is a Games not about good sports and good competition, but about goodness itself.

And 'A Smaller, Better, Faster World' embraces all these ideas.

A Smaller World. Because today the world is better connected than ever before. And because for a few weeks this year Delhi will become the greatest melting pot on the planet. Delhi will be a symbol of a world that is getting ever smaller.

A Better World. Because the Allied Victory Games has its origins in a titanic struggle to save the world. And to make it a better place for millions. And also because one of the important things that make the world a better place for so many is sport.

And finally, A Faster World: Because while we may have our origins in the past we are aware of the realities of the present, and the opportunities of the future. We live in the digital age. And this is why the Allied Victory Games will be the most digitally enabled Games of all time with a comprehensive online, mobile and social media strategy.

To summarize Smaller, Better, Faster is both a statement of fact. And a statement of hope. And it will be the core message of the Allied Victory Games.

By the end even I was beginning to believe the bullshit a little. While the applause died down I hooked up my computer to the projector, opened a picture of one of the Smaller, Better, Faster T-shirts we made for summer internship recruiting and displayed it. I told them that this was just a prototype. But it would adequately show that we at the MURPS have been thinking about this for a really long time.

After that Joyyontoh stepped in smartly and warned the journalists against jumping to conclusions about the Allied Victory Games. Much more was happening than they realized.

And then we dispersed for tea and snacks.

Once the journalists had left we went back to Kedarji's office to figure out how to de-fuck ourselves. Kedarji insists that he had no idea that the Sivaji statues were made from velodrome timber. The minister has this usual guy in the Delhi PWD who procures all such items for him. This time also Kedarji had placed an order for the Sivajis with this fellow. And he delivered promptly on time.

Joyyontoh kept on asking the minister. Was he sure? Did he have any idea at all where the wood had come from? Was he lying to us? Please don't lie to us.

The minister insisted that he would never have sabotaged his own ministry by doing something stupid like that.

We checked the online system and the journalist hadn't filed the complaint yet. But it was inevitable he would. Besides the media already knew about it. So there was no way to avoid it.

I asked Joyyontoh what we were supposed to do now. This was a serious allegation that was made in a very very public scenario. He said that the best way to deal with scandals like this is to use something they taught him during his civil service training called the '10 P + 1 Framework'.

According to this framework whenever an elected representative was caught in a scandal it was the bureaucrat's duty to rescue him using one of the eleven methods that are part of the '10 P + 1 Framework'.

The first ten involve blaming the lapse on, or refusing to respond to the allegation based on one of the following:

- Pakistani conspiracy
- Politically motivated by the opposition
- Politically motivated by your own party
- Police overreach
- Policy misinterpretation
- Permissible deviation
- Pro-poor policy justification
- Press fabrication
- Potential CBI investigation
- Particulars are sub judice

If none of these methods are applicable then there was the eleventh method that was to be used only in cases of extreme crisis:

- Padma Bhushan distribution

(Originally there were only 10 Ps. The latest method, which involves bribing people like newspaper editors or social workers with civilian honours to buy their silence, was added to the IAS syllabus only in 2005.)

Right now we simply did not have enough information to figure out which method to use. Also, he said, there is no point in responding to corruption allegations without facts and details.

The other urgent issue, he said, was implementing my Smarter, Better, Faster plan before people realized it was complete bullshit. I agreed. (However, Kedarji did praise me for my presence of mind.)

I told him that I already had a proposal for a social media campaign from Fundango. I would figure out something to drum up some positive vibes for PIMPAG(E) and SBF (Smarter, Better, Faster).

The last issue was that of the shoe-thrower. They sent him to Ram Manohar Lohia Hospital and he was discharged after a few hours. He is fine. And the minister has agreed not to press charges.

The idiot belongs to some militant farmer outfit in Haryana or something. I don't think he will repeat his performance any time soon. What a counter-attack by Joyyontoh.

The press conference is a huge hit on all the news channels. Unfortunately the shoe-throwing incident has overshadowed everything else. Nobody is talking about any of our initiatives. CNN-IBN is already calling our man Javelin Joyyontoh.

Assuming I must be upset about the whole thing Gouri came to calm me down. She told me that working with the government was always going to be hard. But I just had to remember that I was doing this for the career prospects. And the CEO job.

God only knows how everyone is going to react tomorrow. If John and Joel focus on the negatives I am fucked. On the other hand if they notice my spark of brilliance with SBF . . .

Tired. And no sign of the workload easing off any time soon. Goodnight.

### 3.13 a.m.

CANNOT SLEEP DIARY. CANNOT SLEEP.

Every time I nod off I have the exact same nightmare. I am standing, completely naked, in front of a group of people. Every single one of the bastards in my life is standing there: Yetch, Rajni, Rahul Gupta, Tom, John, Boris, Colonel Kalbag. And everyone is throwing shoes at me. And almost every single shoe is finding its mark.

John keeps saying 'Look at the CEO! HA HA! Look at the CEO! HA HA!' while throwing.

Thankfully Gouri was not throwing anything. But her brother was.

What a terrible nightmare.

## 10 February 2010

**10.03 a.m.**

Humiliation on top of humiliation.

When I reached office this morning everyone, including Joel, was watching Times Now. The imbeciles on TV were discussing how the Allied Victory Games were increasingly becoming a source of international embarrassment.

And who was one of the experts invited on the show?

Think, Diary. Of all the people in the world who would get the most joy out of seeing my downfall?

Exactly. Rahul Gupta. Times Now had invited him on the show because he was an 'Expert on strategy, operations and a major process consultant to the Allied Victory Games'.

(Yes of course. And Ummen Chandy is the Prime Minister of Papua New Guinea. Poda patti.)

Gupta said that much of the MURPS's failings could be explained by one simple fact: The ministry had shown poor judgement in hiring a company with unproven credentials to advise them. The anchor asked him about Lederman. Gupta explained that Lederman was a financial services company with little to no experience in sports events and with a track record of financial fraud and white-collar crime.

You could see the colour draining from Joel's face. (But you had to look very hard. Because . . . you know . . .)

Afterwards Joel asked me for a private meeting.

He thinks that the MURPS mandate is now beginning to bring the company humiliation and nothing else. First there is the ongoing torture of Blunderwatch. Their latest post is about how private companies are cashing into the AVG2010 by posing as independent consultants. There is a small photo of the press conference published along with the post that shows me sitting next to Joyyontoh. This was taken at the exact moment the shoe was thrown at us. I look like an idiot.

Secondly there is the fact that our client just spent the last two months in jail.

And finally there is this new humiliation on TV.

Joel said that usually this humiliation is not a problem if the business returns were adequate. Which is why Lederman was one of the lead private sector supporters for the Muammar Gaddafi Centre for Democratic Reform in Africa. People laughed at us. But we also made 47 million dollars in fees to help find investors for a new port near Benghazi.

The MURPS rubbish, he said, was simply not worth it. Even if the merchandising plan was a success and the MURPS paid us our fees on time we were looking at a realistic business of less than 7 or 8 million dollars. And for that peanut amount we were putting our entire business reputation on the line.

Now I was beginning to get fed up with his moral science class. I told him that things simply did not work like that in India. First of all the government was a huge potential client. But you had to start with small mandates and then work your way to a big one like the privatization of a PSU or something. And then one day, when the government is convinced of our abilities to deliver, they will ask you to find a buyer for Air India. BOOM! Millions of dollars in revenue for basically telling a bunch of lies to some idiot from Qatar.

And as for reputation I told Joel he was reading this all wrong. In India your corporate reputation has nothing to do with your business potential. In the morning you can have an explosion in your factory killing everybody including 150 child labourers. In the evening you make some vague announcement about acquiring some foreign company and everyone will immediately forget everything because of sudden patriotism.

So I told him not to worry so much about what people think. All that is only a problem in other countries.

Joel looked shocked. He told me that he was disappointed at my attitude.

All these months he and John and several other people at Lederman had been under the impression that I was the ideal person to lead our India office. But now, he said as my heart shrank to the size of a small green pea and fell into the pit of my stomach where it was vaporized by my gastric juices, he realized that this may have been a mistaken impression.

He said that I now seemed way too cynical, unprofessional and opportunistic for a major leadership role.

I broke out into very loud laughter. You remember that scene from *Chandralekha* when Mohanlal laughs and laughs and laughs till every single person in the audience has laughed and laughed and urinated a little bit. I was laughing like that. Joel looked stunned.

And then I slowly calmed down. I told Joel that if only he had let me speak he wouldn't have been so disappointed. What I described before was the traditional line of thinking in many Indian companies. What I was going to say next, before Joel interrupted me, was that this WAS THE EXACT TOTAL OPPOSITE of my own line of thinking. If he would have just waited for a moment I would have told him what I really thought.

And that was this: A company is nothing without its corporate reputation. Even here in India the profitability of a company meant little if these profits came from dubious businesses. Do people know how much money the Tata Group makes? Do they even care? No. Why? Because the Tatas are seen as responsible corporate citizens.

I told Joel that like him I was also tremendously troubled by the recent humiliations that Lederman had suffered because of the Allied Victory Games. Like him I was deeply moved by this and intended to rectify the situation as soon as possible.

The next move would be to launch a social media campaign that glorified the benefits of the PIMPAG(E) initiative. Once that took off we could slowly start playing up Lederman's role. By then, hopefully, all these allegations of corruption would have blown over and the MURPS would get back to delivering the Games.

At the same time, now that we have the Games messaging in place, Joel could quickly launch merchandise. This would also help to excite the public, counter the negativity and win us some credibility.

If all went according to plan by the time the Games took place Lederman would be known as the company that helped the government pull off a huge success.

Joel thought for a while and then said that he was still not entirely convinced about me. He was willing to set his scepticism aside. Provided that there were no more public relations disasters. One more humiliation and that was it. He would take over the entire MURPS mandate including PIMPAG(E), bring in Raghu and Rajeev to lead and remove me from any interim-CEO duties.

I again burst out laughing but he got up and walked out.

Right now I don't have the energy to worry about this bastard also. I should have known from the very beginning. Firangs are always trouble. From Vasco da Gama to Greg Chappell. All fuckers.

### 4.13 p.m.

Just got out of a meeting with Harish. Two solid ideas. One for what he calls 'New India' and one for 'Classic India'. (Marketing bullshit.) For New India he recommends a Twitter and Facebook campaign called #TheTruthIsInThere. We will ask people to freely search through the PIMPAG(E) website for any data, quotations or contracts and point out any problematic deals. Someone from PIMPAG(E) would revert with a clarification within twenty-four hours. This way we are showing off our site, connecting with New India, and also expressing honesty and transparency.

For 'Classic India' he recommends a much more conventional strategy: A national integration song. Something like 'Mile Sur Mera Tumhara'. We can play this song on radio and TV and it will reach out to the millions who are not on Twitter or Facebook. This will create a nice positive vibe and also fit in with the idea of 'A Smaller, Better, Faster India'.

(My summer internship campaign is proving to be tremendously versatile.)

The first one is easy enough to do. Harish will take care of opening Twitter accounts and Facebook pages for the MURPS. We should have the campaign up and running in a day or two.

But the song is a challenge. However, Harish says he has some contacts in the music and film industry and has promised to pull some favours.

Fingers crossed.

Both are good ideas.

To be fair, Diary, I may have been too quick to judge Harish. Outwardly he is 100 per cent career criminal. But inside there seems to be some intelligent life.

**6.39 p.m.**

BLOODY!

Why would anybody steal my cufflinks now? They were not even expensive ones. Gouri found them in a gift shop in Bangkok. One link says 'Chick' and the other one says 'Magnet'.

They are my favourite ever cufflinks. And now they are gone.

I've had a word with Sharmila about these thefts.

This is getting out of hand.

**8 p.m.**

Gouri has decided to drop in every night for a few hours till this scandal dies down. She doesn't want me to be alone with all this stress.

**11.09 p.m.**

Diary, one humble reminder: EINSTEIN IS STILL DYNAMITE WHEN IT COMES TO THE HANKY-PANKY BABY!

## 11 February 2010

### 9.12 a.m.

The illegal encroachment has begun.

Today when I came to office Joel was not there. Nobody knew where he had gone. And then, on a hunch, I called up the ministry.

But of course. The fucker had gone to talk to Joyyontoh about merchandising strategy without even telling me. No email. No SMS. Nothing.

Anyway. I am sure Joyyontoh will handle him adequately. I hope.

### 11.01 a.m.

Had a quick chat with Joyyontoh on the phone. Approval for the #TheTruthIsInThere campaign has been secured. Harish will send out the first tweets and pokes and whatever today. There is no time right now for a press release or anything. So Harish has said he will take care of making sure all the newspapers and TV stations are informed online.

He is saying that it will 'go viral' automatically.

Whatever.

### 3.30 p.m.

So far so good. Joel came back from MURPS and gave me a briefing five minutes ago. Of course the ministry has done nothing except allocate a budget for buying stock. Thankfully now that we have the 'Stronger, Better, Faster' theme in place designing the goods should not be a problem.

I've sent him all the designs we made for the summer internship programme. He says that deadlines are tight. But we should still be able to get basic things like AVG2010 T-shirts and mugs in stores in six weeks' time. The faster they go on sale the more revenue we generate. The more revenue we generate the more money the company makes.

Meanwhile press conference clips are slowly beginning to disappear from TV. Anchors are moving on. Relieved.

**7.09 p.m.**

Back home. Gouri coming in fifteen. We're going to cook dinner together.

Harish tells me that the MURPS handle already has over 400 followers on Twitter.

Must check with Ashmath for website traffic details tomorrow. I hope the database is able to cope with the search requests.

**10.16 p.m.**

There is something strange going on with Rajeev.

So after dinner Gouri suggested that we watch *Yes, Prime Minister* on my laptop. I had downloaded some episodes last year for us to watch during our trip to Ranikhet. But we ended up watching nothing. (Wink nudge wink.)

I didn't know where the files were and told her to check on my computer and USB drive. While searching she discovered something strange. There was a folder inside my USB called Prime Minister. It didn't have any video files. Just hundreds of pages of scanned documents. She showed it to me. And I had no idea where it had come from. And then I remembered.

All these files are inside the 'Insurance' folder that I copied from Rajeev's computer. And the stranger thing is that there are hundreds of other folders. There is one for the home minister, the finance minister and I even found one for the minister of urban regeneration and public sculpture. Just hundreds of scanned documents. Nothing else.

Very strange, Diary. Why would Rajeev have all these scans?

I told her that I'd ask Rajeev about it later. Then we sat and saw two episodes.

She left ten minutes ago.

I can sense that she wants to organize another meeting with her parents. But right now I simply don't have the time.

Way too much on my mind.

## 12 February 2010

### 2.02 p.m.

Ha ha ha ha.

PRAISE THE LORD!

For days I've been waiting for some news somewhere in India to push that stupid press conference out completely from the TV. And now it has come. Some nutcase has discovered the home minister's personal mobile phone and landline number. He then sent it to every life insurance company, credit company and auto loan company 'asking for more information'.

Now NDTV is reporting that the home minister and his family are being bugged by phone calls every five minutes.

Major embarrassment for whoever leaked that information. Apparently the HM is livid and has asked some cyber-crime cell to investigate.

Suddenly no one is talking about the wooden statue or the shoe-throwing.

Relieved.

For the first time in my life the home minister has been of some use.

### 3.12 p.m.

Traffic on the PIMPAG(E) site is BOOMING! Thousands upon thousands of people are 'searching for the truth'. At one point this morning over 7000 were accessing the database simultaneously.

The campaign is a fucking superhit. I called up Harish to congratulate him.

### 4.56 p.m.

I AM LOVING IT!

Now even the Prime Minister is getting crank calls on his private numbers. And apparently he is also getting spam on his private email address.

Hilarious. Just when you think this government is incapable of any more stupidity it surprises everybody. How in god's name can a serious government not be able to protect private information belonging to its most senior politicians and lawmakers?

**9.11 p.m.**

DANGER DANGER DANGER

Gouri wants to know if perhaps the Colonel can come and meet me at work if I am too busy to meet the family for dinner. Apparently he is dying to have a chat with me and has been bugging Gouri to arrange it.

I've promised to find a slot this week.

Want to punch somebody or something.

**10.07 p.m.**

*Midday* has a small story on one Mr Karthik Subramaniam who got into a ruckus with the Mumbai Police during the marathon.

Muahahahahaha. Well played, Einstein. Very well played.

## 13 February 2010

### 9.19 a.m.

Harish just called. He has arranged for a five-minute phone call with Shruti Hasaan. (Kamal Hasaan's daughter. Smoking hot.) She may be willing to talk to someone in the film industry to do an AVG2010 song for us for free. Or cheaply.

Why not. Worth a shot.

I asked him if there was any chance Anushka Sharma could be roped in. He has promised to try.

### 2.26 p.m.

Fingers crossed. Initially Shruti didn't seem interested in the concept at all. She said nowadays it is impossible for a song to be popular both in the north and south. And if it is in English then we will immediately eliminate the most of 'Classic India'.

Still I told her to give it a shot. You never know. She asked me if I had any concepts in mind. I didn't. But when has that ever stopped me. Once again I went into 'thinking-on-feet mode'.

What if, I suggested, we wrote a song about getting Indians to set aside our differences and unite? For example we could ask 'Why this Mullaperiyar Mullaperiyar Mullaperiyar scandal da?' with reference to the problems between Tamil Nadu and Kerala. And then 'Why this Cauvery Cauvery Cauvery problem da?' with reference to the problems between Tamil Nadu and Karnataka. Similarly we could write lyrics about the Belgaum problem, Jammu and Kashmir, Bodoland, etc. etc.

Something like that. And if the song works, I told her, we could make a version that handles international problems like Tibet or Siachen.

She has promised to think about it and revert.

I think it is a good idea. But we will have to wait and see if she buys it.

Fingers crossed. A nice peppy number really gets people excited about everything in this country.

**9.12 p.m.**

Back home. Gouri is sitting in the bedroom going through Rajeev's folders. She has been fascinated with them ever since we found them.

Everything with the MURPS is proceeding smoothly. The website is working and Joyyontoh believes that all the projects are proceeding. Everything is behind schedule. But at least some work is going on.

The biggest achievement of the press conference was to kill the enthusiasm on Blunderwatch. Even the BBC is beginning to struggle to find holes in our strategy and the MURPS functioning.

Good job so far, I think. We've had a lot of trouble in the last month. But we've dealt with all of those things nicely. Meanwhile Joel is enthusiastically going about his work.

All systems are go.

**10.10 p.m.**

Breaking news on NDTV: Apparently somebody has applied for a new PAN card using all the personal details of the Prime Minister. Right down to passport details, date of birth, place of birth, identifying marks, permanent address, etc. etc.

Hilarious. This scandal is overshadowing everything else on TV right now.

Gouri is still here. Still in front of the computer. Hasn't spoken a word for two hours.

## 14 February 2010

### 10.03 a.m.

Just got a call from John.

Had a really nice chat with him. Joel has been telling him good things about me.

Even though the MURPS started chaotically, he is now under the impression that I have things under control.

He said that this will be reflected in my appraisal and . . . drum roll . . . 'future job profile enhancements'.

I don't want to jinx things. But it looks like it may be time to order new visiting cards without the word 'interim' on them.

Woo hoo.

### 2.10 p.m.

Crisis. Crisis crisis crisis.

### 3.12 a.m.

Just back from the MURPS. Cannot type. Too tired.
Fucked.

## 15 February 2010

**11.42 a.m.**

The audio is now playing on every channel.

It was first aired on STI News yesterday afternoon. That is the same channel for which that bastard journalist from the press conference works. In the audio you can clearly hear him speaking to someone who works for the Delhi PWD. Some engineer of some kind.

The journalist asks the engineer if he can help him source some cheap high-quality timber. The engineer tells him casually, as if he is a telephone operator for Domino's Pizza, that he can supply not just timber but all kinds of items including plastic seats, CCTV cameras and lighting equipment. The journalist asks him from where he is getting all these items. The engineer shamelessly says that these are all items that have been ordered for the Allied Victory Games. They are lying around in warehouses waiting for the stadium construction to finish.

But won't somebody find out if something goes missing? The engineer laughs like T.G. Ravi in *Chaakara*. And then tells him that so many things are being bought in a hurry to complete projects that no one is keeping track of anything. In fact the engineer himself had already taken one air conditioner, one plasma TV and one treadmill home.

Also, he said, a large batch of timber meant for the velodrome had already been pilfered to make something for the MURPS minister. He didn't know the details. But he said it was for some kind of statue or something.

To make things even worse the channels are now saying that one of the statues had been gifted to the Prime Minister himself.

Clusterbuttfuck.

Every single TV channel across the country has been playing that audio since yesterday. Of course Blunderwatch has already posted a copy online. Just in case you didn't hear it on one of the 400 channels on your TV.

The consensus in the media is that Kedarji will most definitely lose his job and be sent back to Tihar as soon as possible. The MURPS may also be stripped of all AVG2010-related responsibilities.

We spent hours last night trying to figure out a way to escape. Not a single way out even if we use the 10 P + 1 Framework model. The audio recording is just too convincing.

The gossip is that the Prime Minister has blown his top. Not only is the entire AVG2010 falling apart, but Kedarji has also managed to get the Prime Minister involved in the massive scam.

Joel is pissed off. John is pissed off. Everybody in the office is pissed off. Kedarji is shitting bricks. Joyyontoh is probably throwing things at somebody. Gouri is upset.

And Einstein is stuck in the middle of this shit storm. After all it was my idea to approach the MURPS.

Fuck. CEO one day. Close associate of a corrupt criminal the next.

Life is unfair, Diary. UN-fucking-fair.

**4.23 p.m.**

They now have a picture of the Sivaji statue plastered across all the channels. And Rahul Gupta giving his insights into the criminal–politician nexus.

**7.22 p.m.**

First the bad news: There is a TV crew at the reception right now doing a story on our Sivaji statue. Somebody noticed that the 'Velodrome Scam' statues are direct replicas of the Lederman Sivaji.

So far we have not given any comment on this similarity.

WHAT THE FUCK AM I SUPPOSED TO DO NOW? I HAD NOTHING TO DO WITH ANY OF THIS. I DIDN'T TELL THAT IMBECILE TO MAKE STATUES OUT OF PILFERED AVG2010 SUPPLIES! WHY IS MY LIFE BEING RUINED BECAUSE SOMEBODY ELSE IS A MEGA-CHOOTH??

Now the good news: Colonel Kalbag is coming to my office day after tomorrow. At which point I will stab him with a whiteboard marker or strangle him with a LAN cable. Or a little bit of both if I have time. In any case it looks like I will end up in prison for corruption.

Might as well get good value for money.

### 8.09 p.m.

Gouri cooked rajma chawal. We ate in silence. Her family has not taken to all this scandal nicely.

She is very afraid.

I want to be afraid. But I don't have any mental strength left to worry about one more thing.

**16 February 2010**

**10.09 a.m.**

Everybody in the country now believes that Lederman's India office was involved in the Velodrome Scam.

**2.14 p.m.**

Call from Joyyontoh. Emergency meeting in the Prime Minister's Office in one hour. I have to go.
  They can't just put you in jail just like that no?
  Diary . . . What is happening, Diary?

**2.21 p.m.**

Had a chat with Gouri. I have told her anything could happen now.

**7.48 p.m.**

NATIONAL INFORMATICS CENTRE YOU BASTARDS! YOU BLOODY INCOMPETENT BASTARDS! AAAAAAAAAA HOW COULD YOU! WHY DON'T YOU GUYS EVEN THINK FOR FIVE MINUTES . . .

**8.01 p.m.**

Seventeen new blog posts on Blunderwatch. Seventeen. And if the government does something nice? Not even one.

**11.03 p.m.**

Website is being shut down at midnight. Harish has already called off the social media plan. Merchandise plan remains untouched because it has revenue implications.
  John is coming to Delhi sometime this week to take care of transition.
  My career here is finished. CEO finished. Lederman finished. PIMPAG(E) finished. MURPS finished.
  It is all over.

## 17 February 2010

**9.21 a.m.**

So basically this is the latest addition to my catalogue of miseries that is now the size of an encyclopedia. The Encyclopedia Fucktanica.

The cyber-cell tracked down one of the email/phone scam messages to an Internet cafe in Mumbai. Somewhere near the university in Kalina. They went through the logs and discovered that the same person who enrolled the defence minister's personal email for a porno newsletter also spent a lot of time on the PIMPAG(E) website.

And now they know how all those details got leaked. Remember how, to save time, the NIC reused a file format that had originally been designed for the Universal Citizen Database. So those Nobel Prize-winning morons not only used the file format, but they actually used a copy of an original UCD file.

Now you may recall that the original UCD scheme had been called off after just two months. So it only had information about the first set of people who had been signed up. By which I mean the VIPs who attended the UCD inauguration function. By which I mean the President, the Prime Minister and the cabinet.

So the current PIMPAG(E) website not only gives results from AVG2010 documents, but also from all the personal and biometric data collected during that initial UCD period.

Immediately after we launched the #TheTruthIsInThere campaign people realized that searching for the names of the Prime Minister or any other cabinet member conveniently threw up all this UCD data. The patriotic members of 'New India' then proceeded to take this data and fuck everybody's happiness.

You have no idea how PISSED OFF the PM was yesterday. One by one he ripped a new anus into me, then Joyyontoh and finally Kedarji.

Everything is finished. As I mentioned yesterday the PM has cancelled everything except the merchandise mandate. Thankfully he will not be publicizing this lapse. Apparently the UCD had been his pet idea and he doesn't want to take responsibility for our mistakes.

Our mistakes? OUR MISTAKES? IF IT WASN'T THE IDIOTS WHO WORK IN YOUR INFORMA . . .

What is the point in getting angry.

Announcements regarding the termination of the mandate, Kedarji's imprisonment and Joyyontoh's transfer to special fisheries observer in Chandipur will be put out in two or three days.

**11.42 a.m.**

1. Colonel came.
2. Colonel saw me meet Jesal outside the gym that day.
3. He saw us go shopping for lingerie.
4. He followed me to her house.
5. He waited outside for some time.
6. He does not want to hear any explanations.
7. He will never let his niece marry a man with my moral character.
8. He wants me to back out voluntarily.
9. I have twenty-four hours to do so.
10. Nayyinte mone.

Why is he bringing this up now when it happened so long ago? Maybe he was willing to keep quiet but these new scandals have proved to him that Einstein is highly unsuitable. FUCKING DOUBLE STANDARD BASTARD.

Went and sat in the toilet for two hours.

Early this morning a bunch of CBI officers came and took the statue away. Small blessings.

**6.12 p.m.**

Going out for drinks with Joel. He knows my career is finished. But he is trying to be nice about it.

**10.01 p.m.**

HA HA HA HA HA HA HA HA HA HA HA.

OLD LYING BASTARD.

My professional life may be screwed. But I am not going to give up on my personal life just yet. The Colonel is going to get a pleasant surprise tomorrow morning.

Today, for a change, I will sleep well.

## 18 February 2010

### 10.02 a.m.

The phone call with the Colonel took exactly five minutes.

I called up Gouri's house. He picked up the phone. I asked the Colonel when he was planning to go back to New Zealand. As usual he immediately put on his Napolean attitude. He asked me why it was my business.

I told him that last night I went for drinks with Joel Harrison. During the drinks I told him how this professional mess was going to destroy my personal life. I explained to Joel about the situation with Jesal, the mad Colonel and the rest of the Kalbags. Joel sympathized with me. I showed him the last picture I'd taken of Gouri and me. During the lunch with the Kalbags. On my phone.

Joel looked at the photo intently for a few minutes and then asked me if this man in the picture was Kalbag from Dunedin in New Zealand.

At the mention of Dunedin I could hear the air go out of the Colonel.

Turns out that Joel's mother is from Dunedin and buys groceries from the Colonel's shop.

Desperate to sort out at least one issue in my rapidly disintegrating life I asked Joel if he knew the Colonel at a personal level. Did he know anything about the man? Anything I could use to impress him? The Colonel's favourite movie, food, politician . . . anything?

Joel, being the nice man he is, immediately called up his mother to find out.

As I spoke the Colonel slowly began to make a soft whining noise. As if someone had stuck a pin into him and he was slowly leaking air.

What do you think Joel's mom told me, I asked the Colonel.

He didn't say anything. Come on, Colonel Kalbag, I said, at least make a guess no?

He asked me if she mentioned about that minor problem he had last year with health and safety in his store?

No.

Did she perhaps allude to that minor misunderstanding with the tax authorities that led to Kalbag's house in Dunedin being repossessed?

No.

I could sense that Colonel was now panicking. Maybe, he tried again, Joel's mother said something about a family misunderstanding that led to the Colonel's daughter taking a restraining order?

Not at all, I said.

(What kind of criminal mastermind is this fucker?)

No, Colonel, I said, triumph ringing through my voice, this was about the incident in September.

He moaned softly.

In September last year Colonel Kalbag was arrested by the Dunedin Police for harbouring illegal immigrants. Seven out of the nine employees in his shop had come on tourist visas sometime in the 1980s. The other two had no visas or passports at all.

As part of a plea bargain the police agreed to spare him jail time provided the Colonel explained how these illegals were getting into the country. After helping arrest almost two dozen violators his visa was cancelled and he was deported back to India.

This is why the bloody fool has been refusing to commit to when he will go back. He is not staying here because he is some benevolent patriarch and wants to make sure Gouri's marriage goes well.

He is staying back because the fucker can't go back at all.

I asked the Colonel if there were any factual inaccuracies in my understanding.

Sound of crickets.

I asked him if it would be inconvenient if this information somehow reached the ears of the rest of the Kalbag family.

Sound of crickets.

I asked him to ensure that I would never see him, hear from him or hear of him again. He said okay. Irrespective of what happened with my job or my income he would support our relationship. He said yes. I thanked him for his generosity and then informed him that the conversation had been recorded for my private files.

Sound of crickets.

I cut the phone.

*Chariots of Fire* music. Percussion music. Old Spice advertisement music. Overall a triumphant effect.

I am going to savour this moment, Diary. Imagine the pain that idiot has caused me over the last few months. He threw me out of a car. He humiliated me at the airport. He made me join a gym. And then he made me run a marathon.

While the bastard himself is sitting on a criminal record longer than *Jodha Akbar*.

Hypocrite.

**11.23 a.m.**

And in my brief moment of sheer joy who should call me to destroy the moment but Ti . . .

Wait.

**3.13 p.m.**

Done.

**5.02 p.m.**

Diary, if you have NDTV please switch to that channel right now.

'The channel has just learnt that the scam, in which lakhs worth of imported wood was pilfered for the personal use of a cabinet minister, was never actually orchestrated by the minister. Instead the entire pilfering of the wood, and an unknown quantity of other AVG2010 goods that could run into crores of rupees, has been masterminded by a low-profile Delhi-based Tamil politician S.R. Balasubramaniam. Who in turn was reselling the material on the open market.

'Balasubramaniam, previously a member of both the AIADMK and the DMK, had been wandering in the political wilderness for the last few years. He was briefly suspected of involvement in the cash-for-votes scam in 2008. But those charges were dismissed after a brief investigation.

'NDTV has learnt that Balasubramaniam's role in the scam was identified during an internal investigation by the ministry for urban regeneration and public sculpture.

'When approached by the channel Balasubramaniam refuted these charges and said that he was running a legitimate trading business. And that this was a conspiracy to tarnish his political image. The channel has learnt that Balasubramaniam has been taken into custody by Delhi Police for questioning.

'The channel will keep viewers posted on further developments.

'Meanwhile don't forget to tune into a special story at 10 p.m.: Is the clean, incorruptible south Indian politician a myth? Are they as bad as the north Indian politicians? A debate featuring Mahesh Bhatt, Sri Sri Saishankar, and Pratap Bhanu Mehta or Khushboo.'

**7.10 p.m.**

Harish, who no longer has anything to do and will probably never be paid for his services, called to inform me that Shruti Hasaan has backed out of our conversation. She told him we were free to take our ideas to anybody else.

Okay thanks, Shruti.

**8.11 p.m.**

Joyyontoh called to say that Tihar Bala's confession has helped to placate the PM a little. But there will be no change in his plans to wind down everything.

It was worth a shot. At least the world won't label me a corrupt man. Income and position is good, Diary. But one's dignity, that is the most important thing. (This will become a new personal motto starting today.)

Going home now. Suddenly, now that everything has fucking blown up into a million pieces, I have nothing to do any more.

Right now I can look across the office and see Joel in deep discussion with Rajeev and Raghu.

It is as if I don't exist any more.

I hope I get to at least stay on as a senior partner or something. My skills and experience have to be worth something no, Diary?

**19 February 2010**

**10.05 a.m.**

It is past 10 o'clock in the morning. And I still haven't gone to work. And not a single person has phoned to ask why. Not one person.

Last week I was the axis around which Lederman India revolved. Today I am a liability. A nobody. A meaningless has-been who blew up his career by gambling everything on the Government of India.

Good time to catch up on my reading.

**11 a.m.**

Not one phone call.

I think I will order some pizza and watch some *Yes, Minister* and just chill. Maybe I will never again go to office and sit at home and collect salary as long as they keep transferring it.

**11.21 a.m.**

WHAT THE FUCK . . .

**12.09 p.m.**

Everything makes sense!

RAJEEV YOU SNEAKY, DOCUMENT STEALING, LIFE BACKUP PLAN MAKING BASTARD!

**12.31 p.m.**

Joyyontoh will soon call Joel, Rajeev and Raghu to the MURPS for an important merchandising meeting. The Javelin has promised to make up some random reason to get both those bastards to go along.

When they have gone Sugandh will carry out an antivirus update on everybody's machines. When he reaches Rajeev's machine he will delete the entire Insurance folder. Then he will erase the logs. Nobody will ever know.

Meanwhile I have decided to drop everything and focus on a very important project that has just come up.

The Einstein Has Been Unleashed.

### 5.16 p.m.

Diary, please find below copy of an email sent two moments ago to the Prime Minister's Office from the desk of Robin 'Einstein' Varghese:

Respected Sir/Concerned Recipient,

Warm regards from Lederman India.

Sir, you may be aware of our firm as one of the key private sector partners associated with the Allied Victory Games 2010.

Today I write to inform you of an unrelated new initiative that may be of your interest. Ever since you took office your august administration has been working very hard to repatriate Indian black money from banks located overseas. As you mentioned in your last Independence Day speech the return of these illicit funds could infuse the government's exchequer with as much as a trillion dollars in foreign exchange, an astounding boost to a developing nation's economy.

We at Lederman believe that this is a worthy cause. This money belongs to the people of this country. And it must be brought back.

To throw our weight behind your policy we are working on a new white paper titled 'Trillion Dollar Baby: How Did India's Money Get to Switzerland?' We believe this white paper will help to take India's case to a much broader international audience. Thanks to Lederman International's network of global offices and financial experts this white paper will garner unprecedented coverage in boardrooms and newsrooms.

Given the gravity and scope of this burning issue we would like to invite the Prime Minister himself to author a brief introductory note to the white paper. This will help to give our white paper legitimacy and credibility.

We hope the Prime Minister will grace us with his acceptance of this offer.

Please find attached a broad outline of the white paper that we intend to complete in the next two weeks.

Yours respectfully,
Robin Varghese
Interim-CEO, Lederman India Ltd

**20 February 2010**

**11.23 p.m.**

Diary, please find below response to my previous email from an official in the Prime Minister's Office:

Dear Mr Varghese,

Many thanks for your communication dated 19 February 2010.

As you rightly say black money is an important part of this government's Common Minimum Programme. The Prime Minister is committed to repatriating these funds by the completion of this government's tenure. Therefore he wishes to inform you of his appreciation of your initiative. This white paper is a welcome addition to the government's efforts.

However, due to the current circumstances he will not be in a position to provide an introductory note. Given the current enquiries surrounding your firm's involvement with the Allied Games it would be inappropriate for the Prime Minister to associate with your firm at this time.

He conveys his best wishes, regards and appreciation for Trillion Dollar Baby.

Sincerely,
E.K. Kurien
Deputy Joint Under-secretary (PPP)
Prime Minister's Office

**21 February 2010**

**9.09 a.m.**

Diary, please find below copy of email sent to Prime Minister's Office this morning:

> Respected Prime Minister/Deputy Joint Under-secretary (PPP),
>
> Many thanks for your prompt response and your support for our initiative.
>
> We are disappointed that you will not be able to author a note for us. However, we perfectly understand your position. Under the circumstances an association with Lederman India may seem inappropriate.
>
> However, let me reassure you that the company intends to steam ahead with our crusade to bring to India what is rightfully hers.
>
> The Prime Minister will be happy to know that so far we have covered considerable ground. For instance please find attached copies of documents from the records of the Neuchatel branch of BancoGeneve. These documents, just a small part of our vast collection, show considerable secret holdings under the names of several prominent Indian industrialists and politicians.
>
> With access to such reliable information we are confident of publishing a white paper that will be taken seriously and have substantial impact on your government's efforts.
>
> We hope, in time, the Prime Minister will be able to associate more openly with our company. We assure you that all our actions associated with both the Allied Victory Games and the white paper have been conducted to the highest standards of integrity and professionalism.
>
> Sincerely,
> Robin Varghese

**10.15 a.m.**

Diary, please find below an urgent email response from the Prime Minister received a few moments ago:

Dear Robin,

First of all allow me to congratulate you on your recent initiatives to investigate and analyse the reserves of Indian black money currently held by overseas banks. As you rightly pointed out this is a cause of grave concern for this government.

I have followed your recent email exchanges with my office closely.

I request you to kindly excuse Mr Kurien's hasty refusal of cooperation. While it is true that there are some concerns about Lederman's association with the ministry of urban regeneration and public sculpture, these are all within the scope of normal governmental oversight.

In fact, having perused the attachments in your previous email, I would be more than happy to be associated with such an important initiative. When private sector parties such as yourself are willing to put in so much effort on a socially relevant policy it is only right that the government supports you whole-heartedly.

In fact such initiatives must be encouraged. More and more private sector companies must step forward and become a part of our policy ecosystem.

Therefore I have decided to cooperate with Lederman India as much as possible on this white paper. Going beyond authoring an introductory note, which I will do gladly, we would like to also cooperate on the data gathering and analysis. Combining your firm's expertise in analysis with the government's expertise in policy formulation we will be able to author a paper that not only estimates the problem but also prescribes a workable strategy for repatriation.

Not only will this make the venture more meaningful, but it will also be a shining example of the kind of public-private partnership this country needs to cultivate.

Having said that I would like to request you to set aside this white paper for the time being and focus instead on your Allied Victory Games mandate. The Games are a matter of great national pride. The government is not prepared to tolerate any half-measures. Therefore I request you to focus on your partnership with the MURPS.

Collaboration on the white paper can then resume after AVG2010 has been delivered.

This might delay the white paper by a few months. But under the circumstances this is a worthwhile compromise.

I look forward to hearing from you as soon as possible confirming the above-mentioned timelines and our broader cooperation for the benefit of this nation.

Sincerely,
The Prime Minister

**11.23 a.m.**

Diary, in the last one hour I have received at least ten phone calls from the Prime Minister's Office.

However, I have been unable to confirm his request for broader cooperation and new timelines as I am 'currently negotiating this internally with other stakeholders in Lederman'.

Kakkoos. I am actually sitting and watching *Friends* at home.

Rarely do you get a chance to fuck over your government. I intend to savour this moment fully.

**1.14 p.m.**

Diary, the Prime Minister himself called just now. I told him to call back as I am having lunch.

Chumma. Some democracy.

**2.21 p.m.**

Prime Minister called again. I was getting a haircut.

I told him that at that very moment I was in a conference room with several senior Lederman partners. Many of them, I said, were uncomfortable postponing the white paper. We had explosive internal documents from BancoGeneve that implicated many big names. Delaying the white paper could lead to leaks. And some of these guys may relocate their black money.

I promised to call him back when we had a decision.

**3.09 p.m.**

The PM called again. Unrelated call. He wanted to know if Lederman had any expertise in airports. Of course we did. He wanted to know if we would be interested in supporting the government's move to privatize dozens of airports in tier-two cities.

He said the deals could be worth millions of dollars.

I thanked him for the query, told him to give us two to three working days to revert. And then cut the call.

**4.39 p.m.**

You know what? People deeply underestimate our Prime Minister. Some people say that he is too reserved and restrained. Others say that he is too academic. Some foreign people think that he is an underachiever.

I have a different opinion about him now. I think he is a decisive man. A man not afraid to take tough calls. A man who understands a convincing reason when he sees one. A man who, when he sees scans of several years' worth of transactions carried out on his behalf at the Neuchatel branch of BancoGeneve, immediately realizes that there may be merit in not tampering with current arrangements at the ministry of urban regeneration and public sculpture. He realizes that there is tremendous value that an independent subject matter expert such as Robin 'Einstein' Varghese can bring to the MURPS. To this extent the Prime Minister is now willing to not only leave all AVG2010 plans untouched, but also to slip in a kind word or two about Lederman India in his forthcoming speech to the All India Association of Bank Officers. In this speech he will also absolve Kedarji of all corruption charges and ask the police to put Velodrome Balasubramaniam inside the country's premier jail as soon as possible.

This is truly the kind of leader the country needs right now. A man who understands the compromises and the give-and-take necessary to make a democracy functional. And in return for his insight and support he will have access to a vast library of interesting transactional information about a variety of colleagues within the political sphere and outside.

Once the Allied Victory Games are successfully completed the Prime Minister's Office and Lederman India will cooperate on a blockbuster new white paper that will deal with repatriating our precious black money stashed away abroad. The Prime Minister himself will write an introductory note. The white paper will bring together some of Lederman's smartest people and the brightest investigators in the government.

It will be a triumph for public–private partnerships.

AHAHAHAHAHAHAHAHAHAHAHAHAHAHAHAHAHAHA.

Ayyo.

From around 4 p.m. this evening the Prime Minister and Robin 'Einstein' Varghese will be pursuing a mutually beneficial relationship.

**5.43 p.m.**

Joyyontoh just called. He sounded both suspicious and excited. Apparently the Prime Minister has decided not to intervene. Everything will continue as before. He has no idea what has led to this sudden change of mind.

I also sounded excited. But told him I had no idea why.

But then who cares? We get to work immediately.

**22 February 2010**

**1.09 p.m.**

John came in this morning. Just in time to read the latest press release from the Prime Minister's Office. It is a good statement that explains the Velodrome Bala situation, and the status quo with respect to the MURPS and Kedarji. The only mistake in the statement is in the portion where he praises Lederman, Robin Varghese and the other private experts who have been helping the Games function smoothly. Here he refers to me as CEO instead of interim-CEO.

AWKWARD!

John and Joel seem bewildered by this sudden turn of events.

**4.12 p.m.**

Had a free and frank exchange of views with John and Joel. They are both still very upset about the pounding our company's reputation has taken over the last week. However, they are prepared to forgive these as a rookie CEO's mistakes.

As soon as the appraisal cycle is complete John will announce my official elevation to proper CEO.

SUCK ON THIS YOU FIRANG FUCKS.

**7.03 p.m.**

Took a taxi straight to Gouri's house after work. I had turned up without notice. Her parents seemed annoyed. But the Colonel was overflowing with enthusiasm to have me stay back for dinner. Or even overnight if required. Gouri's chin was on the floor.

And then I assembled the Kalbags and gave them the good news.

After years of trying, investing time and effort, and months of dealing with great adversity I had finally made it to the top job. Robin Einstein Varghese had finally made it to CEO.

Now it was time to celebrate.

The Colonel ran and went to buy dhokla.

# BOOK FOUR

# SCRAPBOOK

## Mumbai Mirror

13 February 2010

# Marathon Runner Fiddles w

MATHEW VARGHESE
PARAKKATT. Hilarity
ensued during the Mumbai
Marathon when one of the
runners grabbed a lathi
from a constable and
began running. The
constable, who was taking
care of security along the
running route, radioed
ahead to colleagues. After
a frantic 2-kilometre chase
the runner was finally
apprehended.

It later emerged that the
runner, thirty-four-year-old
Karthik Subramaniam from

New Delhi, had mistaken
the real constable for a
group of fancy dress
policemen who were also
running in the marathon.
Earlier in the race the fake
policemen had playfully
run after Subramaniam
upsetting him

Thinking he had spotted
them a second time
Subramaniam decided to
pull a trick of his own. This
constable, unfortunately,
was 100 per cent
authentic...

Ren
foll
imp

Th
tha
rela
the
beh
of a
exp
in h
beh
cou
or v

It m

245

# The Hindu

27 March 2010

## Allied Games Merchandise

SAMANYU ASHOK. In a spontaneous outpouring of solidarity with the Allied Victory, being held in Delhi, youngsters in Chennai are scrambling to procure the new set of AVG2010 T-shirts launched recently. The T-shirts are available in three sizes (Smaller, Better and Faster) and in a variety of colours and designs. Chennai is only the latest city to see great success for these products. Previously products have sold out in Delhi, Mumbai and Kochi. Minister for nodal oversight, Laxmanrao Badnikedar Dahake, has promised to ramp up production in order to meet booming demand.

**Mint**

3 March 2010

## 'Velodrome Bala' Implicates

VINIFER GANDHI. The 'Scam' Company CEO Ren
tainted ex-minister, S R Rahul Gupta continues to foll
Balasubramaniam, today strongly deny these imp
said that he could neither rumous as a fabrication
confirm not and a conspiracy against Th
widespread rumours that his company's reputation rela
the Indian subsidiary of                              bel
boutique consultancy firm Meanwhile shares in prices of the
The Braithwaite Group company in the parent
may have been involved in 2.4 per cent. the US fell by of
the multi-crore Velodrome                               esp

247

THE TIMES OF INDIA

26 May 2010

# Games a Triumph of Public–Private Partnership: PM

BLOSSOM BABYKUTTY

At his speech during the glittering closing ceremony the Prime Minister had special words of thanks for the numerous public–private partnerships that have made the Allied Games a success.

that stepped in to assist the ministry of urban regeneration and public sculpture with nodal oversight at a time when projects seemed to be slipping out of reach . . .

He had special words of thanks for Lederman Group India

STARLET CONFESSES: I RETIGHTENED MY VAGINA TOO MUCH!

click here to read more.

blunderwatch.blogspot.in

## Games conclude with several open questions

ARSHAD BHATIA

Thursday, 27 May 2010

The Allied Games may have eventually turned out alright. But there are many unsolved questions, mainly revolving around contracts and consultants, that are still an open festering wound.

But now that the event has been declared a success, a relieved national populace will probably brush them under the carpet. This would be a tragedy . . .

THE CARAVAN

# The Social Shaman

24 June 2010

JONATHON SHAININ

Is there a dress code for ace social media consultants?

If not they would do well to adopt Harish Thakkar's now signature style. The effect is both bewildering and striking in equal measure. In his pocket Thakkar carries a Cross pen that he was gifted by an ex-girlfriend. In both ears he wears earrings that don't match at all.

But what will grab your attention and never let it go once you notice them are his cufflinks. One says Chick. The other says Magnet. Together it spells pure audacity . . .

The New Indian Express

7 August 2010

# Kedar splits to form offshoo

ANITA MATHUR: In a
shocking move minister
and cabinet member
Badrikedar Laxmanrao
Dahake has split from the
ruling party along with
four other members of the
Lok Sabha Kedar said that
this was due to
irreconcilable differences
on policy with the Centre
and to help bring greater
focus on the plight of the
people of rural
Maharashtra

The party, which will be
called the Akhil Bharatiya
Sivaji Sena, will remain a
part of the ruling coalition
In a surprise move the
Prime Minister retained
Kedar's cabinet berth and
ministership 'He may have
differences of opinion with
us,' said the Prime
Minister, 'but he remains
far and away the best man
for the job. Let us not let
politics get in the way of
governance.'

Rem
foll
imp

Th
rela
beh
of a
exp
in h
its
beh
con
or

251

19 August 2010

# Government to work with Le...

ANIL PADMANABHAN
Today at the World
Economic Forum India
Summit the Prime Minister
announced a far-reaching
and potentially explosive
white paper that will
outline India's
aggressive strategies so
far, to repatriate black
money The paper, to be
prepared in collaboration
with Ledeman India Ltd,
will combine an accurate
estimate of these funds
along with a strategy to
bring them back

partner will reflect our
commitment, said the
Prime Minister during his
inaugural address

Robin Varghese later told
the press that the white
paper was scheduled to be
submitted for renew to the
ministry of finance in
eighteen months time

"We have often been
accused of moving too
slowly on this matter
Hopefully this partnership
with an aggressive private

Re...
fo...
ung...

Th...
the...
rele...
be...
in b...
its...
beh...
exp...
cou...

The news comes at a time
when there is uncommon
activity in the financial
services space. Just last
week ICICI Bank informed
the bourses that they were
looking to acquire a
controlling in niche Swiss
bank BancoGeneve. This

It...
tot...
thi...
dec...
mo...
reta...

Colonel Jignesh Kalbag
*(Bangladesh '71, New Zealand)*
cordially invites you
to the Wedding Reception of his niece

Miss Gouri Kalbag
*(B.E., M.B.A.-Ahmedabad)*

with

Mr Robin 'Einstein' Varghese
*(B.E., M.B.A.-Ahmedabad, Management Guru)*

at

Hotel Sea View, Connaught Place, New Delhi
on Saturday, 30 April, 2011.

RSVP
EMAIL: SUGANDH@LEDERMAN.CO.IN
DRESS CODE:
MEN: KERALA ETHNIC | WOMEN: GUJARATI ETHNIC | CHILDREN : AVOID
NOTE: ONE PLATE PER PERSON

# Acknowledgements

Ruchika Kapoor: For infinite patience, optimism, inspiration, assorted baked goods and for NOT AT ALL being like Gouri. Fist bump.

Kapoors and Vadukuts: For giving up on the author's social skills without creating too much scene.

Varun Kapoor, Chetna Gulati Kapoor, Sedwin Sunny, Sangeetha Sunny: All of you owe me money.

Gautam Chandrasekharan, Surjo Sinha, Shashank Khare, Ravi Singhvi, Ashwath Venkataraman, Rajjat Gulati, Ankur Goyal, Vanshree Verma, Anjali Grover, Tulika Maheshwari, Shruti Thakar, Chanpreet Khurana, Indhuja Venkatesan, Priya Venkataraman: For paying for dinner and other assorted services rendered to friend with unconventional lifestyle.

Lynn and Merv of the Glendowie Hotel: One day Blackpool will rise again.

Chiki Sarkar: Give me five more minutes and I will send you the acknowledgements page as well.

Paloma Dutta: Please don't tell Chiki, but I need two more days.

Samit Basu: Still the only Bengali I will associate with at a personal level.

Mariana: For ensuring an environment conducive to creative pursuits.

Sukumar Ranganathan, Priya Ramani, Seema Choudhury, Sanjukta Sharma, Supriya Nair, Bhavna Gupta, Siddharth Singh, Pradip Saha, Abel Robinson, the Indulge team and Rakesh Shah: For your patience, support, attention to detail and timely transfer of fees and expenses (Haha). *Mint* is truly an exceptional newspaper.

All you Twitter, Facebook and Whatay people: Please RT/Like/Comment as much as possible. Surprise gifts for everyone.

Everyone who donated money for my charity 10k race: SUCKERS!

Suresh Kalmadi and Lalit Bhanot: For your standards.

The National Health Service: For the C25K podcast.

Anushka Sharma and Raveena Tandon: How you doin'?

And finally, Mohanlal: For everything.

Tuskers Rule.